MW00779645

KIDN
PARALLEL WORLD!

It all happened so fast. One moment she was there, the next moment she was gone! Yes…snatching Ed Langdon's girl was certainly bad enough, but when the "little men" told him flat out that she had no right to be born, it really made him blow his top!

Kidnapped to somewhere in the myriad parallel worlds was this lovely girl from Earth, Freya Haugland. But exactly where she was being held was a complete, seemingly unsolvable mystery. So it was up to Ed to find her, to rescue her—even though the science and knowledge of a different universe opposed him every step of the way.

FOR A COMPLETE SECOND NOVEL, TURN TO PAGE 83

CAST OF CHARACTERS

ED LANGDON
It was a friendly gathering. A few friends watching TV. Ed never dreamed a tiny rocket would come crashing through the screen.

FREYA HAUGLAND
One moment she was sitting watching television, the next moment she was snatched away into another world!

TORSTEIN HAUGLAND
He was Freya's brother, and he knew the best clue to his sister's whereabouts was in the ancient wisdom of an old hag.

COLONEL UTGARD
He was director of inter-level relations. All he was wanted to do was hand over his two Earth visitors to an extermination squad.

MARY LOU SIMMONS
Not what you'd expect for a tough guard. She was slim, pretty, and quite attractive—but she could outfight any man alive.

COLONEL WELCOME
He was one of the few men in the parallel world that had the power to save Langdon's and Torstein's lives.

JUDY HENDRIX
She was just throwing a little house party, but she ended up having one of her guests abducted into a parallel world.

SOMEWHERE I'LL FIND YOU

By
MILTON LESSER
(originally writing as Stephen Marlowe)

ARMCHAIR FICTION
PO Box 4369, Medford, Oregon   97501-0168

*For more information about Armchair Books and products, visit our
website at…*

www.armchairfiction.com

Or email us at…

armchairfiction@yahoo.com

CHAPTER ONE

A BEER commercial lit up the television screen at ten-thirty. Ed Langdon remembered that much distinctly. On either side of him sat Bob Hendrix and his wife—plump and pretty Judy to his right, Bob to his left. Everything was very clear. Except that things started to go crazy right after that.

Because she didn't particularly like television, Freya sat off to one side, her back to the big nineteen-inch screen, her blonde beauty distracting Langdon completely, her radiant smile saying better than any words. We'll be married in a week, darling...

That's what she thought. That's what Langdon thought. No one would have denied it, not even Freya's affable giant of a brother, Torstein Haugland, who liked surprise endings in everything from television to magazines to real life. For Tor liked Ed Langdon even more, and probably now he was busy telling all his friends at the Norwegian Sailors' Home in Brooklyn what a fine young brother in-law he'd be getting, even if the lad didn't have Viking blood in his veins.

But at ten-thirty-one Langdon remembered the time because the announcer had predicted a one-minute commercial—things went crazy.

The beer commercial flared up brilliantly, so brilliantly that you couldn't see the commercial at all. Instead, a bright light pulsed on the screen, throwing its glow across the room.

A droning sound unlike any television disturbance. Langdon had ever heard rumbled up from somewhere deep within the mahogany console.

Judy Hendrix said, "Bob dear, we'll have to get a repair man in the morning."

Her husband did not answer. He yelped instead.

The nineteen-inch screen shattered.

Flying shards of glass shot out in all directions, one sliver grazing Langdon's forehead and cutting a deep gash.

Something zipped out from the shattered tube, a gleaming teardrop no bigger than your index finger when it first appeared. In a fraction of a second it passed just overhead between Judy and Freya, and by then it was bigger than a baseball bat.

5

SOMEWHERE I'LL FIND YOU!

By Stephen Marlowe

Snatching Ed's girl was bad enough; but when the little men told him she had no right to be born—he really blew his top!

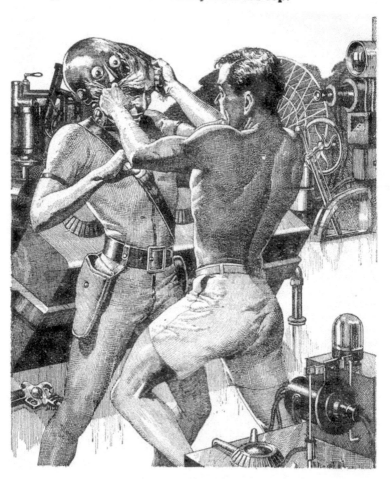

Langdon's groping fingers, seeking Utgard's eyes, found yielding skin instead. A savage wrench—and the man's entire face collapsed!

A BEER commercial lit up the television screen at ten-thirty. Ed Langdon remembered that much distinctly. On either side of him sat Bob Hendrix and his wife—plump and pretty Judy to his right, Bob to his left. Everything was very clear. Except that things started to go crazy right after that.

It grew.

By the time it reached the far wall it was as big as a good-sized bathtub, only it didn't look like a bathtub at all.

Langdon had visited the Planetarium, had seen what spaceships might one day look like. The thing which exploded from the Hendrix television set could have been a pint-sized spaceship, with peaked prow, stubby wings and a cabin from which Langdon thought he saw three heads peering.

The gleaming blue teardrop came to rest at the far wall, exhaust smoke curling lazily from a bank of tubes at its rear. Judy whimpered softly, her auburn head slumped down over her chest. Tall and superbly formed, Freya stood with hands on hips, surveying the thing. Hendrix looked at Langdon. Langdon looked back at his host, shrugged foolishly. "What the hell," he said, "let's see what that contraption is."

He got up and strode across the room, a lithe, athletic figure of a man, six-foot-two and broad of shoulder, yet carrying himself with the effortless grace of a jungle cat. Like his wife, Hendrix was built along stubbier lines, and he didn't seem in any great hurry to poke his nose around the miniature spaceship. Langdon reached it first—and a door in its gleaming hull popped open.

THREE FIGURES stepped out jauntily, alighting on the floor. Langdon squinted down at them in the dim glow of the television lamp. He'd have accepted three little bug-eyed horrors more readily. Each no more than a foot long, the figures were tiny men!

Briefly, Langdon stood in the way, and neither Freya nor Hendrix could see the spaceship's occupants. By the time Langdon moved aside, the figures made like their spaceship.

They grew and grew.

They did not stop until they had attained normal proportions, each one nattily attired in a bright orange uniform. They waited patiently for the metamorphosis to take place, as if it were the most natural thing in the world.

One looked around, scratching his bare head. "Uh-huh, this is the place. Third Level world—"

Langdon failed to hear the rest of it. Judy stood up, took one quick look at the three men. She screamed before she fell to the high-pile carpet in a dead faint.

The first of the three figures seemed utterly unperturbed. He took a white card from his pocket, read it briefly, jabbed a gloved finger at Langdon's chest. "Which one of the women is Freya Haugland?"

"I'll answer that when you tell me who the devil you are." Langdon did not feel nearly as brave as he sounded. More than anything else, he felt stunned. But that seemed the thing to say, despite the fact that he'd have preferred a good stiff shot of whiskey. Men just don't come popping out of television screens in little spaceships. Men who grow bigger right before your eyes. Only they did—

"Please! Which one is Freya Haugland?"

"I said—"

But Freya came forward, taking her stand beside Langdon. "I'm Freya."

"But of course. Your Scandinavian ancestry certainly asserts itself. Well, come along."

"What do you mean come along?"

Langdon bristled, stepping between Freya and the orange-uniformed man.

BY THEN Hendrix had regained some of his lost composure. With the help of a glass of cold water, he'd revived Judy, who sat on the floor with her legs crossed under her, slightly disheveled. Now he said, "See here! If this is some kind of an advertising stunt—if it is, I'm going to call the police."

"My friend, does it look like an advertising stunt?"

Freya smiled. "You never know what's liable to come out of a television screen. But it sure looks more complicated than an advertising stunt—"

"I'll say," Judy chimed in. "They ruined our television—" And then she started to blubber again.

The second orange-uniformed man said: "We're getting nowhere fast, Captain Adams. May I suggest that we take the woman and go?"

"Naturally. But it is a bit awkward. We were supposed to come upon her alone, not in the company of three other people."

"What's the difference? If they tell what they've seen, who will believe them?"

"Umm-mm," Captain Adams considered. "A good point. All right then. You guard these three while I take the woman."

"If I may suggest, sir, while we get smaller they might try—"

"Again a good point. Very well, then—paralyze them."

Langdon had listened in silent disbelief to the dialogue, but now he began, "Listen, you—"

He stayed that way, mouth open, ready to form the next word. The second orange-uniformed man had removed a slim metal tube from his belt, had pointed it first at Langdon, then at Hendrix, at Judy, and finally at Freya.

Langdon could not move a muscle! He strove mightily, but he could not even move his little finger. He could only stand there and watch while the third uniformed figure slung Freya over his shoulder like a big beautiful rag doll. After that, the three figures commenced to shrink.

And Freya with them...

Langdon could not blink his eyes, which began to sting and tear. Dimly, he was aware of four-foot-long figures entering the little blue ship, the fourth one a tiny immobile statue, which had been Freya.

The door swung shut. The ship shuddered, rose off the floor—began to shrink.

A TINY mote again, it plunged back within the television tube and disappeared. Nothing remained to remind them of the visit but the shattered screen. Not even their paralysis, which disappeared abruptly with the ship.

Hendrix's fingers shook too much, and he dropped the cigarette on a table after two unsuccessful attempts to light it. "You want me to call the police, Ed?"

"What for? What'll we tell them, that a little ship blew in out of the television set and took Freya?"

Judy bent over and peered within the shattered screen. "I don't see anything," she admitted. "Don't worry, Ed; it's probably somebody's idea of a big joke. Hah hah…" Her laughter trailed off, lamely.

"I still say the police," Hendrix persisted. "Look, Ed—you don't want to play around with a thing like this—"

"Damn it, don't you think I know that?"

"Hey, take it easy—"

"I'm…sorry, Bob. But they took Freya, just like that. Where or why, we don't know. Neither will the police. They'll ask a lot of pointless questions, waste a lot of time, bury us in heaps of red tape…no, we don't want the police."

"What can you do?"

"I don't know. I don't know! Maybe if I told Tor—"

"You mean Freya's brother Torstein? Yeah, he's quite a guy. I've never seen anything he couldn't handle when he really set his mind to it. And what an imagination."

"Yes, Torstein," Langdon mused, liking his idea better every moment. He crossed into the foyer, picked the phone off its cradle, and dialed information. "I'd like the number of the Norwegian Sailors' Home in Brooklyn. What? No, my directory isn't handy. Uh-huh, thanks."

He dialed the number, waited. Then:

"Hello? I'd like you to page Torstein Haugland. Haugland, H-a-u-g-l-a-n-d. Yes, it's important. I'll wait…

"Tor? Yeah, Ed. I've got to see you at once…you're damned right it sounds like a matter of life and death…sure, take a cab. I'd ask you to fly if you could…Right."

Langdon lit a cigarette and paced about. Three quarters of an hour before he could expect Torstein to arrive from Brooklyn. But what could Torstein do? What could any one do? Well, it was a final straw to grasp and he knew he'd feel a lot better when Tor's giant figure squeezed in through the apartment doorway.

SIX and a half feet of Torstein Haugland joined Langdon in his pacing, topped by rugged features, icy blue eyes and a blond crew cut. "So that's your story," Torstein grunted finally, after Langdon had finished talking. Even as Tor said it, Langdon realized how ridiculous it all sounded, and he half-expected Torstein to burst out laughing. But the Norseman took it all very seriously.

"Ed, if it weren't you, and if the girl it happened to weren't our Freya—"

"What then?"

"I think I would squash your face a little for making me run all the way up here."

"Well, do you believe me?"

"You ask a man to believe a lot, with no proof beyond a smashed television set."

"Do you believe me?"

"Ed...yes! But that's not important. We've got to get Freya back. You know I would die for my sister."

"You talk like you know where she is."

"I didn't say that. But I know something." Torstein stopped his pacing long enough to tamp the bowl of his pipe full of tobacco and light it. He sighed, blew a great cloud of smoke to the ceiling, muttered, "Freya, Freya," under his breath.

Then he said, "Ed, may I tell you a story? Good. Years ago, when Freya was just a little sapling, not the tall strong maiden of the Valkyrie that she now is, she had dreams. Night after night they came, not the sort of dreams that may strike the mind of any youngster, but wild, impossible nightmares. Little Freya would wake up red-eyed and screaming, and it would be long before my mother—Lord rest her soul—could croon her back to sleep.

"Now, at that time there lived with us in the Fjordland an old hag, my mother's cousin's great-grandmother. Old she was, so old that all had lost count of the years. She would shake her shaggy gray head and grin her toothless grin and we would all listen, for she was what the Indians of this country would call a shaman. I won't pretend that she had any ancient wisdom that is lost to this generation, Ed. I don't know.

"BUT I DO know this. She claimed that ancient wisdom, whatever it was, for her own. And whenever little Freya had her dreams, the hag could quiet her. Dream no more, my child, she would say, and then Freya could sleep the sleep a babe is meant to have. And there by the fire while the winds howled in among the fjords outside, the hag would talk of another world, of many worlds as far removed from this one as the farthest star, and yet not removed at all.

"One day soon after Spring had come to the Fjordland with the fresh smell of growing things, Freya disappeared. She—"

"What? Did you say she disappeared? Like this time?"

"I don't know. The aurora was on that night, I remember, bouncing lances of fire from crag to crag down by the sea. And Freya...vanished. Without a trace, Ed.

"For two weeks she was gone. My mother wept, the whole village wept, for little Freya was beloved of all. Only the hag did not weep, the hag who perhaps loved Freya more than us all. She said our worry was foolishness. She said—but I do not recollect too well, because I was no more than ten. Anyway, after a fortnight, the old hag joined Freya. Without warning, she vanished. And perhaps the queerest thing of all was this: the aurora had returned to the Fjordland!

"We never saw the hag again. But a few days later, thunder and lightning rocked our village, a very unusual thing in the Fjordland in early Spring. When the storm subsided, we found Freya sound asleep in her bed..."

"That's all?" Langdon demanded.

"All that matters." Soon after, we left the spot as a place cursed by devils, by Loki's brood or worse. We came here to America, and nothing like that ever happened to Freya again. Until what you just told me. Freya remembered nothing of it; she was only three. I am the last alive perhaps who knows, because my father took ill and died on the crossing, and my poor saddened mother followed to her reward soon after that."

"You say you're the last. What about the old woman, the hag?"

TORSTEIN shrugged. "Ah, what about her? Who knows, who can say? I only know that while we lived in the Fjordland she never came back. It was as if she had substituted herself for little Freya—wherever Freya went—to a world as far as the farthest star, yet not distant at all, as the hag would say. As for her—I don't know. Perhaps, after all, she has returned to the Fjordland. Perhaps she lives there even now, a hundred years old if she is a day. Perhaps she is dead. Perhaps...well, wherever she went, if the place wanted one and she traded herself for Freya..." Torstein spread his hands out eloquently enough.

Judy Hendrix frowned. "If you don't mind my saying so, Mr. Haugland, it sounds a little cockeyed."

Her husband did some frowning of his own, but Torstein chuckled softly. "We live in a cockeyed world, Mrs. Hendrix. Not many years ago, a cousin of mine went with some men across the Pacific Ocean on some logs to prove a theory. That is cockeyed, but it also is wonderful. Who's to say what is crazy and what isn't?"

Getting some glasses and pouring drinks for all, Hendrix said, "I'll swallow that. But even assuming there's some connection between what happened when Freya was a girl and what happened now, what can you do about it?"

Torstein slapped his palm hard on his thigh. "We can go to the Fjordland and find out. I can sail in a week on a Norwegian freighter, and I know the company well enough to see that Ed books on with me as a deck hand. That is, if you want to, Ed—"

"If I want to! I want Freya, Tor. I want to know she's safe, I want her in my arms where she belongs, I want—listen. Why wait a week? If I take the money I saved for our honeymoon, we can fly BOAC to London, and from there to Oslo. We can step off in your Fjordland tomorrow..."

"Your savings, all your savings—"

"So what? They were for Freya and me. They are still for Freya and me. Shall I call the airline terminal, Tor?"

Torstein stood up and banged the ashes from his pipe. More to himself than to anyone in the room, he mumbled, "The Fjordland after all these years. And Freya...little Freya whom we must find," He placed a huge hand on Langdon's shoulder, looked for a long moment into the eyes of the man who would be his brother-in-law.

"Call them."

CHAPTER TWO

NORWAY. LATE afternoon of the next day, they stepped out of the airliner in Oslo, a crisp, clear early Spring day. Torstein had wired ahead and a tall, angular man with the bluest eyes Langdon had ever seen met them at the administration building.

"You are little Torstein!" he cried tremulously in English, embracing the Norse giant. "Ah, but you are not so little any more. I would know you anywhere."

Torstein smiled. "It has been a long time, Uncle Leif. This is Ed Langdon, who would marry a Haugland woman."

"Our Freya," the old man said, pumping Langdon's hand warmly. "And how is she? Tan and strong and beautiful as the mists that rise up from the Fjords on a good Spring morning, I'll wager. Tell me, lads, how is she?"

Torstein said solemnly, "It is because of Freya that we came to Norway. I suggest that you take us someplace where we may drink and talk. But first answer a question; you remember the ancient hag, Olaf Erickson's great-grandmother I believe she was?"

"Of course I remember her—the cackler."

"Is she here, in the Fjordland?"

"No, lad. She's not. She never returned after that day...that day long ago when—"

"I know what day you mean, Uncle. Yesterday Freya vanished again, and now there is no hag to bring her back..."

Leif Haugland swallowed hard, his Adam's apple bobbing up and down. "I think we'd better find that place to drink," he said, while Torstein and Ed got their luggage.

It was several hours of hard driving from Oslo to the northern Fjordland, with the small fishing villages flashing by one after the other. A stiff breeze blew in from the sea and low, fleecy clouds scudded along the horizon, sparkling like a string of pearls against the deep blue sky.

When old Lief Haugland pulled the car off the macadam road and drove for a time along a winding dirt path, Torstein was amazed. "But where's our village?" he demanded.

"Didn't you know, Tor? When the hag failed to return, the villagers left the spot, their simple souls thinking of curses and the Elder Gods. Left alone for twenty years on the Fjordland, a village does not stand unchanged. Look now..."

THE SITE of the deserted village swept from the road down to the sea, but nature had encroached everywhere, leaving only a few scattered huts in one piece. Walls had disappeared as if by magic, hardly a roof still stood, cobbled streets were broken and torn.

"We had the pride of the village," Torstein sighed. "A stone cottage. Surely it yet stands?"

"I think so," his uncle admitted, driving their car down one. of the narrow cobbled roads that twisted its way between the fallen, broken huts. "There, you see?"

Alone of all the village, the neat stone cottage by the sea had withstood the fury of the elements. Now it waited for them, silently, as if it had been only yesterday that a bright fire roared on its hearth, sending a cheery curl of smoke out against the sky.

"What a world we live in," Torstein mused. "All that red tape yesterday, Ed, so you could get us here with official sanction from the two governments. And today—what is government, what is all the red tape and politics and science of the world? Today we stand in the Fjordland, near a cottage where I was born, where Freya...Freya..."

The door squeaked open on its rusty hinges and a musty smell greeted them from within the cottage. "Here we sat by the hearth," said Torstein, "while the old hag wove stories of the old days and the olden magic, and here—" opening another door"— here I slept in this bed with little Freya in the next room. See? Sometimes I remember our mother would stand in the doorway and croon to both of us at once."

Ed cleared his throat impatiently.

"I know you have your memories, Tor, and I don't like to intrude...but we came because Freya—"

Torstein shrugged, peered from a window. Outside, the sun was falling below the horizon, turning the fleecy clouds to scarlet fire. "Don't you think I know that, Ed? I am thinking. Yes...there was a place here that the hag had for her very own, and no one in all the village could go near it. Often we heard rumbling noises, and as children we were frightened. In the cellar, come."

THEY OPENED a trap door in what had been the living room, and before they went down the rickety wooden stairs, Leif Haugland ran out to the car and returned with a flashlight. Soon the light cut a swath for them through the inky darkness and they poked around curiously in the damp place. From somewhere, water seeped down slowly. It must have trickled in like that over the years, for the stone floor was covered with a thick carpet of moss.

Said Leif Haugland, "Would you think me a fool if I told you I was frightened? Even when I was a child—and that is a long time ago, Tor, Edward—even then, the hag seemed old as time itself, and she went about her mysterious way frightening all the children, and the adults as well—What was that?"

"By the Elder Gods now, will you relax?" Torstein chuckled. "I merely scraped my foot against the wall, Uncle." Then he grunted, playing the light along the far wall. "What have we here?"

"It looks like a lever," Ed told him, padding across the moss and examining the huge metal arm that protruded from what looked like a shield hanging on the wall. "But what for?"

Torstein grunted again, touching the thing with his fingers. "This is steel, I think. But what is steel doing down here in this ancient place? And that thing on the wall—it's no shield, Ed. Here, try to move it."

Ed nodded; grabbing the edge of the shield and tugging. He pulled with all his strength, pulled until the veins stood out on his forehead, but he did not move the shield-like slab of metal one inch.

Torstein ran a hand through his short thatch of blond hair. "Now that lever, maybe the lever moves."

His Uncle placed a trembling hand on the giant's forearm. "Naturally, Torstein. That is what levers are for, to move. But this one, must you move this one?"

"Apparently the hag used this thing, long and long ago. We're here for just that reason, Uncle, to see what powers she had. If you want to run upstairs like a craven—"

"Hold your tongue!" the old man cried. "I was a captain in the Norwegian Navy before you were born! I merely joked…" He sighed and then stood there, waiting for Torstein to make the next move.

TORSTEIN took the lever between his two hands and yanked at it. He yanked again, and this time furiously. In the light of their flash, rust flaked off and settled on his forearms like the plague, but the lever failed to stir.

"See?" Leif Haugland told them.

"The hag could move this thing because she knew its magic. But you cannot, Tor. Perhaps if we leave now and return later with the tools we need—"

"Quiet, Uncle! No hag with all the magic in this world and others is stronger than Torstein Haugland. No…"

If anyone else had said that, Ed knew, it would have sounded mildly ridiculous. But Torstein made that declaration quite seriously, and no one thought it was funny.

"…not that all," Torstein was saying. "Rust has made this thing stiff, that is all. Ed, if you'll lend a hand—"

Together they grasped the stubborn metal arm, and Ed crouched, his knees bent, the muscles on his back flexed, until Torstein shouted, "Heave!" Then they were pulling at the thing together, while old Leif Haugland stood off in a corner, holding the flashlight and muttering to himself.

It wasn't doing any good, Ed thought. The metal arm could have been part of the wall for all their tugging. Besides, what on Earth could they expect to happen, even if they succeeded in activating the ancient machinery…?

Abruptly, with a loud scraping sound, the lever came down a full two feet.

Something clanged and rumbled and Ed got the impression that it was far, far away. After that, only their harsh breathing cut through the utter silence.

Something whispered over and over again in Ed's mind: go upstairs, upstairs…

"Let's get out of here!" Torstein roared. And when Ed nodded: "Oh, you hear it too, eh? Come on!"

The three of them clambered up the rickety stairs, stalked through the living room and out into the gathering night.

DESPITE THE final flickerings of sunset, the aurora already had come to the Fjordland. It formed a great canopy of wild, pulsing light across the sky, hiding the stars and the crescent moon. Lances of light touched each other playfully, crashed together with silent thunder, darting and twisting and eluding one another in a game that belonged to the Elder Gods.

"By the brood of Loki!" Leif Haugland cried passionately. "I've never seen it like that before! And this so early in the evening."

"I wonder," said Torstein. "I wonder. Did pulling that lever have anything to do with the aurora— Hello, what's that?"

A bright note seemed to detach itself from the flashing canopy and then plunge Earthward like a shooting star. Down it came and down, and when its brief glowing faded away, something had alighted near their old automobile.

Torstein took the flashlight from his uncle's nerveless fingers and played its beam at the car. "Loki's brood is right," he said.

"Hold it steady," Ed pleaded.

"Yeah, like that. I'll be damned!" Together, they ran forward, and Ed was half aware that Leif Haugland hung back near the stone cottage by himself, trembling and afraid.

A blue ship like the one, which had come through Bob Hendrix's television set rested idly not half a dozen steps from their car!

Ed examined its smooth blue surface curiously, not even thinking that the impossible had happened again. You accepted something like this, or you went off your rocker trying to ponder the reasons for it. And overhead, the aurora began to fade from the sky, as if it had come with but one purpose, and that to deliver the ship...

"I'd like to go inside," Torstein said. "I'd really like to do that."

"How can we? First place, there's no opening I can see. Also, it's too small, maybe as big as a good-sized barrel, that's all."

"No—look. It's growing!"

It was, or that's what Ed thought at first. But then, so was the old car, the cottage, the nearby trees, even a now-monstrous Leif Haugland who had crept forward to watch.

Ed felt oddly removed from the whole affair. It couldn't be happening to him, not this. And so when he spoke it was in a very level voice. He said, "That thing isn't growing, Tor. *We're* shrinking."

Leif Haugland shouted something, but his voice came out too deep for them to hear. If they stood next to him, Ed realized, they'd hardly reach up to his knees. The blue ship had become huge, as large as the BOAC Constellation, which had taken them across the Atlantic. Something big and brown and hairy brushed against Ed's shin and he kicked at it, watching it scamper away. A beetle—

At that moment, a door in the side of the blue hull popped open, exactly as it had done in the Hendrix apartment. Ed smiled grimly. "You've got your wish, Tor. Let's go." But he thought: *maybe this will take me to Freya.*

THEY STEPPED through the portal, into a square cubicle about half the size of the cottage living room, relative to their new proportions. Several panels glowed dully in its walls, casting a feeble illumination that was sufficient to show them that the cubicle was empty. No furniture. No instrument panel. Just a bare room. Off to one side, up near the ceiling, a row of windows broke the wall's smooth surface. And that was all.

Torstein shrugged. "I guess we just wait for something to happen." Then, an instant later: "Lord, what was that?"

Something huge and watery and blue had flashed briefly by the row of windows.

"I'd say that was your Uncle Leif," Ed told him. "Or that is, his eye. Probably he looked in through those windows."

"Yes!" Torstein cried. "And that means we're still shrinking, but along with the ship now. You remember, you said it got very small before it went back into the television tube."

A stirring came from someplace beneath their feet, deep within the core of the ship. Bank after bank of machinery might reside below them and all around them. Ed couldn't tell; the four walls of their little cubicle effectively blocked them from everything else.

Especially when the door snapped shut with complete finality, and when the panel lights winked out...

Standing in total, complete darkness, Ed reached into his pocket, feeling for a crumpled package of cigarettes. He took one out, lit it, relieved by the brief flare of the match before it too went out.

"I generally smoke a pipe," Torstein whispered. "But better give me one of those, Ed, I think we're moving."

Ed didn't have time to reply, could not even find the strength to light Torstein's cigarette. Gravity crushed them down helplessly against the floor as the ship gained acceleration. Crushed harder, flattened them, pounded in Ed's ears, took the ability to see from his eyes—

The last thing he remembered was Torstein's muttering, "Maybe that—old—hag wasn't—a fake—after all…"

Then the aurora flashed in all its brilliance, this time inside his head.

"AMAZING!" TORSTEIN said. "No broken bones."

Ed got to his feet groggily, leaned heavily on Torstein's arm for support, then backed away. "The door is open, Tor. How long have you been up?"

"I don't know. Twenty minutes, maybe half an hour. Wherever we went, we've arrived. The door was ajar as soon as I opened my eyes. And you should see it outside, really nice. Just like a park."

"You been out?"

"Hell, no. I want to find Freya just as much as you do, but I think wherever we are, the two of us can do a lot better than one. I hope it isn't a fight we'll have on our hands, Ed. Between us we haven't got as much as a toothpick. No knives, no gun. Nothing. Shall we go?"

"Yeah, sure." Ed bit his lip. "Where on Earth can we be?"

"Friend, if you think we're on Earth, you've got less of an imagination than I thought—"

"I didn't mean it that way. Just an expression, Tor. If we're still on Earth, I'd be plenty surprised. But where…"

Torstein muttered something about there being only one way to find out, and then they crossed to the door.

They climbed out of the ship and into a park.

A fountain bubbled gaily nearby.

Birds chattered overhead, calling to one another. Small, stunted trees stood about on all sides, neatly groomed, each one clustered with giant, sweet smelling purple blossoms.

Torstein laughed. "If I were old Leif, I'd say Valhalla."

"If you were yourself, you mean, you superstitious old—"

And then Ed shut up, fast. Someone ambled up the tiled path toward them, a well-built young man in a bright orange uniform.

"Where'd you check in from?" he demanded. "Oh, you just got here?" Then, when he was met with blank stares: "You haven't checked in yet? Say, where are your uniforms?"

"As you can plainly see," said Torstein, "we haven't got any. What is this place?"

"What is this place? By the dimensional gods, who are you two? Colonel Utgard must hear of this. Will you join me, please?"

Did the simple question veil some threat? Ed couldn't decide for sure. He cast a questioning glance at Torstein, who merely shrugged his shoulders and followed the uniformed figure. Ed looked once behind him at the strange blue ship, which now had assumed a size in logical proportion to the surrounding landscape. Well, at least they seemed to be done with this size-changing. Ed fell into stride beside Torstein and followed the man in orange.

For perhaps five minutes they walked through the park, the man ahead of them cutting across easily from one path to another.

THEY entered a plaza, crossed it to a low rambling structure with gleaming white walls and a terrace girding its middle some twenty feet overhead. Ed saw several other orange-uniformed men idling about, saw more of them when, with Torstein and their guide, he had entered the white building. Frowning, Ed found himself wondering if Freya had trod this same path the day before.

Inside the building, they climbed one flight of stairs and came out in a blight hallway. Off to the left should be the terrace. And to the right were a row of doors, all shut, each bearing a name prefixed by a military rank. They stopped in front of one marked: COLONEL L. UTGARD, Director; Inter-Level Relations in English. Everything in English, with the possible exception of Colonel Utgard's name. But the names on the other doors: Peters and Smith and Wanewright and Clarke.

Just where the devil were they? "Yes?" the receptionist asked. She stood at a railing inside the office looking them over curiously. She wore a trim, tailored orange uniform, the sort of masculine outfit that enhances rather than diminishes feminine appeal. And of that, Ed thought briefly, she had plenty.

Their guide told her, "We have no appointment, but this is something unusual, Ma'am."

"Really, Private," the girl said.

"You know the Colonel sees no one, except by appointment. I think he's out sunning himself now, anyway. But, of course, that's confidential between us, eh? Now, would you like to make an appointment? Say, for some time next week?"

"Next week? Will you give the colonel a message for me?"

"Of course."

"Tell him I have reason to believe two men, probably third level, certainly no higher than second, somehow got hold of one of our inter level ships and came here in it."

The girl licked her lips, gazed long at Torstein and Ed. "Is that so? Positively incredible, Private. But—wait. I'll see the colonel."

"She doesn't like non-coms," the orange-uniformed man said while they waited. "Well, sometimes women get cocky because they know of the reversal of sex-roles on the Fourth Level, but still..."

In a moment, the girl returned.

Their guide saluted her smartly this time, and she smiled a little. She said, "Colonel Utgard is annoyed, Private. If what you say is true, you should have had the men exterminated at once, he said. But now that you're here, he'll see them before they're killed."

"Be quiet, Ma'am," the guard hissed. "They can understand."

"Goodness, you didn't tell me they came from an English-speaking level!"

"Aren't most?"

"Umm-mm, true. Well, come along."

Torstein planted himself firmly and did not move.

Ed told the woman, "I think we'll stay right here, thanks."

But their guard, who until this moment had been a guide, took what could have been a pistol from his belt and said, "No you won't. Come on...move."

CHAPTER THREE

COLONEL UTGARD turned out to be a striking figure of a man garbed in the inevitable orange uniform. As tall as Ed but not so broad across the shoulders, his dark eyes stared out intently from under a generous brow. He had a straight, handsome nose, but flabby jowls and sensuous lips told of a soft life for all his military bearing.

"These are the men?" he snapped at the woman.

"Yes sir, Colonel."

"All right, you two, let's hear it. That is, if you have anything to say before we send for an extermination squad."

Just like that, as if they were vermin, Ed thought.

Growled Torstein, "You might find us a little hard to exterminate."

"Suppose you let me worry about that. I said, let's hear it."

"He's Torstein Haugland," Ed told the colonel, "and I'm Ed Langdon. One of your blue ships came yesterday and took Freya Haugland, Torstein's sister and my fiancé. We came to get her back."

"Don't just say it, man. How'd you come?"

Ed smiled blandly. There was the rub, he knew, and maybe if they could keep this Colonel Utgard guessing, there'd be no extermination squad. At least, not for a while. "Why," he said, "in our own little blue ship."

"In your...listen, you idiot, I want the truth."

"That's the truth. We found a ship and came here."

"No one finds a ship. Who took you? If that decadent Colonel Welcome had anything to do with it..."

"I know no Colonel Welcome. But if you think he's on our side, we'd like to meet him."

Utgard threw his hands up into the air, stalked across the room and prodded the girl's shoulder. "You—fetch me Colonel Welcome."

"Sir, like you, he'll see no one without appointment."

"By the First Level, he'll see me. And tell him I said so."

"Yes sir," she said, a little doubtfully. But she departed on her errand.

She returned in five minutes, and Ed thought she was trying hard to hide a smile. "Sir, Colonel Welcome gives me this message to relay: he is extremely busy, but if you really must see him, you know where to find him."

"Damn that insipid oaf—damn him. Very well. We'll all pay a visit to Colonel Welcome."

At Utgard's directions, the guard marched Ed and Torstein out the door.

WELCOME was a little round Colonel whose shining bald dome wouldn't come up to Torstein's shoulders and whose face seemed set in a perpetual jovial grin. "Hello, Utgard," he said after they'd barged into his office. "Just what does the Director of Inter-Level Relations want with me?"

"You're the Third Level expert, aren't you? We've got two specimens from that level, I think."

"So?"

"So I want to know how they got here. Talk..."

"Don't tell me when I can talk, Utgard," Welcome was still smiling, but his icy tones made the smile meaningless. "You're a colonel, I'm a colonel. I am not one of your subordinates. If you want any information, suppose you fill out the usual form in triplicate."

Utgard turned red, then blanched.

"Very well...I'm sorry. But this is the problem, Colonel. Somehow, these two came here. Unauthorized, of course. The penalty always has been and must be extermination. But first, I want to know how they got here."

"That's easy," Ed persisted. "We're looking for Freya Haugland. A tall blonde girl, very lovely."

Utgard slammed his open palm down on Welcome's desk. "I don't care who you're looking for."

"Just a moment," Welcome told him, chuckling. "If they came for the Haugland woman, I'm glad. I never approved of the whole thing, anyway."

"You never approved!" Utgard stormed. "That's my responsibility, Colonel, not yours."

"I know it. But now that the case has reached this point, I think I'll call in the Regent for a decision. Do you know what's behind the Haugland case, Colonel?"

"Naturally, naturally. It fell in my department, did it not? Of course, there are so many, and—"

"Then you don't. Simply put, the mistake that placed the Haugland woman from birth on Level Three was utterly without consequences, but since law dictates that all such mistakes must be rectified when discovered, she's been sent to the Fourth Level, where a new life has been prepared for her."

"You mean she's not here?" Torstein demanded.

"Keep quiet," said Utgard. "Naturally, she had to be sent to Level Four. Welcomed. She might alter a Probability Curve, and—"

"That's just what I was trying to say. She'd not be doing that at all, not according to the Logic Division. Only tradition demanded her removal. And I believe it a foolish tradition."

"I don't need you telling me how to run my division."

"I'm not. I'm merely going to request a decision from the Regent. Meanwhile, I suppose you'd better keep these two confined—"

"No, I've decided to have them exterminated."

"I'll see that the Regent holds you responsible if you do. Until he makes a decision, these two are prisoners of the State."

"I refuse."

"Very well," Welcome smiled, "you give me no choice. We're in my quarters now, Utgard, remember that. I'll keep the prisoners, and you'll see them step toward the little round man, but again when the Regent summons us."

Thoroughly flustered, Utgard took a step toward the little round man, but two guards stood between them. Utgard snorted once, then turned on his heel and left the room. The girl followed him, smiling lightly, but the guide who found the men from Level Three looked very pale.

The flesh on his cheeks bounced merrily as Colonel Welcome chuckled. "I really enjoyed that. But did you two know you were very close to death?"

"I got that impression," Torstein admitted dryly.

"LET ME say that I'm quite amazed," Colonel Welcome told them two hours later, as they entered the Regent's quarters. He must think it terribly important. A summons within two hours. Are you two frightened?"

"Might be," Ed admitted, "if we knew what was going on."

Colonel Utgard was sitting nearby, fuming, biting his lower lip between sharp white teeth. Two dozen uniformed officials sat around him, mostly men. Far off at the end of the long silent hall, the Regent paced back and forth, a wrinkled, white-haired little man in his seventies.

The whole scene appeared theatrical, almost like a movie set from some fantastic epic, with the bright, mirrored columns supporting an arched roof high overhead, with the scores of guards standing stiffly at attention, strange weapons loose in their holsters, with three or four kirtle-dressed girls serving food and drink to the officials. Theatrical, lurid—but Ed knew this room might see the pronouncement of his and Torstein's death sentence.

Finally, after a lengthy time, someone came forward, placed trumpet to lips, blew ore long strident note. Then he cried:

"The Regent has decided! The Regent's word is Wisdom!"

Forcing wind through a dry reed, you might be able to imitate the Regent's shrill voice. Bending that reed almost in two, you might be able to mime his posture. "Here on Level One it is indeed a rarity to receive two unescorted visitors from a lower level. But such has happened this day."

Muttering among the officials, and then the Regent went on: "I have received the intelligence reports from Colonel Utgard, I have weighed them against the contrary opinion of Colonel Welcome. I have this to say: there should be no question. Death to intruders stands out as a paramount necessity of the order of things."

Utgard's smile was a cold thing now.

He was sure of himself, and did not hesitate to show it in his expression.

TORSTEIN whispered, "Listen, Ed, I don't know how far we can get, but if his decision is death, you want to make a run for it?"

Ed let his glance rove over the many uniformed guards. He shrugged. "I sure as hell wouldn't like to die lined up against a wall with a blindfold on my eyes. But running away and getting shot in the back wouldn't do Freya much good, either. Let's wait and see."

"...however," the Regent's shrill voice continued, "there are extenuating circumstances here. Will the two Third Level men come forward?"

"That means us," Torstein muttered, and with Ed siding him he stalked grimly down the length of the long hall. The last mile?

"Young," said the Regent, surveying them. "I did not realize you were so young. Do you know where you are ?"

Ed said the one word, "No." Then he added, "But we're not on Earth, that's for sure."

"Don't jump to conclusions. You are on Earth. A different Earth. There are, you see, many Earths."

Torstein looked puzzled. "Better repeat that."

"Consider," explained the Regent, "At every moment in history, a decision has to be made. One decision means one sort of world, another means something else again. Did you know that a world exists on which the conqueror—what's his name, Hitler?...enslaved all Earth?"

Torstein started to say something.

"Wait...don't interrupt," continued the Regent. "What I mean is this: space curves back in on itself along with the whole universe, interlocking bubbles curved in four-dimensional space. In each bubble there is a different Earth, the point of departure being a complete break in historical continuity."

"Hold on." Torstein held up his hand. "Hold on...please. I read something like that once, long ago. Worlds of If, you mean. If such-and-such happened, we'd have a world like this, but if something else happened—"

"Now you're getting the idea, young man. Here on the first level, a scientist named Isaac Newton did not stop with his laws of gravity. You know of Newton?"

"Sure," Ed told him.

"Well, he went much further here, discovering several centuries ago what Einstein discovered only recently on your world. And that led us to the interlocking dimensions, as it will probably lead your version of Earth in another two hundred years. It also gave us a multi-dimensional headache."

"OH, I won't deny it. We receive a lot of valuable commodities from the many cultures on the various Earths. But secretly, because our paramount rule is lack of detection. The whole economy would be unbalanced if the other levels knew, which is why Colonel Utgard wants you destroyed." The Regent's stern face creased a smile. "I think he feels responsible. You see, years ago his division—under the original Utgard, his grandfather botched things up terribly, taking people from one level, placing them on another, that sort of thing. You'd be amazed at the havoc that could wreak with the probable sequence of events. You'd be—"

"That's very interesting," Torstein grunted. "But what I want to know is this: do we get killed, or don't we? And if we don't, can we take Freya with us and go home?"

"Patience, young man, patience... You'll have me believing Utgard is right. Did you know that your sister Freya belongs on another level? Now, the law states that if a man lives on the wrong level—and, mind you, that has happened in several cases because of the botch-job done by Utgard's grandfather—he must be returned instantly. We've been cleaning up on that for years now, with still a lot of work to go, the theory being that the curves of Probability in each dimension can be altered by such dislocation.

"However, Colonel Welcome has proposed an interesting theory. He does not think we are ethically justified in our action. Someone lives all his life on one level and, right or wrong, that is his home. Nothing, he says, gives us the right to upset all the people involved—the families, the friends, you know, that sort of thing. You, my young friends, will be a test case."

By now, Ed's brain was whirling.

He couldn't deny, he could only believe, and belief left a jumble of impossible concepts...

"What do you mean, we'll be a test case?"

"This, our decision is not immutable. The girl Freya has been returned to her true level, where a life has been prepared for her. We will give you one of our ships—and you may try to find her."

Ed leaped forward impulsively, shook the withered old hand. He'd expected death—and got this instead. "Thank you, sir. On which level can we find Freya?"

"On the Fourth."

"Thank you. That shouldn't be too hard. We'll have a whole Earth to search, but there should be some hints." A different Earth among many different Earths in a universe of probable worlds. But there it was...

"It isn't as simple as that, young man." There exist on each level a dozen Earths. The level merely designates the cultural status of the world in question."

"Okay, which world?"

The old man shook his head. "Oh, no. You're on your own. You find out, then you try to get her. With these conditions, too, I might add: First, if you find her, if you can return her to your own Earth, I think we will agree to open up inter-dimensional travel for your people. Second, if you cannot find her, the whole adventure is forgotten, the events are erased from your minds hypnotically, and that's that. Third, if you find her and she refuses to go with you; she remains on the Fourth Level, you return here so that Colonel Utgard may dispose of you in any way he selects."

And, when Ed started to say something: "Enough, young man. You have received my decision. No more! I have spoken."

Something told Ed the third condition might turn out to be the sleeper. Why on Earth—why on multiple Earths—would Freya refuse to return once they found her? And where did the old hag fit in? No one here on Level One had even mentioned her. Yet, except for her mysterious understanding of the whole setup, they wouldn't be here at all.

As he strode back across the hall, these thoughts chased one another around inside his head. But they cleared out fast when he spotted Colonel Utgard standing off by himself in a quiet but all the more furious rage.

Said Torstein, as they left the hall with a smiling Colonel Welcome, "I don't think we've seen the last of that devil."

Ed agreed, and it didn't make him happy.

CHAPTER FOUR

"GOODBYE, my young friends," said Colonel Welcome, leading them to their ship the following day. "Searching one planet would be a life's work, and you have *twelve*. Good luck—"

"We owe our chance to you," Ed told him. "If there's any way we can repay—"

"Ridiculous!" Welcome roared. "Payment enough, if you succeed, if I can see that Utgard knocked down a peg or two. But a warning, lads: watch him. He has freedom between the worlds, you know. He can travel back and forth at will. And he may give you trouble."

"Don't I know it," Torstein nodded. "We'll look out—"

"And listen," Welcome confided.

"I'm not permitted to tell you where you can find Freya Haugland, but that is the only restriction. Would it perhaps help if I informed you where you might find an old hag who lived on your Earth once, but who was relocated to a Fourth Level world? Not necessarily the same world as Freya's, but Fourth Level nonetheless?"

"Would it!" Ed cried. "You're damned right."

"Well, you'll find an instrument panel in this ship. Four big levers, one for each level. Twelve notches on each one, each notch for a known world. There are others between the notches, an infinity of unknown Earths, unexplored. The work is slow. At any rate, you will find your hag's world if you use the fourth lever and its ninth notch. Again—good luck..."

"One thing more," said Torstein. "That is, if you can answer it. What causes a change of size?"

"That's simple. You'll observe that strong electromagnetic energy is needed to activate the ships. The aurora, an electrical storm, the inside of a powerful electrical device: That energy is merely for relocation in space. Infinitely more is needed for dimensional hopping, as we call it. The atoms of your body must be squeezed together, temporarily, yielding the energy of the inter-atomic forces, which bind them together. Do I make myself clear?"

"No," Torstein laughed. "But forget it. We'll see you again, Colonel Welcome?"

"I hope so."

"Goodbye," Ed called, climbing within the ship.

"Goodbye, and don't forget Utgard..."

Ed pulled the circular door shut, bolted it, and turned to face the same bare cubicle—except that this time a series of levers hung from the far wall.

"What are we waiting for?" Torstein crossed to the wall, examined the instruments. "Twelve on each one, ah, here we are, last lever, ninth notch. You know, I'll feel strange seeing the hag again after all these years."

"The hag, sure. And after that, Freya. Pull that thing whenever you want, Tor."

Torstein did, and a giant hand slammed them both down into a black pit as the ship gathered its tremendous energies and roared away from the First Level.

THEY LEFT the ship behind them in a forest glen, bright sunlight shining down on it through the foliage in fantastic patterns. The ninth world out of twelve on the Fourth Level. But, Ed wondered, how do you go about finding one ancient woman on a totally new world?

"Don't worry," Torstein advised cheerfully. "The hag has a way of making her presence felt."

He failed to grasp the magnitude of the problem, and Ed told him that. "Look—this is an alternate Earth. Seven continents, millions of square miles of land. Back on our Earth, did anyone in New York ever hear of your Norwegian hag?"

"I did."

"Sure, but you're an exception. Anyone else, except for Freya? All I want to know is this: how do we even start looking for her?"

"Why, we simply ask the first person we meet. The hag has a name, and that should help. She's Elsa Thorssen." Torstein began to whistle an old Norse tune.

Dust appeared on the road far ahead of them, a small swirling cloud of it. Soon they descried an old horse-drawn cart, its driver perched high on a pile of colorful cloths. Torstein hailed him, but it wasn't necessary. With much swearing at his horse, he pulled the cart to a stop when he reached them.

"Can I deliver you anywhere?" the middle-aged merchant demanded, smiling out at them from under a mop of unkempt hair and a great bristling moustache.

"That depends," said Torstein.

"We're looking for a hag, upwards of a hundred years old, perhaps, who calls herself Elsa Thorssen."

The merchant laughed. "Well, I suppose you wayfarers must have your little joke. Magitrix blessings on you then, if I can't take you anywhere."

"Who's joking?" said Torstein. "I only asked—"

"Don't they all? A cousin of mine, on my mother's side, waited for an audience with the Magitrix for five years. Far as I know, he still waits. You have to know someone who knows someone who…well, you get the idea, I think."

Torstein placed his big hand against the side of the cart. "I take it you know Elsa Thorssen?"

"No. But I know of her. Everyone does. Say, are you serious? I'm heading for the city of the Magitrix myself."

"How far?" Ed wanted to know.

"Just four or five miles up the road. But everyone also knows that. Just who are you two, with those foolish questions, and that clothing?"

What was it the Regent had told them? Above all, this matter of parallel worlds must be kept a secret, else a serious disruption of economy on all worlds might result. "Like you said," Ed told the merchant, "we're a couple of wayfarers, new in this part of the country. Will you give us a lift to the city?"

"Give you a lift? What does that mean? Oh, will I take you? Certainly, certainly. Climb in."

The cart groaned and creaked its protest as they did so, and the stout horse strained at his harness, but soon they went bumping and clattering down the uneven road. "Magitrix blessings on us all," intoned the merchant as they started on their way.

THEY STOOD in an anteroom, lavish, richly furnished. "So he brings us here, says this is the Palace of the Magitrix," Ed muttered. "What does that mean? Will we find your hag here? Will we come any closer to Freya?"

"If you have some patience—" Torstein began, but then they had reached a large circular desk, and the matronly woman behind it said, "Magitrix blessings, young men. May I help you?"

"Does anyone here know an Elsa Thorssen? Torstein scowled. "I was led to believe we might find her here."

The matronly woman's face split into a broad grin. "Some people will try anything to get in. Don't tell me you don't know whether she's here or not?"

"I merely asked a question."

"Very well." The smile vanished.

"She is here and I know her. Now what?"

"We'd like to see her."

"So would a couple of hundred million other people. But few ever do. I could arrange an appointment with one of the acolytes—"

"Madam," Torstein broadened his A-vowels and sounded almost fawning; Ed tried to hide his smile, had to cough to cover up his laughter. "Madam," said Torstein, "have you access to Elsa Thorssen?"

"I do."

"Will you be good enough to inform her that Torstein Haugland has arrived to see her? Please?"

The woman snapped her fingers and a youth hopped up to her desk, after parting a curtain and stepping quickly out of an alcove.

"Torstein Haugland here," the woman told the boy, who skipped back inside his alcove again. They waited five minutes, and then ten.

Fifteen.

The boy came out again, flushed of face and panting. "Magitrix blessings, all."

"Magessings." The matronly woman rolled it all together.

"Torstein Haugland may enter, with this reservation: if he is not Torstein Haugland but merely claims to be, his head will find itself on a refuse dump."

"You mean if he's who he says he is she'll see him?"

"That's what they told me."

"Twenty years behind this desk," the matronly woman mused. "I've seen them come and I've seen them go—the rich, the poor, people who thought they had influence, people who just hoped— and she saw almost no one. Now these two...well, Magessings, I always say. You may follow the boy."

THEY DID, through the heavy draperies and into his alcove. Inside, he opened a door, bowed low and ushered them into a long, well-lit tunnel. Ed got the impression that the way wound underground and since the building had seemed quite unimposing on its ground level, he did not know what to expect.

The tunnel opened out on—splendor.

A great, high-vaulted chamber, its upper walls lost in haze, its ceiling only half-seen through flitting, coruscating swirls of light. Great marble columns soared up toward the haze, lost themselves in the curtain of light. Ed's feet sank almost to the ankles in rich carpeting which could have been one incredible expanse of ermine, kept somehow virgin white.

"By the Elder Gods!" Torstein swore. "Someone sure knows how to live in style."

"The hag? You think it's your Elsa Thorssen?"

"Bah! How could that be? I remember she used to like the simple things, except when it came to magic and witchery. The hag wouldn't know what to do with all this luxury."

Ed chuckled. "You know, if this is where they took Freya, I almost wouldn't have the heart to ask her to leave."

"I doubt it. Remember, Colonel Welcome said that while he couldn't tell us that, he could tell us how to find the hag. No, I think my sister lives elsewhere."

The boy led them to a door at the far end of the huge wall, said, "Magitrix blessings. You go in there."

Ed tried the door, opened it, entered with Torstein. A simple room, sparsely furnished, and another door. No, Ed observed two of them. Two doors, half a dozen paces apart, identical in every respect. Strange, the boy hadn't given any instructions. And had he been laughing at some secret joke when he scurried away?

A little doubtful, Ed hung back, but Torstein boldly tried the right-hand door.

A FURIOUS growling issued forth. Came a clanking of chains, and something hideous peered out at them. "Close the damned thing!" Ed cried, rushing forward and putting his shoulder to the door. It refused to budge, even when Torstein added his great strength.

Warily, they backed away, observed that the chained monster couldn't fit through the aperture. Its neck, however, could, and it was endowed with plenty of neck, a dozen feet of great serpentine muscles, ending in a flat head with red-rimmed little eyes. A tongue flicked in and out of the foot-long jaw as the neck wagged back and forth, sending the head out exploring in all directions.

Torstein picked up a chair and hurled it. It struck the beast squarely across its snout, and it growled indignantly, searching about with its tiny eyes.

Fascinated, Torstein stood and watched, but Ed grabbed his arm and pulled him away. "If you want to be that thing's dinner, stay right here!"

"What can we do? Don't tell me you're going to leave."

"There's another door, remember? Maybe we'll find your hag through there. Of all the crazy receptions…"

They skirted the dragon-like thing, and Ed got a brief glimpse of its monstrous bulk through the partially opened door. Only its girth and a taut chain which Ed could see at the base of its neck, prevented it from coming all the way out. Still, that neck could rove the entire antechamber…

"Okay," Torstein said grimly when they reached the other door. "My luck seems to have petered out on the last one. Suppose you try."

For a moment Ed waited. Could that monster be a prelude to something more fearful? But why? They'd merely asked to see Elsa Thorssen, and although the matronly woman had displayed considerable surprise, Tor's name seemed capable of opening all locks. Further—but Ed stopped his pondering and flattened himself against the door when the monster head flicked close, weaved away for a moment, then started to come back.

He pushed the door in.

The woman who shrieked, "Come in, come in!" and then shut the door against the extended head of the monster could have been Methuselah's grandmother. A black cowl framed her withered face with its shrunken cheeks and slit-like mouth. The deep-set eyes alone appeared young, staring out anxiously from their skin-folds.

SHE HOBBLED about them for a time, chattering meaninglessly to herself. Then she said, almost merrily, "Torstein, which one is Torstein? Of course, I'd recognize you anywhere. My, you've grown."

She prodded Tor's ribs with a boney paw of a hand, then began to cackle. "Did you come here just to find me, Tor? And how is little Freya, eh?"

Torstein growled, "Do I say 'Magitrix blessings' first? Everyone in this crazy place seems to say it."

"That's up to me in this room," the hag confided. "Do you like the way I speak English, Tor? Everyone speaks it here, and so I had to learn it. Now, what did you say? Oh—no one has to say it in this room. You see, I am the Magitrix. I rule this world."

"I give up," Torstein said. "Better explain."

"There's nothing to explain, young Tor. I belong here, I never should have been on your Earth at all. I came of my own free will, and so they didn't have to strike any memories from my mind. Everyone laughed when I knew the old magic, eh? Everyone doubted, but I have flitted about among the parallel worlds, and I know how to summon the First Level ships. Now, what are you here for?

"Wait…I hope the reception outside didn't frighten you. They run everything on this world by chance. If someone's granted an interview with me, he still must run the risk of becoming an appetizer for my little dinosaur outside. You see, they put every-thing to use, and dinosaurs still live here. It's a crazy, superstitious world, Tor—but don't go telling that to my subjects."

Tor said, "This man here is Ed Langdon. He is to marry our Freya."

The hag circled Ed two or three times, looking at him from every direction. "He's not a Norther," she muttered. "Do you approve, Tor? I'm glad you brought him here for my approval."

"Yes, I approve. And I didn't bring him here for any such thing. Listen." Quickly, Torstein sketched in all that had happened.

When he finished, the hag shook her head sadly. "So they took her back. They took her once, you remember, long ago. What would you have me do? Because I rescued her once, it doesn't mean I can do it again. Travel between the parallel worlds is a strain, as you must know, and now I am well past fifty."

"I'll say," Tor grinned.

ED SPOKE for the first time. "We came for one reason only. If you rescued Freya once, then you know where they took her. We want you to tell us what you know."

"Well, she's here on the Fourth Level."

"You mean right here on your world?" Ed demanded.

"I did not say that. There are twelve worlds on the Fourth Level of culture. This is the ninth. Freya's—"

"Yes?" Torstein leaned forward eagerly.

"I don't know if I should tell you. If I do, you'll only go scampering off again, before I've even had time to appreciate your visit, young Tor. Maybe I ought to tease you for a while."

"If you do—remember when I used to go around chasing you with a broomstick when I was a child?"

"Heh, heh—and did you think I cared? I enjoyed it. You can't use coercion, Torstein. Perhaps I may suggest a compromise."

"Go ahead," Ed suggested, but Torstein was fuming.

"Well, when you find her, why don't you all come here to live? After I die—I'm well past fifty, you know Freya can become the Magitrix."

Torstein seemed too angry to speak, but Ed told the hag, "That's ridiculous. We came to bring Freya back to Earth, to our own Earth, and that's what we'll do, with or without your help."

"I like him," the hag cackled. "He may not be a Norther, but he acts like one."

For a while it looked like Torstein had swallowed his tongue, but now he managed to say, "What's your answer?"

"I will suggest another compromise," the hag said brightly.

"Bah, you senile—"

There was no stopping the hag. She laughed and stamped her foot up and down. "That's wonderful. Did you know that your grandfather called me that, too?"

Torstein smiled in spite of himself. "How can that be? You're only past fifty." Then he sobered: "Listen, we don't ask much. I want my sister, Ed wants his sweetheart. You know where they've taken her. Talk."

"I said I will suggest another compromise. If you two will agree to stay for dinner, then perhaps I will tell you. Perhaps."

"Of all the bothersome old hags," Torstein began, making Elsa Thorssen grin from ear to ear, "you are the worst. Every moment might be important, and you—"

"It's only a few hours," Ed admitted. "We'll stay, provided you take the maybe out of your conditions. You'll tell us, definitely."

"We-ell—all right. Agreed."

"By the Elder Gods!" Torstein cried. "She likes you. I never knew her to make a definite statement to any man…"

The dinosaur head and neck had vanished from the anteroom when they crossed back through it with Elsa Thorssen, and the hag merely went to the second door and bolted it, chuckling something about a mighty hungry critter. They'd fit that description too, Ed realized. It'd been a long time since they'd sat down to a decent meal. And just how long had it been since the Hendrix television set acted as a conductor for the blue ship? Not long, not really, but it could have been years since last he'd seen Freya…

CHAPTER FIVE

THEY ATE dinner in a huge hall, although the original high-vaulted underground chamber would have dwarfed it. With them at the table sat a dozen other black-cow led figures—acolytes, as the hag explained. And even in the brief time it takes to eat a meal, Ed could see just how much living on this particular alternate Earth depended on chance.

The main dish came in individual platters, each covered by a shining metal dome. When an acolyte lifted the dome, he found either a savory slab of roast ham or a mess of gruel! Maybe the gruel was nourishing, Ed didn't know. But it looked terrible. And the acolytes who received the substitute didn't bat an eyelash. That was the way you lived—according to a chance. Afterwards, performers trouped out into the hall, and once a young dancing girl tripped and fell. She regained her feet almost immediately, and slunk off into a corner while the nearest acolyte grunted something to a waiting guard. The man nodded, led the girl away.

"She'll be imprisoned for five years," explained the hag.

"What for?" Ed wanted to know. "Well, it depends on the disposition of the nearest acolyte when such an accident occurs. Had he inclined himself toward mercy, she'd have continued dancing. But, you see, that particular acolyte received a plate of gruel instead of his roast ham, and he wasn't feeling too happy about it. So he took it out on the girl. Of course, it could have worked the other way, but then all things have a way of equalizing."

"Just what do you do here?" Torstein asked.

"Once in a while someone balks at the system. When that happens, he applies for an audience with me. But I can always refuse, which I often do if I feel that chance alone had brought on the man's troubles."

"She wanted us to bring Freya here," Torstein said. "She's crazy!"

"Perhaps, perhaps. Anyway, that is past, for I said I will tell you how to find the girl. Are you sure you won't stay another day?"

"We're sure," Ed informed her.

And Torstein said, "Talk..."

"First world of the Fourth Level, my young friends. I suppose this is goodbye..."

Tears welling up in her eyes, she led them back through a tunnel, through the first great hall, and finally up to ground level. She prodded a uniformed man with her knobby hand.

"You!"

"Ye-es, Magitrix!" Apparently Elsa Thorssen didn't make a habit of hob-nobbing with common soldiery.

"You are to take my two friends where they direct you. After you leave them, you are to forget what you see."

"How can I do that?"

IT WAS important, Ed knew, because the hag alone on this world knew of the parallel Earths. And she must keep her secret.

"Oh, you will do it. And I grant you an audience in advance. Next time chance plays you a mean trick, I will see you and pass judgment. Now, go."

"Magitrix bless—"

"Poo! Don't give me my own blessings. Begone. Get your horse and carriage ready." Then, after he had departed: "Goodbye and good luck, my two young friends. And Edward?"

"Yes?"

"When you find Freya—if you find her—make her happy. Do that, or I promise I'll find a way to haunt you."

"Oh, he'll make her happy, " Torstein grinned. "You should see how in love they are..."

The hag wiped a tear from her cheek with a corner of the black cowl. "Is there something you'd like to know before you leave?"

Ed nodded. "On the First Level, a Colonel Welcome told us that even if we found Freya, we might have trouble taking her back. Why?"

"Colonel Welcome! Ah, yes—a nice young man, if a bit on the portly side. I know him well. I remember—"

"Ed's question," Torstein suggested. "What about that?"

"Well, Colonel Welcome is right. First, they will erase the memories from Freya's mind and, while dim shadows might remain, she may not know you at all. But more important than that, the first world on the Fourth Level is an Earth ruled by women! It parted from your own world an age ago, when a decisive battle was fought between the ancient Greeks and the mythical Amazons. Except that in the world where they have taken Freya, the Amazons won. So they rule, and don't ask me what it is, but something on that world makes women a match for men physically. Some men are stronger, some women are. It depends entirely upon the individual, but the women have ruled for thousands of years, and they intend to keep things that way."

Ed frowned. "Why should that make our job more difficult?"

"Well, add it to the fact that Freya won't remember you. She's liable to get angry, blacken your eye or have one of her friends do it, mop up the floor with you, and send you off packing! Well, goodbye—and don't say I failed to warn you..."

"Parallel worlds," Torstein mouthed his disapproval. "Women should stay at home, caring for the young ones."

Outside, their coach and driver waited for them. As they clattered away, Elsa Thorssen waved goodbye in the gathering darkness.

ED ORDERED their driver to stop a few hundred yards short of the grove of trees that hid their ship, and with Torstein he waited until the man had driven away. Night had come, but a full moon hung high in the heavens, lighting their way.

"Here we are," Torstein said after a time. "See how the moonlight gleams on that blue hull. See—"

"Shh!" Ed raised a finger to his lips for silence. Strange, the door stood ajar, but they'd left it closed. Something appeared briefly in the doorway. A dim shadow, hardly more than that. But the shadow of a man...

Ed ran forward, saw the shadow dart away and plunge into the woods. Ed followed, hunching his shoulders and forcing his way through the thickets and dense undergrowth.

Closer, closer...he dove, grabbed running legs, and brought the cursing man down. They rolled over and over, struggling, striking out blindly in wooded darkness that the moon failed to penetrate.

"Where are you?" Torstein called, crashing through the undergrowth. "I can't see you..."

The man got to his feet, but Ed clambered up after him, and they locked together once more. Strong, whoever he was, and grimly determined to get away.

For a moment, Ed lost his footing in the tangled matting of vines and creepers. But it was enough. The man probed out in the darkness, touched his face briefly. Ed still swung his hands out wildly to regain his balance, and an instant later a fist crashed against his jaw.

Ed toppled, fell, heard the man scurrying away. He started to get up, more than a little groggy, but Torstein chose that moment to discover the scene of the fight, and plunging in blindly, he stumbled against Ed and they both fell in a heap.

""There is he!" Tor cried. "I don't hear him now!"

"No." Ed rubbed his jaw, which had begun to throb. "He got away, whoever he was."

"Well, we'd better see."

THEY FANNED out through the woods and searched, but in the darkness it proved a hopeless task. Wearily, Ed led the way back to their ship. They entered, found the wall panels glowing with dull light.

"At least we can see what damage has been done," Torstein said.

"Yeah? How? We don't know a thing about this ship, except what levers we have to press. We won't discover anything, Tor, not if we search from now till next week."

"Well, if the hag hadn't detained us—"

Ed shrugged. "What's done is done. And she sure as hell had nothing to do with it, Tor. Remember Colonel Welcome's warning. Utgard didn't like us one bit, and he liked even less what the Regent had decided. It would be easy for him to send a man here and foul up our ship."

"Yes? How could he know where we went? Certainly Welcome would not have told him."

"So what? Don't forget, we don't know a thing about this. Maybe they have a way of tracing ships between the parallel worlds, something like radar. I don't know."

"Then the important thing is this: shall we just forget the whole thing and set out for Freya's world? We could call the hag to look at the ship."

Ed shook his head. "No, we've spent enough time here already. Besides, that guy is liable to return."

"You want to go?"

"I want to go," Ed nodded eagerly. Maybe someone had tampered with the ship. Well, that was a chance they would just have to take.

Ed crossed to the controls, pulled the fourth lever all the way down to its first notch.

The now-familiar force of acceleration gripped them, crushed them to the floor. Even the blackout became familiar...

"HERE WE are," Torstein said later, opening the door. "See, you were right, we didn't have anything to worry about."

Anxiously, Ed stuck his head outside. Bright sunshine greeted him, and he saw a fertile plain rolling to the horizon in all directions. A nice world—

Abruptly, he pulled his head back inside and slammed the door.

"What's the matter?" Tor demanded.

"Nothing much, damn it. Except that this isn't the right world."

"How can you tell so quick?"

"Well, I poked my head out and things looked real nice. But then something came bouncing up over a low hill, and I knew we got the wrong address."

"Something? What?"

"A grasshopper."

"A grasshopper?"

"That's what I said, a grasshopper. Only it was about as big as the two of us, standing end on end, and we aren't exactly shrimps, Tor."

Torstein scowled. "Wait a minute. Wait a minute, don't get excited. Couldn't that mean that we merely remained small? You must get smaller, you know, along with the ship, to release inter-atomic energies."

"Sure, but you also have to get larger again. That's the way it works. The last stage is automatic, Tor. Welcome told me that, so we'll have to let it go."

"Then what do you think happened?"

"I don't know, but I can guess. If something as peculiar—and probably dangerous—as grasshoppers twice the size of men…"

"I see. If something like that existed on Freya's Earth, the hag would have warned us."

"Sure. And you know what that means? Whoever tampered with the controls fixed it so the ship wouldn't go where we directed. This world outside, Tor, is a place where insects and not men became the dominant creatures. Let's take a look."

They opened the door for only a few moments, but it was enough. Another giant grasshopper came bounding into view, chasing a tiny furry creature for dinner. Great wings droned overhead, and a flight of bees as big as men, striped brilliant yellow and black, flashed down at them.

Torstein slammed the door and turned to the controls as the bees drummed against their ship, shaking it. "What now? There are four levers, twelve notches on each. Forty-eight possible worlds. Do we have to stop at all?"

Ed shrugged hopelessly. "I guess so. It—it's worse than that, Tor. Remember, Welcome said that the notches stood for known worlds, but there might be an infinity of unknown ones. If the guy did a good job on this crate, we may have to look at a thousand worlds. Maybe more. And it won't be this easy each time to tell we're at the wrong place…"

Torstein paced back and forth. He smiled, but weakly. "Well, we're young. Want to start now?"

"I don't see there's anything else we can do. Lord, what a mess. And Freya—"

"Take a number," Torstein said.

"Any number. Third lever, seventh notch—coming up!"

A CLOUDY day. The outskirts of a small city. An orchard, with lush apples ripening on the trees. They appeased their hunger, found a brook and did the same for their thirst, and then a man approached them.

"We're strangers here," Ed began.

"You're telling me, fellow! What the devil is that blue contraption?" The thickset man pointed at their ship.

"Never mind," Ed told him. "I have a question to ask you, and please answer it, no matter how strange it sounds."

"What's this? You from a quiz contest or something? Okay, okay, I'll answer."

"Well," Ed felt foolish asking it, but they couldn't waste the time it would take to explore around. "Who's boss in your family, you or your wife?" If the latter alternative proved the correct one, the man would not be ashamed to answer that way, since it followed in accordance with the cultural pattern.

"Ho-ho! That's rich," the thickset man roared.

"What's so funny?"

"Who's boss, me or my wife? Son, I have sixteen of 'em, sixteen wives. Which one did you have in mind?"

"Forget it," Torstein said, turning back to the ship. "Wrong world." Scratching his head, the man watched them climb into the sleek blue thing. Thunder and lightning darted down from the sky quite suddenly as the ship grew smaller and then disappeared. Shaken and afraid, the thickset man returned to his home and his sixteen wives.

UTTERLY FLAT, the gleaming whiteness stretched off in all directions, dotted here and there with circular pits. From one of these pits, a long, cigar-shaped projectile pointed straight up at the sky. Abruptly it flashed up and away, leaving a glowing mass of slag in the white pit. A car whisked up, and attendants sprayed the slag, which hissed violently.

Ed stood at the portal of their blue craft, mouth agape. "You see that, Tor? Know what it is?"

Torstein shook his head, shrugged his giant shoulders.

"A world where they've conquered space travel." Ed spoke in an awed, husky voice. "How I'd like to see—but it's the wrong place, Tor. Again, the hag would have mentioned it..."

They re-entered their ship, and the thunderstorm that followed made the spraying of the pit-slag unnecessary.

"HEIL HITLER!" The black-shirted figure raised his hand in a stiff salute.

Torstein grinned wearily. "Here's the world where old Adolph got his way. It's hard to believe, isn't it?"

"What did you say?" The soldier saw their ship for the first time and mouthed an unknown command in German. Shrugging, Ed and Torstein turned away, but the man whipped a revolver from its holster, motioned them to stand still.

Torstein dove at him and the gun went off wildly, creasing a furrow along the side of the ship. The struggle was brief and, when Torstein got to his feet, the soldier lay there without moving. Torstein picked up the gun, strapped the holster and cartridge belt around his own waist. "These might come in handy," he muttered, and they were on their way again...

A HIGH, rocky crag overlooking the sea on one side and stretching out to a barren, desolate wasteland on the other. Not a single tree, nor an insect. Not even the faintest odor of growing things. Nothing...

"What the hell is this place?" Torstein demanded. "How did we wind up over a desert? We haven't moved in space, Ed. We should come out over the same spot in each of the parallel worlds."

Below them, the surf roared against the foot of the crag, pounding out its fury in white froth.

"Geography might be different," Ed said doubtfully, looking about the drab surface of the promontory. A natural fault in the rocks had formed where it jutted out over the sea and, although the going proved difficult, they climbed down it, half-sliding from rock to rock, and finally reached the narrow beach.

Ed strode out across the sand, waded into the water. He bent and cupped his hands, brought them to his face and sniffed. "It doesn't even smell like it should." He tasted it.

"Good Lord, Tor! Try it."

Torstein did, then scratched his head.

"It isn't the slightest bit salty," Ed told him.

"I don't get it."

"Wait...I think I do. This place is dead, completely dead. Probably we're the only living things on this Earth, Tor. Maybe here, in this parallel dimension, Earth didn't get born till a lot later. It's a new Earth, Tor. No life, no time yet for salt in its oceans."

"Maybe," Torstein grunted. "But one thing's for sure; we won't find our Amazons here."

"Nor Freya," Ed nodded, leading the way back up the rocky crag.

A FLAT plain, and off in the distance what looked like a race-track with its long low grandstand and rambling stables. A strange, saurian smell came to their nostrils. "I don't know why," said Torstein, "but I don't think I like this place." He patted his holster, loosened its cover as they stalked out over the plain. They reached a grove of trees, entered it. From its other side, but still hidden by the foliage, they could see the racetrack.

It wasn't right. Ed didn't get it at first, because they still were far away, and the audience in the grandstand consisted of many thousands of tiny dots.

They crept closer, out of the woods altogether. But as the saurian smell grew stronger, Torstein's caution was somehow conveyed to Ed. They crouched as they moved forward, finally reaching the oval track itself at a point directly across from the grandstands. A race was in progress and, obscured by dust, the riders came thundering toward them.

Closer—closer—and Torstein let out a yelp!

The steeds were men and women.

Five sweating, struggling men, as many women. All naked, all with bridles and saddles and bits in their mouths. Strange reptilian things clung to their backs, used tiny whips to goad them on.

Her long legs flashing, a female steed took the lead, but a male, goaded on by the alien jockey, closed in and boxed her against the rail. She missed stride, stumbled—and the male went on to win by a considerable margin. Just like at the pony-tracks...

"All right," said Torstein. "I'm dumb. But I don't get it."

"I think I do," Ed told him as, a little sick over what they'd just witnessed, they stumbled back through the woods and toward their waiting ship. "Human animals, and creatures who rule over them. But did you ever see creatures like that, Tor?"

Torstein shook his head in bewilderment.

"Alien, that's what. Completely alien. Creatures from another world, coming to Earth in this parallel dimension and conquering us completely..."

THEIR SHIP was surrounded by a tight little ring of the green saurians!

"Want to become a thoroughbred?" Torstein grinned.

"It isn't funny, Tor. Do you think they'll go away?"

"They don't give any signs of it.

What do we do, hide in the woods?"

"I don't—uh-oh! They've spotted us."

The dozen saurians, each no more than four feet high, walking upright on incredibly bow-legged limbs, peering out of huge lidless eyes, approached them. Two or three of them held whips, long, lead-tipped things, much larger than those Ed had seen at the track. One flicked his whip, and it streaked out with a vague hissing sound, curling around Torstein's shoulder and bringing blood to his shirt before it was withdrawn. Torstein roared his rage. But he also dropped the gun.

Ed darted forward, picked it up, and said, "If you went to the races, even if you were an official, you wouldn't carry a weapon, would you? Maybe a whip for the horses if you worked in the stables, but that's all."

One of the creatures flung its forelimb back, prepared to use the lash again. Ed pumped a shot at him, felt the gun snap back against his palm. The slug blew a hole the size of a baseball in the creature's gut. It slumped to the ground, green liquid oozing out.

The other creatures grunted and hissed among themselves, but when Ed snapped off two more shots and when two more of them fell to the ground, they backed away.

Another shot—and they were running.

"They'll come back..." Ed panted. "With some kind of weapon, I think. Let's get the hell out of here."

Tor needed no prompting. They ran to the ship, reached it just as the last of the saurian masters of an alternate Earth disappeared within the woods.

It had been a long time since Ed felt anything better than the crushing force of acceleration...

CHAPTER SIX

NIGHT. DULL fires glowed far off on the horizon, and overhead they heard a roaring of planes. Something white mushroomed up many miles away, something brighter than the sun at high noon. Temporarily, it blinded them, and the roaring concussion that followed threw them flat on the ground.

Dazed, Ed crawled to Torstein, began to see vague shadows through his tearing eyes. A dull silhouette, the ship loomed before them.

"Atomic war," Torstein said as they staggered back inside. "By the Elder Gods, how I hope it stays right here. I'd hate to see that on our own Earth."

"It's bad enough either way," Ed agreed. "Same Earth, really. Same kinds of people. Maybe if some of those Ruskies on our Earth could see this, they'd cool off a little…"

A HUGE metal thing lumbered forward as they came out of the ship. Its arms clanging against its sides, it stopped before them. "Greetings, masters. But I thought all the masters were dead."

"A robot!" Tor cried incredulously. "A robot that can talk and think!"

Ed addressed the metal monster.

"What do you mean, all the masters are dead?"

"They killed each other off with a plague," the hollow voice boomed. "We robots weren't affected, of course. But we don't know what to do. Can I serve you in any way? Here, tell me where you're going and I'll carry you. I can bring a companion to carry your friend," the monster added hopefully.

"Keep away," Ed told him. "We're not going anyplace. We're leaving right now."

The robot looked hurt, blinking metallic lids over its eyes. "Are you sure, master?"

"I am sure."

The robot clanked off slowly, its metal shoulders slumped.

"So here man's work lives after him," Torstein said, shaking his head sadly.

DAYS PASSED. Weeks. They lost all track of time. World governed by a great cybernetics machine. Decadent world where men and women mated quite dispassionately when their eugenics agency prescribed it. Earth of hairy, squat sub-men. A world where the United States had never fought its revolution against England, where Britain still ruled supreme. A place in which Christ had not been born, where men still worshipped idols and pagan gods. A world—all the worlds of infinite possibility.

Sometimes they stayed long enough to eat. Sometimes they remained in their ship for hours on end to rest. Three or four more times, the German gun stood between them and death, but they reached a point where they had to count out the cartridges and, finally, in a peaceful garden of a world, where men had not known war or a lethal weapon for five hundred years, they discarded the revolver and threw away the empty cartridge belt. Idly, Ed wondered what the denizens would think of the ugly snub-nosed thing.

Their beards grew, and Torstein looked more like a Viking every day. He shook his head in mock horror at the black stubble on Ed's chin and told him that a Viking would rather shave his face bare than stare in the mirror at a black beard.

Torstein's beard grew curly, and he said, "You know, for years I wanted one of these things, but every time I started to let it grow, Freya would march in on one of her visits and produce a razor and a shaving mug. My sister is pretty set in her ways, Ed."

"Yes...Freya," Ed mused. "I wonder, will we ever see her again...?"

"Cut it out. Stop that. Of course we'll see her, Ed. We'll find her if it takes the rest of our lives!"

"I don't want any octogenarian wedding, thanks. We'll find her, and soon."

"Attaboy," Torstein roared his approval, sounding utterly unlike the Viking he looked.

A BARE grassland without trees. A hot sun overhead, and scores of men, bare to the waist, digging a long slit-trench and piling a high embankment up in front of it.

"They look like they're preparing for war," said Torstein.

"Uh-huh. And look at those weapons, will you?" Off to one side of the embankment lay piles of spears, of javelins, bows and arrows.

"Primitive," Ed grunted. "So at least we know we're back on the Fourth Level."

Beyond a low hill was their ship, and the profusion of great trees there made up for the lack of them on the grassy plain. The blue hull would be well hidden, Ed was thinking. And then he forgot all about it.

Someone approached them.

A woman, quite beautiful, and dressed so they could see it. Tall and lithe and sun-bronzed, she strode forward, garbed only in a brief kirtle, which fell from navel to mid-thigh. Her shoulders were strong, but gently curved and feminine. And still more gently curved and more feminine were her bare breasts...

"Just what do you two think you're doing, loafing like that?" she demanded, a quiet authority in her voice.

"We're new here," Ed began. "We'd like to—"

"Bah! No one is new here. Just who do you think you're kidding?"

The girl strode forward, her bare limbs flashing in the sunlight. Suddenly, she reached out, grabbing Ed's now-long shock of hair in her strong fingers. She did a quick half-pirouette, spinning a completely startled Ed around and sticking out her long, shapely leg. He stumbled over it and at the same time she let go of his hair. He fell in a heap at her feet.

Dazed, he looked up. She stood with hands on hips, glaring down at him insolently.

A broad grin split Torstein's face.

"Ed," he said, "I think we have arrived."

"NOW WILL you two get back into line and dig those trenches?"

Ed got to his feet. "Look at our clothing," he protested. "I said we're new here. And we'd like some information."

"Don't tell me what you'd like. I ordered you to dig those trenches. I meant it."

Ed faced her squarely. "I'm looking for a girl who—"

The woman moved with lightning speed. One moment she stood with hands on hips, apparently cocking an ear and listening to him. The next, her right fist flashed out and struck the point of Ed's jawbone. It hurt. It hurt a lot, but he wanted to stand there as if he could take it—and more of the same, because he had the feeling that they had to assert themselves now if they were to get any place. But what was it the hag had said? On Freya's world neither men nor women are the superior sex physically. It depends entirely on the individual.

Ed rocked with the blow, staggering back three steps, and the girl, smiling now, moved in on him. He couldn't fight with her, not with a woman. Yet that was what she wanted as she approached him. She hit him harder this time, again with her balled right fist, bringing it up from someplace below her waist.

The green plain, the men in the trenches, the wildly staring Torstein, the woman—all spun crazily. When they returned to normal, Ed sat on the ground with blood trickling from his nose. Torstein stood rooted to the spot, but the girl did not. She launched herself down at Ed, hitting him squarely with the force of her leap and stretching him out flat.

"Hey, cut it out," he pleaded, still unwilling to fight. With the advantage that she now had, he began to doubt that he could do anything about it even if he had wanted to. Something in the air, the hag had said, and, women are men's equals...

The girl sat astride his midsection, pumping lusty blows at his face with both fists. He squirmed, tried to get away, purely defensively, but she leaned forward and pinned his shoulders quite effectively with her knees, still striking trip-hammer blows at his face.

It couldn't he happening, he thought dimly. Except that it was. Left and right, left and right. His senses swam, and he heard the beautiful Amazon shouting, as if from far away, "Enough?"

"By the Elder Gods, enough!" Torstein cried. "You'll kill him if he doesn't fight back."

"Doesn't?" the girl laughed. "You mean can't." Nimbly, she jumped to her feet, and Ed lay there panting and thoroughly exhausted.

The girl grabbed Torstein's shirtfront and brought his face inches from her own. "Do you want more of the same? No? Then pick up your friend and march over to the trenches with him. Come on now. I want to see both of you digging inside of three minutes."

She released him and, shrugging, Torstein helped Ed to his feet, supported him with a shoulder as they walked to the trenches. The girl stood off to one side, looking very trim and lovely, and as completely feminine as any woman Ed had ever seen.

"HOW DO you feel?" Torstein asked, shoveling some dirt up on the embankment.

Ed leaned on the handle of his shovel. "Lousy, thanks."

Torstein laughed in spite of the situation. "She really gave you a licking, that slim girl."

"Slim, maybe. But her muscles were like iron, Tor. And—"

"You didn't want to fight back, did you? I mean, if you did, if you'd forgotten chivalry—"

"I don't know. I won't make any excuses. But she was strong, Tor. Maybe it would have been a good match, I don't know. But what the hell are we going to do now?"

"Don't look at me, Ed. But one thing I want us to decide. If it comes to fighting these Amazons again, we won't hold back. We can't. We want to find Freya, remember? And if on this world there is no sex distinction when it comes to physical activity, we're liable to get into a lot of trouble if we don't act accordingly. When you're in Rome, Ed—"

"Sure, sure." But Ed didn't feel that way at all. It was one thing to say it, and quite another to throw away a lifetime of tradition. Yet, that was exactly what they had to do, because the next time it could turn out to be a knife instead of bare fists, and if they didn't fight, they must at least protect themselves.

A whistle blew. Lunchtime. Kirtled girls, most of them pretty, came through the trenches, bringing buckets of some gruel which was ladled out into tin cups. Ed ate his gratefully, watched big Torstein take a second helping.

A man shuffled over to them, thirtyish, stoop-shouldered. "Mind if I join you, friends?"

"Not at all," said Torstein, introducing himself and Ed.

"Me," the little man said, "I'm Johnny Greengate. They captured me in their last attack on Pine Bluffs City. What about you two?"

"We're new here," Ed told him. "We come from far off."

"Oh," Johnny Greengate grunted. "I see. Maybe that explains why you didn't give up right away when Simmons—"

"Who?" Torstein demanded.

"The guard, Mary Lou Simmons. I was saying, maybe that explains why you tried to fight—"

"I didn't try to fight. It was all her idea."

"You coulda' said you surrendered. Anyway, you're new here, like you say. But lemme tell you this, brother—better keep outer her path. They say Mary Lou Simmons is a nice gal when she likes you, but otherwise—thunder and lightning, brother!"

"Go ahead. I'm listening."

"Not much more to say. Last week they held the Games. Once every full moon, you know. When it came to gymnastics, Mary Lou didn't do so hot. But fightin'—wow! I remember in the semi-finals she faced a big guy—big as your friend Haugland here--but she cut him down to size, all right, and they hadda' stop the carnage after a time. He was the hope of the men, too. If he won, we coulda' taken the trophy, first time in six months. Anyway, Mary Lou lost in the finals, but it was a close fight, and the gal who beat her was one o' them tall, graceful Nordic types. You know, beautiful as can be, but strong. Anyway, brother," he finished, as the whistle blew and the lunch buckets were removed, "better watch your step. I wouldn't want that Simmons gunning for me, nossir!" Then he quickly retrieved his shovel and began to dig furiously. "Speak of the devil…"

THE BRONZED girl, Mary Lou Simmons, stood at the lip of the trench. "You…"

"Me?" Greengate demanded, paling. "No, that one. The guy I had to hit. You."

"Yes?" Ed raised his head. He hoped she wouldn't want to start all over again, because he knew he'd not be able to follow Torstein's sound advice.

"I—I'm sorry about before. Maybe I should have noticed your clothing, I don't know. Shake?"

She leaned down…extended her hand. Ed took it and she shook hands with him gravely, man-to-man fashion. "Are you really new here?" she wanted to know. "I can believe it, looking at your clothing."

"That's what I tried to tell you. We just came, and before I knew it—"

"I said I was sorry. I meant it. You two Gold or Black?"

"Huh?"

"Are you Gold or Black? A simple question. Don't you know anything?"

"Like I told you, we're a long way from home."

The girl frowned, jumped down lithely and joined them in the trench.

"Where on Earth are you from?"

Ed felt like saying: *Yes, we're from Earth, all right, but a different Earth.* But he couldn't, for they had to keep that secret or forfeit their right to search for Freya. Besides, this business of parallel worlds still left him a little confused. Mary Lou Simmons, that was the girl's name. A nice name, a perfectly ordinary name, but only because the English-speaking peoples had spread all over the globe on this world too. A Mary Lou Simmons, slim and pretty, who could hold her own in a fight with any man, because here something added strength to the smaller-boned, smaller-muscled bodies of women.

"...where we come from," Torstein was saying, "there is no distinction of Gold and Black. I don't know what you mean."

"Well, that's hard to believe. Everyone knows that the city-states have divided into two armed camps, those of the gold banner, those of the black. We're Gold here in Crescent Village. But what we do with you depends on your own banner."

"I said we have none," Torstein insisted.

"Umm-mm. That makes it difficult. You see, these men in the trenches are Black-banner prisoners. We wouldn't have them digging our fortifications otherwise."

Torstein said, cheerfully, "Well, I guess that leaves us out. I guess we can go from these trenches and—"

"Don't get smart, wise guy. I didn't say that. I'm captain of the guard in Crescent City, so it's up to me. Maybe we can work out a compromise."

Ed nodded his battered face. "What do you mean?"

"Well, once a month we hold the Games. Black-banners aren't eligible, naturally, but all Golds and neutrals can compete. The higher you rise in the Games, particularly in the fighting, the further you can go in our military system. Would you like to try that?"

GINGERLY, Ed felt the bruises on his cheek, his puffed lips, his swollen eye. Well, he'd refused to fight back. Besides, some of his opponents, at least, would be men, and he'd feel no qualms about matching blows with them. "Yes," he said. "I think so."

"Good. Then it's decided. Full moon comes in three weeks. So, until then, you two will dig fortifications, but I'll enter your names on the fighting lists right now."

Ed gave her their names, which she wrote on a slip of paper, then she jumped out of the trench and walked back across the plain toward Crescent City, which looked like a cluster of white dots on the horizon.

"Games," snorted Torstein. "Bah!"

Ed grinned. "Better change your attitude, Tor. She didn't say it, but I think she meant that if we don't do well, it's back to digging trenches for us. And we're not going to find Freya, digging trenches. No, our only hope is to do well in the Games."

Now Torstein was grinning. "Yes? Well, what will you do if they put you up there against Mary Lou first thing?"

Ed grunted, picked up his shovel, started digging.

After three weeks, it seemed that all he'd ever done all the years of his life was this digging. But it was heavy exercise out in the strong sunlight, and what little softness city life had brought to his frame melted away. By the end of the third week, he could feel the smooth muscles rippling under his sun-bronzed skin with every stroke of the shovel. Physically he hadn't felt so good in years. But his thoughts were on Freya, somewhere in this world—possibly nearby for all he knew.

The day before the Games, Torstein had an accident. He stood on the lip of the trench, turned to tell Ed something. He lost his balance, swung his hands out wildly for a moment, then plummeted headfirst into the trench.

He hit with a thud, and half a dozen of the prisoners came running, led by Johnny Greengate.

"He don't look so good," the man said.

"Damn it!" Torstein gritted. "I don't feel so good, either."

Greengate nodded. "I sure can see why; brother. They made me a medico over in Pine Bluffs, 'fore I got captured. Know what's wrong?"

"What?" Ed demanded, bringing water for Torstein to drink.

"Broke his collar bone, that's what. Yessiree, neatest break I ever saw. I tell yuh—"

Ed looked. Tor's shoulder seemed somehow twisted, and when the big man tried to move it, he couldn't.

"What happened?"

Ed turned, saw Mary Lou and an older woman he didn't know.

"He fell."

"Umm-mm." The older woman knelt by Torstein's side, probed around a while, then let her fingers stay on his shoulder. "It's broken, Captain Simmons."

"Hell, that's a shame. He was going to enter the Games."

The older woman, who evidently was a doctor, shook her head. "Maybe next year, you mean. I'm going to make a splint, but this man will need a lot of rest."

"Damn it!" Torstein swore. "That puts me out, Ed. You've got to enter those fights yourself, and you've got to do a good job. Feel up to it?"

Ed shrugged, watched while the doctor began to tape Torstein's shoulder. "I can try," he said.

"I," Torstein kept repeating over and over, "am a clumsy oaf…"

CHAPTER SEVEN

THE DAY of the Games. Excitement had come to Crescent City, but Ed had seen only glimpses of it. He'd been ushered down to a little dressing room below the arena. A couple of cots, a first-aid cabinet, a shower. And Torstein pacing back and forth angrily, still fuming over the plaster cast on his shoulder.

"They said you go on right away tonight, in the preliminaries. Nervous?"

"You bet I'm nervous. I've got to win."

Mary Lou peered in through the half-open doorway. "You decent? Ah, okay."

Ed wore a pair of white shorts they'd given him. No gloves. Apparently you could box or wrestle.

"I thought I'd give you a pointer or two," Mary Lou told him. He supposed she felt responsible for them in a way, and he certainly needed all the help he could get. He nodded eagerly.

"First," said Mary Lou, "they don't let you see your opponent until the fight. You'll find a circular ring, so does your opponent. You grope around, find his shoulders, place your hands on them. He or she will do the same, and then the lights go on. That's the signal to start, and you fight. No holds barred. The fight ends when one of you is unconscious, or surrenders. Is that clear?"

Ed nodded. "Sure. But let's get one thing straight. Just how successful must I be to get us out of those trenches?"

Mary Lou smiled. "Whoever becomes champion can name his own ticket. That's the way it works.

"Meanwhile, all the contestants will probably fight twice each night, because rumor has it that the Black-banners are on the march, and we'd like to get the Games concluded before they come. Well, good luck."

"Will you be fighting?"

"Me? Naturally. I lost in the finals last month, but we'll see about it this time. Again, good luck." And Mary Lou was gone.

"Better hope you don't draw that tigress in the prelims," Torstein muttered.

"Or any other girl, Tor. I still can't get used to it. Probably I'd take what she had to offer without fighting back."

"By the Elder Gods, don't be a fool! In a sense you're fighting for Freya. We've come a long way for her, Ed. So if they put one of those Amazons in there with you, you'd better ram her pretty teeth down her throat before she does the same to you."

"I don't know," Ed admitted, slamming fist into palm. "It's easy to say, but..."

SOON AFTER that, a girl in pigtails led him up a flight of stairs and out into the arena, Torstein following behind. Ed could not see much in the darkness, but as he walked down the aisle he was aware of a babble of conversation all around him. Finally, his palms sweating and his mouth very dry, he climbed up into the circular ring. Just a raised platform with no ropes. Apparently, if you were hit hard enough and fell off, you had to climb back—if you could.

Remembering Mary Lou's instructions, he walked out into the center of the ring, stiffly, his heart beating a mad dance inside his chest. He groped out with his hands, found wide, hairy shoulders on a level somewhat under his own. A pair of hands fell heavily on his own shoulders, and something made him look up in the darkness.

Overhead, brilliant lights flashed on, half-blinding him.

Splat! Something crashed against his jaw and he felt himself falling. He blinked his eyes, began to see again, heard the roar of the crowd. A squat, muscular man with a bull-neck and beady little eyes stared down at him, then lumbered forward.

Ed rolled away, got to his feet. The man came on, his arms outstretched, ready for an embrace that might end with half a dozen of Ed's ribs broken. He darted away, then in, ripping three quick jabs to the man's face, and three more without a return.

He felt good. He felt quick, and he almost wanted to thank Mary Lou for his three weeks in the trenches. Again he flicked out with the left, and again, watching a red welt grow on his opponent's cheek.

It turned out to be no contest. Ed danced in and out, keeping away from the great hairy arms, striking at will with a short left jab, hooking from the outside when the man covered up. The bruising contact hurt his knuckles, but his opponent's face took on the semblance of raw tenderloin.

The man cowered away, bringing both hands up to protect his head, and Ed lowered his attack, shifting it to the body, throwing hard lefts and rights which caught the unguarded midsection. Down went the guard, covering chest and stomach now.

A good left hook set the man up, and when Ed followed with a right cross, it was over. Slowly, his opponent fell. First to his knees, then all the way down, flat on his face.

WHILE THE crowd thundered its approval, two attendants came with a bucket of water, splashed the man's face, and helped him to his feet. They took him from the ring, still dazed, and Ed prepared to leave.

Torstein met him, pumped his hand vigorously. "Three minutes, Ed! That's all it took. Well, let's get you rested."

A woman attendant jabbed Ed's chest with a thin forefinger. "Where do you think you're going?"

"Why, to get some rest."

"Uh-uh." The woman shook her head. "Two bouts an evening, young man. Stay right where you are."

"You mean now, right after that—"

"That's what I mean. Now."

The lights went out, and Ed heard someone else shuffling into the ring. Wearily, he made contact, waited. When the lights went on again, it turned out to be another man who could have been a carbon copy of the first.

He lasted half a minute longer, but the results were the same. His face glowing, Torstein ushered Ed away from the ring. "How you set him up with that left hook, man—it was perfect! You'll mow your way right through these Games."

Ed grinned boyishly, blew on his knuckles and said, "I hope so, Tor."

He fared as well in the quarterfinals the following evening. His two opponents were tall and lanky, men who'd probably used his own tactics of hit-and-run to win the preceding evening. But now Ed changed his style, slugging away in each bout until he slugged at nothing but air. Again, two quick knockouts. Total time, less than ten minutes.

Torstein's enthusiastic optimism must have been catching, because Ed began to feel it the following evening as he prepared for the semi-finals.

But it didn't last. He got out into the center of the ring, found a pair of shoulders in the darkness. Smooth, well rounded.

The lights glared forth.

Her body gleaming under the lights, Mary Lou smiled at him, then backed away and raised her fists.

"You've done better than I expected, Ed. You surprise me."

"Thanks," he said lamely, circling away as she shifted toward him.

"Well, come on. Won't you fight? The crowd won't like it if you don't..."

Try as he might, Ed couldn't hit her—it was against the entire culture of his people.

ED STOOD there, backed away again, heard the catcalls from the audience and Torstein's groan. Hell, Ed knew he'd never felt so strong in his life. Probably he could take Mary Lou—if he could bring himself to fight her.

But now he said, "I can't fight with you."

"Why not? Because I beat you once? I promise to make it fast." She had a cocky grin on her face.

"No. Because you're a woman. I can't fight a woman."

"But why? Of all the silly things—can't fight a woman! Why on Earth—"

Ed knew he couldn't explain. Different cultural patterns, and there it was. Meanwhile, a loud stamping of feet came to his ears as the audience grew restless. And if he didn't win, he might find himself back digging trenches, with no way to look for Freya.

"Well," Mary Lou frowned, "that's enough talk. I said 'good luck,' Ed. I wasn't joking...but you can't win by standing still."

Ed stood off near the edge of the ring, and she came in slowly, cornering him. He had no place else to go, unless it was back and off the ring. But that would only delay...

Still two strides away, Mary Lou lowered her fists and hurled herself through the air, arms outstretched, ready to drag Ed down when she hit him.

He did the only thing he could do.

He ducked, fell flat on the edge of the ring. Completely surprised, Mary Lou sailed over his head, hurled headfirst off the raised platform, and struck—still head—first against the cast on Torstein's broken shoulder.

Tor yelled his pain, and Ed knew they'd have to set his shoulder all over again. But it didn't matter. Mary Lou lay there at Torstein's feet. She breathed regularly enough, but she didn't try to rise. She'd knocked herself out with the force of the blow and, according to the rules, that made Ed the victor. A moment later, three officials signified that by placing a wreath over Ed's shoulders while the crowd hissed and booed.

"Okay," said Torstein, grinning in spite of his pain, "One way is as good as another, and you'll enter the finals in a few minutes. Don't complain."

"Who's complaining?"

CHAPTER EIGHT

HALF AN hour later, Mary Lou came into their dressing room, a bandage wrapped around her forehead. "Hello," she said. "It sure was a rotten piece of luck, Ed. But maybe I'll do it next month. Meanwhile, I sort of feel responsible for you, so—"

"You mean you're not mad?"

"Gosh, no. That's part of it—luck. It could have happened to you just as readily, but it happened to me. Now I'd like to see you win. Except that I doubt it."

"Yeah? Why?" Torstein demanded. "I'd say Ed is doing all right for himself."

"I suppose he is. But do you know who the other finalist is?"

"How should I know?"

"The one who beat me out last month! Good, too. Strong and fast and tricky."

"A man?" Ed wanted to know. Mary Lou shook her head. "A girl. So—"

"That does it. What the hell, I'll just walk up there, but I won't be able to fight."

"I don't understand you at all," Torstein said. "What, precisely, does Ed get if he wins?"

"Why...anything. Anything at all."

"For example, if he wanted to look for someone, could he have help?"

"Lord, yes. We'd give the champion anything. The key to every city under the Gold banner. Like I said, anything."

Torstein thumped his hand against Ed's shoulder. "You hear that? Damn it, if you win, we'll have enough help to find her, Ed. Don't tell me you won't try."

When do you forget all about ethics, Ed wondered? Wasn't it a question of determining what factor weighed more heavily? Didn't he want to find Freya, wouldn't he risk his life over and over again for her? Wouldn't he?

And now all he had to do was throw a meaningless cultural pattern to the winds. "I'd be a jackass if I didn't," he said.

Chuckling, Torstein led him upstairs while Mary Lou whispered instructions in his ear.

Again, the dark ring, the groping for his opponent's shoulders, placing his hands on them while the hushed crowd waited.

After his first fight, Ed had learned to look down when the lights flashed on. The first thing he saw was a pair of sandaled feet, shapely legs, with white shorts above them. His gaze roved further. A bronzed torso, long and lean, but perfectly proportioned. A tall girl and a beautiful one, with proud breasts and shoulders and a billowing mass of blonde hair.

He looked at her face. "Freya!" he cried.

"THAT'S my name," she said haughtily. "But I don't think I know you."

Of course. Something about stripping her memory from her and planting a new one, making her think she had always been on this Earth. Freya...

She looked a little puzzled. "I don't think I know you, but you do look...familiar."

"Familiar? I'm Ed...*Ed*—"

"All right, Ed. Hello. But let's save the formal introductions for after the fight. Okay?"

She walked in toward him, but she failed to raise her hands. "What's happening to me?" she said to no one in particular. "I don't understand it. I—"

"What's the matter?"

"I can't fight. Something tells me not to fight with you. Yet—why? What's to prevent it? You're Ed, you said that. And yet, it seems to me—oh, I don't know. It seems to me I must have known an Ed once. Ed..." She rolled the name around on her tongue, flavored it, then shrugged hopelessly. "I don't know. I don't know."

He tried to drive the point home through the apparent chink in her mental armor. "Remember the Hendrix apartment? The television set, and a little blue ship that got bigger? Remember, Freya?"

"I..." She paused, ran a hand over her eyes, shook her head furiously. "You're using witchcraft, that's what. I don't know you. I don't remember any of those things." Slowly, still unsure of herself, she lifted her hands to fight.

65

Ed heard the angry roar of the crowd, worse than last night. Angry, and he couldn't blame them. Here in the championship, the contestants refused altogether to join battle. The volume of sound increased, and he could not hear Freya, who was talking again.

Angry—no. Frightened perhaps. Men and women milled about in the aisles, clambered over the chairs, yelling and fighting one another in their haste to get away.

Torstein bellowed something, but Ed couldn't quite catch the words. Even Torstein seemed alarmed, and Mary Lou was pounding his back and shouting advice in his ears.

Ed backed to the edge of the ring and leaned down. "What the hell's the matter?"

Mary Lou's voice was a piercing shriek. "The Black-banners, that's what! They've overrun the city while we were all busy with our final night of Games. They've got the arena surrounded now, and with almost our entire military force inside—"

"Can't you fight your way out?"

"How? Our weapons are in the armory."

FREYA joined Ed, reached impulsively for his hand. She whispered fiercely, "I'm glad our fight will be postponed, Ed. I don't know why, but I'm glad. But now—what can we do now?"

Ed looked about wildly. A confused throng, the Gold-banner warriors, women and men, seethed and tumbled through the arena, running and pushing aimlessly. And far off to the right, a compact wedge of armed women streamed in, brandishing spears and swords. One defiantly carried a banner overhead, a banner black as night.

Still numbed by the sudden attack, those within the arena hardly offered any organized resistance. Closer to the ring came the stream of warrior women, not fanning out, but seemingly intent upon Freya and Ed.

It didn't make sense, not at first. You'd think they would exploit their advantage to the hilt, spreading out and killing the Gold-banners in droves. Instead, they maintained their battle wedge, hacking their way through the crowd, battering down only those who stood in their path, pushing their wedge ever closer to the ring.

And then, abruptly, the cloud of mystery lifted. There, in the rear of the wedge—a man, tall, dark, garbed all in orange.

Utgard!

Colonel Utgard who'd stop them from returning Freya to her own world at all costs.

Ed spun around and faced the girl.

"Run! In the confusion, you could get away!"

"Why should I do that? What's so special about me?"

"No time to explain. Just believe me—and run!"

"That's silly. I'll stay right here and I'll fight if I have to. I'm no different from anyone else."

Ed flung his hands up in a shrug that was more eloquent than any words. By now, the vanguard of the wedge had reached the first row of seats and Torstein had spotted Colonel Utgard. "Ed, do you see who I see?"

And Utgard's voice, booming above the roar of the crowd. "That man will be dangerous. Get him. But I want him alive, and the girl, too."

Alive? Why? Ed didn't feel like looking a gift horse in the mouth, but Utgard's behavior failed to jell, especially when he shouted his next orders. "The man in the ring—you may kill him! But the other two I want alive!"

Torstein stood up as they surrounded him. He shouted, "By the Elder Gods, I can't even fight, not with this arm..." He swung ineffectually with his good left arm, and the lithe girls evaded his clumsy blows. One of them wrapped herself firmly about his legs as he climbed up and stood on his chair. He reached down to strike her away, lost his balance, tumbled over her shoulder and down to the floor. After that, they swarmed all over him, striking with the hafts of their spears. When they were finished, Torstein lay there unmoving, and two of the warrior women picked him up and began carting him off.

Mary Lou was on them like a fury. From somewhere she'd taken a sword, and she swung it in a great arc, plowing into them like it harvester into grain. For a brief moment, the wild attack almost turned them away, but the two women had dropped Torstein, and Mary Lou tripped over his unconscious body. She struggled to rise, got up to her knees and no further. Someone struck her from behind with a sword-hilt and she slumped across Tor's chest.

"THE RING is surrounded," Freya admitted, confusion in her voice. "But I don't know why they want us particularly."

"You heard what the man said. They want you alive. They want me dead."

"And we have no weapons. Ed, I wish I could remember the thoughts which clamor just out of reach. Someday, perhaps, I will remember them. But I don't want them too late. If they want me alive, and if I make things a little rough for them, maybe you can get away. Maybe—"

"Hey, wait a minute. I'm supposed to be rescuing you."

But Freya didn't hear him. She also didn't wait for the warrior women to reach her. The first of them had climbed halfway up to the ring, and Freya reached out and helped her. The surprised girl came forward, was spun about by Freya and deposited in a heap on the surface of the ring. Freya dove down after her and came up with a sword in left hand and spear in right. She flashed by Ed so rapidly that he had no time to question her intent, but he saw it for himself a moment later.

Freya met the other warriors before they could climb up, swung a continuous loop of flying metal overhead and kept them at bay with it. She turned briefly, cried over her shoulder. "Run. Run!"

"Ridiculous! I intend to help you."

"That's what ridiculous. Live today so you can fight tomorrow. I'm safe; they don't want to kill me."

"Still—"

But that ended the conversation, for Freya had turned back to her foes. Aware of noise from the other side of the ring, Ed whirled around. Two of the women had fought their way around through the first row of chairs, now stalked Ed with raised, bloody swords.

One panted, "That's the one! He's the one we kill."

"Umm-mm, yes. You don't know why, do you, June?"

"Who cares? That Colonel what's-his-name is paying us enough money to choke an ox."

"Yeah, and we've been mercenaries all our life. Okay, let's get him!"

They came forward. Two beautiful—if sweat-streaked and disheveled—women garbed only in black kirtles, their swords flashing overhead, each a messenger of death for Ed!

BUT THE times when he wouldn't fight back against Mary Lou were over. Now it meant life or death—and upon life depended his chance to fight again for Freya. He gave a wild war-whoop, which he thought would have made Torstein proud, and charged the women.

So startled were they, attacked by an unarmed man, that they didn't have time to bring their swords down. He bowled them over, saw them fall one in each direction. But the force of his lunge carried him on beyond the edge of the ring and he plunged down into the seats.

When he got up, two of Utgard's orange-uniformed bodyguards met him, swords drawn. Apparently they couldn't bring their more lethal weapons here to the Fourth Level, for that would smack of another world, and it might lose Utgard his job. Bellowing, the men closed in.

Ed ducked under a wild blow, felt sword-point swish through his hair. He piled his right fist into the man's stomach, saw his face go suddenly gray, and heard the sword clatter to the floor. He scrambled down after it, swung around and up in time to parry a blow from the other man's weapon which, had it landed, could have split him from crown to navel.

Together clanged the two swords, but the orange-uniformed man took the force of the blow down near the hilt of his weapon, and the sword clattered from nerveless fingers. Ed smiled grimly and said, "You don't know how to use that thing any more than I do, huh?"

He turned away from the man, faced again the fighting in the ring.

Except that there was none.

Freya had been conquered—he could draw no other conclusion. Ed found himself wishing now that Utgard's command had been followed. Freya a captive would fare far better than Freya a corpse, but in the heat of battle anything could have happened.

All about him in the arena, the fighting had almost come to a standstill, as if the Black-banners had had but one purpose, and that to take Freya. From outside, he could hear shouts and an occasional scream, but within the arena, except for a few individual combatants paired off one against the other, Gold-banners milled about in confusion, licking their wounds.

Mary Lou stood up groggily. "What happened? Where's Tor?"

"They took him, alive I think. And Freya too."

"Freya? Oh, the girl you were to fight. But you sound more worried about her than you do about Torstein."

Ed smiled weakly. "There's something you don't understand. Tor and Freya are brother and sister. I came here with Tor to find his sister, whom I am to marry."

MARY LOU allowed herself no more than a brief instant of startled surprise, then said, "Well, I know where the Black encampment is. Want to go there—with warriors?"

Ed shook his head. "Wouldn't do any good. They're heading elsewhere, and I'll have to travel that road alone. If I can."

"Alone! That's what you think. Something's been happening right under your nose while you were busy with the Games. Something—Tor and me, we—" She blushed, looked exactly like a shy maid of Ed's Earth. "We—well, Tor says he loves me, and I...anyway, if you know where to find them, I'm with you."

He certainly could use her, but it would be a clear-cut violation of the First Level Regent's edict, and Freya might be forfeit as a consequence. On the other hand, Colonel Utgard had violated that edict himself, and Ed had a hunch the coldly logical Regent would let one factor balance out the other. "Okay, Mary Lou," he said. "But I'm warning you in advance, you're going to see a lot of strange things where we go, and most of what happens won't make much sense to you."

"Who cares? If we can find Tor. If we can..."

It hit Ed suddenly, like a thunderbolt. Utgard would take his captives back to the First Level. Fine, so they could follow in their own blue ship. Could they? No! They might not be so lucky this time with a ship that didn't work, and except for that stroke of fate, Torstein and Ed might still be hopelessly visiting one parallel world after another. If it happened this time to Mary Lou and Ed, Utgard would find himself with years—and certainly months—to dispose of the two Hauglands as he saw fit.

"What are you stewing about now, Ed? I thought you said we could find..."

"I said a lot of things, but I left out the complications."

"You mean it might be a difficult journey to where we're going?"

"That's putting it mildly. That's—hold on!"

Of course. He'd failed to see this thing out to its logical conclusion. Colonel Welcome had spoken of trade between the parallel worlds, trade carried on for the benefit of the First Level. Naturally, the people of other levels did not know at all that interlocking dimensions were involved. Still, there should be something, and this Gold-banner city was one of the capitals of Mary Lou's Earth.

"Everything depends on what I'm about to ask you, Mary Lou. So think, think like you never did before."

"I'm listening."

"There should be some strange people here in this city, people who don't belong. Traders maybe, or businessmen. They act peculiar, maybe they don't know your customs, maybe they live entirely different than you do. Do you know of any such people?"

"What a strange question. Well, let's see. No, no, I can't say that I do."

"Think!"

"I said I don't know. And listen, while you're asking these foolish questions—"

"They're not foolish. Try again, Mary Lou. Anything. Wait...did you see those orange-uniformed men with the Black-banner warriors—"

"What is this, a color game or something?"

She still didn't take him seriously, but he ignored the question. "Did you ever notice anyone like that, here in this city before?"

"You mean dressed all in orange? N-no—no, I didn't."

ED FELT himself sweating. The lead was there, somewhere, waiting for them to take it up. And it might be their last chance. "Well, knock this around then. All government activity and most business enterprises are carried on by women, right?"

Mary Lou nodded.

"Can you think of one important business organization here that is run by men, maybe a business outfit of some kind?"

Mary Lou smiled. "Sure, that's easy, World-Wide Enterprises, that's what they call themselves. Big business, they'll buy anything from native weaving to pottery to—well, you name it." Mary Lou was still grinning, "A queer outfit. I don't know why I didn't think of them before, because they're mighty peculiar. All the owners are men."

Men, business magnates in a woman's world, First Level tycoons unwilling to accept the strange cultural pattern of a Fourth Level world? It could well be, and Ed's heart began to feel lighter.

"Okay, take me to them."

"Now?"

"Yes, now."

"Cool off, Ed. It's after midnight, so World-Wide Enterprises is fast asleep for the night."

"I don't care. You're military boss here in Crescent City, aren't you? All right, dream up some excuse to enter the place, just you and me. And I don't mean tomorrow."

Mary Lou shrugged. "Suspicion of alliance with Black-banner city-states. That's easy. Want to go now?"

For answer, Ed grabbed her hand and started running from the still-crowded arena.

MARY LOU took a badge from inside her kirtle-pocket, showed it to the night watchwoman, but the old lady shook her head, and planted herself firmly in the long, low doorway. "You got a warrant?"

"I told you this was an emergency," Mary Lou insisted. "Of course, if you want to lose your job and maybe go to jail as well..." She paused momentarily, then said, "How do I know you're not involved in this Black-banner thing?"

The woman jumped away as if she'd poked her feet down on a bed of hot coals. "I don't mean no trouble, Miss. Honest. And if you want to go inside—here, I'll open up."

Mary Lou grumbled her satisfaction, and with Ed she followed the watch woman inside. Ed whispered, "We'd like to see the owner's quarters."

"That bad, huh? All the way up at the top, mister. You think the boss is a spy?"

"I didn't say that. We just want to see his quarters."

Mary Lou nudged his ribs with her elbow. "I sure hope you know what you're doing."

They followed the watchwoman up a flight of stairs and then across a hallway dimly lit with night lamps. She paused at a doorway, fumbled with a ring of keys at her girdle.

The door swung in noisily, and as it did, bright lights flashed on in the room.

Mary Lou leaped back. "What happened?"

But Ed was smiling at her. "That's easy. The door hit an electric eye, closed an electric circuit. But that's something unknown here on the Fourth Level."

"I hope you realize I don't know what you're talking about."

"Forget it. Point is, I think my hunch is paying off."

Ed's optimism soon received a severe jolt. They found a suite of offices, three elaborately furnished rooms, the chairs and desks and fixtures smelling quite evidently of another world. But that wasn't enough. Ed didn't seek proof of what he already knew. He sought a blue ship that could take them to the First Level. And if he didn't find it...

CHAPTER NINE

AFTER SHE'D taken them around the offices, the watchwoman demanded: "Well, and did you find what you wanted?"

"As a matter of fact," Ed admitted, "we didn't. But that doesn't mean it isn't here. Has the owner—the big boss himself—got a special retreat here? You know, a little hidden office where he can get away when he wants to be alone; maybe a bar stuck off in the wall somewhere?"

"Well…" the old watchwoman began doubtfully.

"Well what?"

"He—listen, mister. He pays me to forget about that; yeah, and to have one of the char-boys clean it, too. But I can't go poking around and showing it to you."

Mary Lou said, "You got a family?"

"Yes'm."

"Want to keep supporting them?"

"Yes'm."

"Then you'd better show us what we want to see. Get a move on."

The old woman shrugged, cursed softly under her breath, and led them through the first two offices and into the third. She stopped at the far wall, did some tricks with the frame of a rather drab landscape painting.

The wall slid back, revealing a bare room.

Almost bare.

A bank of machinery jutted out from the left-hand wall. What could have been a model of a blue spaceship, certainly no more than two feet long, rested on the floor.

"Nothing here," Mary Lou said. "Except those silly gadgets."

Ed ignored her, spoke instead to the watchwoman. "All right, you can leave us now."

"You mean in there? No sir."

Ed took her arm, high up, and led her gently from the room. "Look, you'll argue and then you'll agree with us. But we haven't the time. So get out—now!"

The woman began to grumble, but she uttered no other discernable protest. And she didn't resist when Ed parked her outside the hidden office and slid the door back into place from within.

"Now what?" Mary Lou wanted to know.

Ed got down on hands and knees, opened the door of the tiny blue ship. "Might as well have it waiting for us," he muttered.

"You sound as if we can squeeze into that tiny model of—of something."

"There won't be any squeezing at all," Ed assured her as he crossed to the wall. He understood nothing about the complicated bank of machinery, but it did not matter. Protruding from its center was a large lever, and this he pulled all the way home.

Nothing happened. Nothing—except that from far away outside the building, Ed heard the booming drums of a sudden thunderstorm.

A FEW moments later, Mary Lou clutched his hand in fear. "Ed...Ed, I think this room is—growing. How can that be? And yet, and yet—look! The blue thing is as big as you are, and the walls drop back further and further..."

She looked half-hysterical, and Ed tried to comfort her. "I've been through this before, and trust me, you really have nothing to worry about." Then he added, under his breath, "I hope."

Sure, he'd try to comfort her. But every time this happened, he couldn't prevent the hackles from rising on the back of his neck. And he wouldn't bother to tell Mary Lou the room wasn't growing at all. No, they were shrinking, but probably, she wouldn't believe her eyes either way.

Gigantic now, the blue ship loomed up before them. "We're going inside," Ed told Mary Lou, but she hung back, clearly frightened.

At that moment the door to the office slid open ponderously. A huge figure stalked inside, flesh wrinkled on the great columns that were legs.

The watchwoman.

She looked about for a time, then fell to hands and knees. Her scream was a deep-throated roar, and Ed knew she'd spotted them. A gnarled hand, each finger as big as a man from crown to toe, swept out across the floor and slammed down, inches from them.

"The ship!" Ed cried, pulling at Mary Lou's arm. "Come on!"

"Lord, what's that? A giant, a great, huge—"

"Come on!" Half-dragging her, he led the way toward the ship. The hand swung down again, pounding the floor and shaking them like a miniature earthquake. Maybe the watchwoman didn't recognize them, Ed could not be sure. Perhaps her eyesight was myopic, perhaps she saw two somewhat oversized insects on what should have been a clean floor, and so she wanted to exterminate them...

She changed her tactics, standing up and bringing a tremendous foot down toward them. It slammed against the floor as they scurried away, and then it lifted again.

Ed pushed Mary Lou ahead of him, clambered into the blue ship right behind her, shoved the door shut. He ran to the far wall while the girl cowered in the center of the chamber. He found the first lever of four, depressed it, stood back, panting but happy.

But he felt a giddy, spinning motion, was flung about wildly, colliding with Mary Lou and tumbling in a heap with her against one of the walls.

That hadn't happened before, no!

Then did it mean that the watchwoman had raised the ship on high, even now prepared to hurl it away, to crush it against the floor?

Mary Lou was whimpering, but Ed ignored her, climbing to his feet and running to the string of windows high up on the wall. He peered out, thought he saw the palm of a giant hand. Holding them.

And then, something forced him down flat against the floor, crushing bone to muscle. Acceleration.

As they blasted off the Fourth Level, he wondered dimly if the sudden explosion of energy had killed the old woman.

THE SHIP came to rest in the park-like garden with its stunted trees. First Level, and the ruling world.

Mary Lou was still frightened, but she gained some courage when Ed assured her the journey had ended. She got to her feet doubtfully, but stood far back from the door when he opened it.

Ed walked out confidently—into the arms of three orange-uniformed guards!

"He's the one."

"Yes, no doubt. Matches the Colonel's description. Well, let's take him."

"Careful, he might be dangerous." Ed struggled furiously, but he'd have had his hands full with anyone of the big guards, and the three of them soon had him down on the ground helplessly.

They did not know of Mary Lou, and Ed smiled grimly when the warrior-maid launched herself from the ship, her sword brandished high overhead. For all her slim grace, Mary Lou's tremendous strength might turn the tide.

One of the guards rose, parried her sword arm as it came down. The weapon clattered away, and Mary Lou struck out with her fists. Her right hand landed flush on the man's jaw, but he shook it off without any trouble, and soon he'd slung a dazed Mary Lou over one shoulder, and for all her writhing and kicking, she could not do a thing about it.

Ed couldn't believe his eyes, not immediately. And then he remembered what the hag had told him. Something on their Fourth Level world makes the women strong. But Mary Lou was out of her element, and whatever unknown radiation played about that Fourth Level Earth did not exist here or anywhere else. Mary Lou was just an ordinary girl now, and a very bewildered one.

Mary Lou still clawed and bit and kicked as they led her away. Two guards prodded Ed along warily in front or them, their strange pistols in their hands. The third still carried Mary Lou over his shoulder and, walking thus, they came to the long low building Ed remembered from his last visit.

"In five minutes, they stood before Colonel Utgard, a coldly handsome man, impeccably attired in his orange uniform. He scowled darkly, then said: "I never have any rest here. I gave you men orders. Why didn't you carry them out?"

"Here are your prisoners, sir."

"I DID not request prisoners. I distinctly told you to kill this man at once if he appeared."

"Sir," one of the guards apologized, "we respect your orders. On the other hand, Colonel Welcome has been firm about this thing too. The Regent wants to review—"

"I don't care what the Regent wants. I gave you orders, and I'll have you stripped of your rank if—"

"Sir, the Regent—"

"You're demoted, all of you. Better still, I'll see you before a tribunal of your peers. I'll—"

On and on ranted the Colonel, a bitter, resentful, angry man. He almost seemed like a mechanical figure, with but one purpose in life—and that to be evil. Too mechanical. It struck Ed that way, oddly. Something didn't fit...

"...you have one alternative," Utgard was saying. "Kill him now, and kill this girl as well."

There was silence. The guards shuffled about uncomfortably, their pistols raised.

Suddenly, Utgard moved. He tore the weapon from one of the guards' hands, swung about with it and faced Ed. "So you perish—" he said, and fired.

Ed dove in, felt something hiss over his head, a seething stream of raw energy. Then he was grappling with Utgard and together they crashed into a desk, plunged to the floor, rolled over.

One of the guards would have stopped them, but his companions held him back. One of them said, "The Regent would probably like it better this way. After all, don't you think he'd blame us if this man ended up being killed in cold blood? I say let them fight."

And thus they fought. Utgard seemed possessed of an inhuman strength, ripping blow after blow into Ed's face with his free hand, clinging to the pistol with his other hand. Ed fought defensively, used all the strength at his command to keep the weapon averted. But Utgard forced him down and back, bringing the pistol in toward him. Closer...

The crushing acceleration had left Ed weak, had tired his muscles with the tremendous burden forced upon them. Now he kicked out with his legs, saw Utgard totter above him for a moment, then fall away. The weapon went off, hissing into the floor and carving a chunk out of it.

Ed fiercely threw himself on top of the Colonel. He then struck out with his fist and heard the pistol clatter away. They both scrambled after it and reached it at the same moment. This time Ed got it and heard Mary Lou shout triumphantly. But Utgard reared back and kicked him as he crouched on the floor, the toe of his sandaled foot catching Ed's abdomen and forcing all the air from his lungs. Lances of pain coursed up and down his body, streaked red before his eyes. His limbs felt numb as Utgard swung down at him again.

Somehow he caught the foot and twisted. Utgard tumbled down beside him. Ed swung the gun up, brought it down on the man's head. Over and over again he raised his hand and let it fall, the heavy weapon pounding against Utgard's skull. Over and over...

"STOP IT, ED! Loo—look—" Mary Lou crouched by them, fear in her eyes. "I said, look!"

Ed blinked. Wearily, he tried to rise. He couldn't make it his feet, not quite. Then his legs gave out. But he saw what had been Utgard.

The skull was impossibly crushed, dented, broken—but no blood covered it.

No blood...

And dents that looked like dents in metal, under a thin coat of what could have been artificial skin!

Still dazed, he ripped away Utgard's orange shirt, saw under it only gleaming metal.

Even the guards cowered in one end of the room. One of them shook his head from side to side numbly. "I don't get it. I don't get it."

Neither did Ed.

LATER, HE stood before the Regent, Freya's hand in his. They'd put Freya back through their device—whatever it was— which had taken her memory from her and put a new one in its place. The process had been reversed, and Freya remembered only as a dream all that had happened since that evening with Bob and Judy Hendrix.

Torstein and Mary Lou stood there too, gazing into each other's eyes, refusing to see or acknowledge anything else about them, very much in love.

The Regent's high voice spoke a glowing tribute to them, to all of them. He spoke eloquently and told them that the past was forgotten, that Freya could return to the world where she'd spent her entire life. As for Tor and Mary Lou, he said they could decide for themselves where they would prefer to remain. Of Colonel Utgard he mentioned not a word, and presently he drew the interview to a close.

Outside, Colonel Welcome greeted them. He took Ed's hand and shook it heartily, a widening smile on his face. "My boy, you've done it," he said happily.

Ed nodded. "Yeah. Yeah, I guess so. But I don't really understand…"

"You mean about the late Colonel Utgard? That's easy. Remember that talk about his grandfather, the one who'd caused all the trouble in the first place?"

"Yes."

"That was Utgard, his grandfather."

"I don't get it."

"Look: the grandfather disappeared. He didn't die. He just disappeared. Fifty years later, a younger edition of him returned, claimed to be his grandson. Only—it was a lie.

"The original Utgard had caused a lot of trouble and knew it. Also, he'd passed the prime of life, and he wanted to do something about it. There's a Third Level world—not your own, naturally— where the natives know how to build robots. Not just mechanical toys, but synthetic men of metal, metal bodies that can last hundreds of years.

"Utgard had one fashioned for himself. That was the man you fought with and destroyed, only it wasn't a man, it was…a robot. Further, the original Utgard was bad enough according to the records, but this man was worse. Why? Because there exists one flaw in the robots. Human character is not transferred perfectly to the metal bodies. Something is lost. That is, the main trait of the individual becomes the only trait in the new metal man. So Utgard, who claimed to be his own grandson, was all bad. A hundred percent evil…"

WELL, THAT was just the last of a long string of improbabilities, and Ed couldn't doubt it. He shrugged. "The hell with it," he said aloud.

"What say?" Freya demanded.

"I said I want to forget all about this."

Torstein grinned. "That won't be easy, especially since they'll be opening inter-dimensional travel for our Earth. The Regent wants you in charge of it, you know."

"Me? What about you? I thought both of us—"

Torstein was still grinning. "There are complications, Ed. You see, Mary Lou wants to return to her own world, and you can't blame her, not if she's strong as a man there, and just an ordinary girl elsewhere. But you and Freya can visit us whenever you want."

"That's crazy!" Ed cried. "You can't leave this whole job in my hands, teaching Earth how to fare among the parallel worlds."

"Sorry, I said you can visit us. Mary Lou insists."

Ed smiled in spite of himself. Maybe with Freya's help he could get Earth ready for its new role, and anyway, looking at Mary Lou, he knew there was a girl to tame the wild Viking in Torstein's nature.

"I tell you what," Ed suggested. "We'll compromise, like the old hag, remember? You're getting married, we're getting married. Let's spend our honeymoon on the hag's world. She'd like that. Then, afterwards, we'll see about all this."

Torstein nodded. Then, when Mary Lou poked her elbow against his rib-case: "That is, if it's all right with Mary Lou."

She smiled up at him, said she agreed.

Ed squeezed Freya's hand. "It's been a long time, kid. It's—"

His musing was interrupted by Freya's arms thrown around his neck, her lips pressed to his in a passionate embrace.

"Oh darling, let Mary Lou boss Tor. With us—let's go back to our own Earth and be just like we always were."

"You'll get no argument from me there," Ed promised, "and once a year we can fly over and watch Mary Lou and Tor stage a match." He winked at her before his lips found hers again.

THE END

If you've enjoyed this book, you will not want to miss these terrific titles...

ARMCHAIR SCI-FI & HORROR DOUBLE NOVELS, $12.95 each

WHEN PARALLEL WORLDS COLLIDE

They say that the blending of politics and science isn't always a good mixture; sometimes bad things can happen. Unfortunately, Congressman Blair had the habit of dabbling in physics. That was how it all started, the beginning of an incredible journey through time and space—a journey that ended on a parallel world in a completely different dimension…

Trapped in this parallel time world, was an Earthman, Douglas Blair. Blair knew nothing about the world he had been thrust into; but he soon came to play a key role in a twisted society that killed children to discourage wars—all the while not knowing that his own two sons were scheduled to die!

CAST OF CHARACTERS

CONGRESSMAN BLAIR

A respected political leader who liked to "putter" around with physics. He was nearly identical to his parallel world counterpart.

SENIOR QUADRATE BLAIR

The ranking military leader in his world. Would his experience at manipulation help him find a place in a parallel world?

LARSON TAYNE

Being the Director's little brother was not good enough for this military strategist. He wanted it all!

MRS. BLAIR

Loyal wife or loving mother? How far would a woman go to make her children's planet a safe and nurturing place to live?

TERRY AND MIKE BLAIR

Ten-year old twins trying their best to survive. Was this a dream...or had their dad's "contraption" actually worked?

CARL GRAYSON

This reporter was the confidant of a powerful U. S. Congressman—but loyalties can sometimes change.

THE TIME
ARMADA

By
FOX B. HOLDEN

ARMCHAIR FICTION
PO Box 4369, Medford, Oregon   97501-0168

For more information about Armchair Books and products, visit our website at…

www.armchairfiction.com

Or email us at…

armchairfiction@yahoo.com

PART ONE

CHAPTER ONE

5:20 P. M., April 17, 1958

CONGRESSMAN Douglas Blair shivered a little and turned up his coat collar against the gray drizzle that had been falling like a finely sifted fog all day. His head ached, his nose felt stuffy, and he was tired. It was good of Grayson to pick him up.

The front seat of the dark blue sedan was soft and reassuring, and the warm current of air from the heater beneath it felt good. He let his spare, barely six-foot body slump like a bag of wet wash and pushed his hat back with the half-formed thought that it might ease the dull pressure behind his eyes.

"Rough going today, eh, Congressman?"

Grayson twisted the blue sedan into outbound Washington traffic and turned the windshield wipers to a faster pace. *Click-click, click-click.* Blair wished someone would invent windshield wipers for the brain, to be worn like a radio headset, maybe with a hole in the top of the head.

"Hey, buddy! Republicans got your tongue?"

"No, sorry, Carl. Just tired. It's that damned McKenny bill."

"Off the record?"

"I'm afraid so for now, Carl. He can get the thing through—he's so damn clever he should've been a woman. Got the steel men eating out of his hand. Made no bones about telling the rest of us today that what the hell, the people never had anything to say about it, anyway. The work of government is up to the professionals. The sooner the people get their nose out of it, the better off they'll be. He said that, Carl; right in front of everybody. And nobody so much as blinked."

The drizzle started to develop into a dark blue rain as they headed toward the suburbs.

"What's going to happen, Carl?" Blair said after awhile.

"If I knew, believe me, I wouldn't be sitting here! I don't know, Doug. We'll all cook in Hell together I guess. Here, have a cigarette."

"Thanks. No, dammit. That's just it—if they'd take this going to Hell business and forget about it—sink it, scuttle it. Nobody goes to Hell, he makes his own if that's the way he lives, or he makes his own

personal Heaven or Paradise or whatever you call it if that's the way he lives. Most of us are in between someplace, a little scared, mostly indifferent, and too mixed up to see the fact that the life style we've

THE TIME ARMADA

By

Fox B. Holden

got in this country isn't so bad but what just plain honesty and a little intelligence couldn't run it right side up."

"Sure, sure, I know and you're right, Doug. But take it easy... Things aren't always as bad as they look."

BLAIR inhaled on the cigarette, laughed a little and felt better. Sometimes he knew he sounded like a college kid trying to tell his father what was wrong with the world, but that was why he liked Carl. Carl let him talk, knew it was his way of blowing off the pent-up steam.

"You know what, chum?" They were running smoothly along the highway now, the engine a reassuring hum of power, the interior of the sedan warm and relaxing. The rain was letting up a little, but dirty banks of fog had started gathering at the roadside like ghosts of all the work of the day, tenuous, without substance.

"What, Carl?"

"You should've stuck with the M. I. T. degree after all. Hell with your brain you'd've made that try for the moon a success last month instead of another near miss."

"Maybe you're right. Those boys know what they're doing though.

I'll stick to puttering."

"Puttering the man calls it. 'He hath a lean and hungry look—such men are dangerous…' Myself, I think that gadget you 'putter' with in that cellar of yours is some kind of a gismo to hypnotize all the states-righters into doing something intelligent like dropping dead without being told!"

"With ingenuity such as yours, my friend, I think I could really accomplish something in that cellar of mine at that! That's the trouble. You writers and newsmen have all the good ideas—slide-rules don't think worth a damn! Instead of a wonderful creation such as you suggest, what have I got? A pile of junk that may, if it works in any degree at all, turn out to be a fairly good television set…"

"You wouldn't kid an old friend. That martini you were putting away the other night said that it was an experiment with something called tired light."

"Exactly. Television."

"Look, the quality of curiosity is not strained, it droppeth as a gentle ten-ton truck from twenty stories up! You said—or the martini said anyway—that if this little gimcrack of yours works, it'd be able to bring back pictures of things that happened in the past. You're guilty until proven innocent, Galileo. Start talking."

"Off the record—"

"I should broadcast it and get dunked in a witch's chair."

"Well—the martini had it a little balled up, but the essential idea's there I guess. Anyway, it isn't everybody who has a space-warp for a household pet."

"Or Einstein for a hobby."

"Blah, this is strictly Blair. That's why it won't work, and I'd be only sensationally nuts if I ever thought it would. But some men take Scotch for their nerves, and I take Scotch with electronics. More of a jolt that way."

"Yuk, yuk."

THAT was why it was good to have Carl for a friend. No matter how sorry you got to feeling for yourself, he could usually snap you out of it one way or another. Right now, Doug thought, Carl was diligently at work with that peculiar brand of psychology that all newspapermen strive ceaselessly to acquire that makes people blab when they ought to keep quiet. But why not—Carl wouldn't know what the hell it was all about and he wouldn't care if he thought it would take some of the pressure off.

"Well, listen then. Ever look through an observatory telescope and have somebody tell you you were focused on some star or other a couple of thousand light years away? Maybe it was in the process of blowing up and becoming a nova or something like that. Anyhow, it would be explained to you that you were seeing that star as it was two thousand years ago. You were seeing, for instance, an explosion that happened twenty centuries in the past. Reason, of course, is that it took the light that long to get from the star to you. More simply, the light that strikes your back porch in the morning left the sun about nine minutes before."

"Very clear. Only why if the universe is a closed form of infinity like it says in all the new books, this light never doubles back on itself—gives you two or even a million images of the same star?"

"That's where the tired light comes in. After a certain length of time—unthinkable aeons of it—it, like all other forms of energy, peters out. Runs down. Quits. Kaput. They call it entropy. It constitutes, actually, a gradual running down, growing old of the universe. As far as anyone knows, this happens before it 'doubles back' on itself, as you put it. You can't catch it coming around the second time to see what you looked like umpteemillion ages ago. So, if you want a second look at yourself, you've got to go out and catch the light which you reflected in the past—"

"Oh brother. You mean anybody on a planet, say, forty light years from Earth with a super-telescope looking at us would be watching the battle of Chateau Thierry and Belleau Wood! A hundred and eighty light years away he'd see us slugging it out against King George III at Saratoga and Valley Forge!"

"You've got it. In other words, the light reflected from Earth then is somewhere deep in Space now. If you could haul it in on some kind of a receiver, you could see everything all over again—you could watch the land masses of Earth as they shifted to form the continents as we know them today."

"You'd need something faster than light to trap the light itself—and I thought that was against Fitzgerald or somebody."

"If you followed the same space warps the light did, it would be. But if it were possible to operate your receiver *through* the fabric of space-time, instead of *along* it—a kind of short-cut—you might turn up with what you're after."

"I am sorry I got into this."

Blair smiled tiredly. "Me too. Hell, I'm fooling around with things I don't pretend to know anything about. Just enough to putter. Just enough to keep my mind off all day long. God knows what I'll get when I turn the damn thing on. Probably not even snow so I'm not worried. Turn left at the next stop-light—they've got that new cut-off finished." He started buttoning his coat. Grayson turned left as ordered.

"But suppose it works?"

"Wow. Then the steam-fitters would envy me."

"Well it sure oughtta do something. You've been tinkering with it for—how long? Couple years?"

"About four I guess, off and on. Sometimes I get to wondering what it'll do if it does do anything."

"Show us Lillian Russell, maybe, or Little Egypt!"

"There's a million possible results when you go fooling around with the structure of the universe, Carl. I guess that's what fascinates me. A little learning is a dangerous thing, they say. Dot's afraid I'll blow us up."

"Well—she could have something there!"

"The thing probably won't even toast a piece of bread. But I'd rather fool with it than collect buttons or play bridge or some other damfool thing, so…"

The blue sedan sloshed up the puddled driveway to the new nine-room bungalow and at the porch Doug Blair got out. A wind had sprung up and the dampness suddenly grasped his body, clung, as though he were naked.

"Time for a drink, supper?"

"No, thanks, Doug—gotta see a man. Now take it easy—let the state of the nation go bury its head for tonight and you have some fun blowing fuses!"

"Yeah, yeah! O.K. and thanks."

The blue sedan sloshed its way back to the highway, and Doug went into the house.

DOUGLAS Blair kissed his wife and, as he did every time he kissed her, wondered how he'd been so lucky. He preferred to think as seldom as memory would permit of how close he'd come on a couple of occasions to marrying a country club, a bridge deck, a women's society, an Emily Post book. And when Dot had given him Terry and Mike, she'd topped off the miracle of herself with the added one of two healthy young minds that had already learned to say "prove it!" Some of the tiredness left him, a lot of the aching discouragement was brushed away.

"Tired, Doug?"

"I was."

There was a sudden thundering which grew quickly into the crashing noises often made by wild elephants getting exercise in a native village.

"The patter of little feet," Dorothy said.

"Oh. For a minute I thought it was termites. Hi, fellas! What kind of trouble did we almost keep out of today?"

"Hi, dad! Hey, Mike says you aren't ever going to try it out. You are, aren't you?"

"I didn't say not ever. I said *maybe* not ever. Things like the Contraption take years to develop, don't they, dad?"

"Well," Doug said, doing what he could to stem the onslaught and still stay on his feet, "what's the source of all this wisdom, *Mr.* Scientist?"

"Some day I'll be a scientist. Mommy said so, didn't you, mom?"

Every so often Doug wondered where they got that solid healthy look, and if either of them would ever faintly resemble the Cassius after whom even Carl thought he should have been named. The red hair of course was Dorothy's. The blue eyes were Dorothy's. Even the brains were, he sometimes suspected, all Dorothy's. But the dormant challenge that grew, not yet quite fully awakened, somewhere behind the freckled, ten-year-old faces—that, if it matured well, would be his.

"If," Doug said then, "you three will let a hungry man eat his supper, he'll let you in on a little surprise before hand. That is, if anybody's interested—"

"Tell us!"

"Is it, Doug?"

"Your brilliant father has exactly three connections to solder on the Contraption, and then—well, after supper, we'll all see together." He laughed, Terry and Mike hooted. Dorothy looked a little worried, and told the boys to wash up.

IT covered half the ten-foot workbench, its large screen a huge, lens-like square eye as it glinted beneath the glare of the cold-cathode lights that lined the ceiling of the laboratory-like cellar.

Doug put the cooling soldering iron back in its place. Dorothy had her Christmas camera mounted on a tripod a few feet back, "Just in case," she said, "it does something before it blows up."

Terry and Mike were silent, eyes wide, not quite behind their mother.

"We shall now," Doug said, "see if we can get a look at Hop-Along Cassidy the way he looked when I was a boy. Better yet, maybe Jack Benny when he was 39...and Valentino..."

He closed the switch, and the cathode lights flickered, went out. There was a humming sound that seemed to come from all sides of the cellar rather than from the Contraption, and the bluish glow emanated from the square convex eye. Directly before it, they watched.

The light shimmered, gave the illusion that the Contraption itself was shimmering, fading. The workbench became indistinct.

"Doug—"

And then the workbench and the Contraption were gone, the overhead cathode tubes were gone, and daylight was filtering through a cellar window that had moved about four feet along the wall—which was now made of glass brick instead of concrete.

Doug and his wife stood rooted. Terry and Mike were gone, too.

CHAPTER TWO

SHE was clad in superbly tailored cream-colored slacks of a material that was glass-like in sheen, an equally well-fitted blouse of forest green hardly a shadow less than opaque, and sandals of a soft, flexible texture slightly raised at the heel. The wide cummerbund of silken flame that circled her slender waist was her only ornamentation.

Doug's pastel shirt felt like a feather; it lay open at the throat and clung comfortably about his chest and shoulders, then tapered leisurely to his waist. The trousers were of the same weight and of a darker hue somewhere between the blue of midnight and cobalt; the sandals were like hers.

He did not understand.

"You—I know you are not—"

Her face was not the same; her hair was the deeper red of mahogany, her eyes as large, but of green, not blue. Dorothy's mouth was wider, her cheeks not quite so shadowed. Yet now her face was drawn in the look of bewilderment that he felt on his own.

"Doug?"

"Dot! For God's sake!"

"Your voice is the same—but you don't look like—"

"Don't get scared, take it easy. It's me. You're different too—all but your voice. I've got to figure it out. Everything's all wrong. Wrong as hell—"

He found a chair of light metal that felt like foam rubber when he sat on it. Dorothy—and he knew somehow that it must be Dorothy—was looking around her with quick, nervous glances.

"Doug, the boys—where are the boys?"

"Terry! Mike!" He called again, stood up. "Oh, God—"

"They were just behind me, Doug, they couldn't have run—"

"No I think—I think they must've stayed with—with the Contraption. We were in the blur light. It wasn't. They must've been just beyond its effective range. That must be it. It just got *us*."

"Got us—you mean we're—"

"No, no of course not. Alive as we'll ever be. But where—"

"Wherever we are, I don't want to be here, Doug. I want to be back..."

"Easy, honey." He put his arm about her, drew her to him, and he could feel her taut muscles relax a little. "I'd like to say it's a dream, but two people don't dream the same dream at once. And I'm not the type to think up clothes like these all by myself... Somehow, the Contraption did it. I was monkeying with a theorem I got interested in once in space-time mechanics. But it was all on paper—just something to fool with. It was impossible for the Contraption to really do anything." He sat down again. "Impossible."

"Like flying, my mother used to say. What do we do, Doug?"

"That's my gal..." He got up a second time, forced a smile. "Let's go upstairs and see if anybody's around."

There were stairs. Wide and gently curving and constructed of a light, lusterless steel.

Architecturally, the house was little different from many of the expensive-looking California-type affairs he had seen in the women's

95

magazines that Dot bought every so often. Yet there was something about its interior, a certain grace combined with a subtle simplicity that made it a work of art as a good painting or sculptural piece is art. There was rebellion in it—a gentle rebellion against the eye-aching extremes of artificial modernity, yet at the same time a freedom of execution that made the confines of formalized pattern seem childish.

The pastel carpeting was of a deep, soft substance that Doug recognized as a masterpiece in plastic; the furniture was simple, casual, but not stark and starved-looking. The rooms themselves were ample and were as bright in the far corners as in those nearest the wide, sashless windows. They were not separated by partitions, but divided instead by a fragile-appearing tracery of latticework in which a decorative motif was woven with an almost fairy-like geometrical magic. The air was cool and fresh.

"Now I know I'm dreaming," Dot said in a low voice. They walked quietly, from room to room, listening, half-waiting. "I expect any minute to find three bowls of porridge somewhere."

"I wonder..." Doug said. "What's here is—I think its ours. I think we live here."

"Doug look—through the window!"

HE saw a broad lawn of carefully trimmed yet almost ankle-deep grass, inset at the edges with a running garden. And the street beyond was wide, and there were other houses at its far side that looked much as he knew this one must appear. Roofs of tinted tiling, walls of delicately toned glass brick, wide, gently curving windows.

These Doug saw in the first instant, and then there were the soundless vehicles in the street.

"Like smooth, transparent walnut shells," Doug said. "Cooling louvres in the back—engines in the rear. They know their engineering, too. Wonder if the body is some sort of transparent steel—"

"The people in them, Doug! Did you see them? Just like—"

"Like us, of course. Still expecting the three bears?" He laughed a little. They were like children in some new fairyland, half-afraid, half-unbelieving. "Wherever we are, it's populated by humans—if it weren't, we may not have come out this way..."

"Doug, do you know?" She turned, faced him, and there was still fear deep in her eyes. Not the stark fear of terror, but the bewildered, uncomprehending fear of disbelief.

"No I don't. But these clothes aren't ours—even our faces, our bodies aren't. Just our actual selves came through unaltered. Our egos—personalities—whatever you want to call it that gives a human being his identity. The rest we've—moved into, I think. Anyway, it's a theory to go on. I wonder what our names are—"

"Doug, don't."

"I wish I were trying to be funny. But don't you see?"

"Whatever happened to us—couldn't that have changed us? Our—our atomic structure, couldn't that have been changed or altered somehow? It's all so crazy—"

"It's easy to see, m'girl, that you don't spend your time at a bridge table all those hours I'm slaving away on Madhouse Hill! But if that had happened... I don't know. It's the clothes. Too completely different—not just out of shape, or an altered shape, but of a fundamentally *different* shape. We got—we got transplanted."

"But then what of—"

"Thinking the same thing. Suppose the Contraption, whatever it's done—suppose it works *two* ways? A swap, a trade?"

"But Doug that's—"

He smiled. Dot was suddenly silent with the knowledge that whether she liked it or not, she could no longer refuse to accept the facts as they were, could no longer cross off their implications for want of bolder imagination.

"Are we—is it the...the future?"

"Maybe. You could even ask 'is this Earth?' and I couldn't tell you. I wonder what *they* think where *they* are... I wonder if they know."

"Doug, would they—do anything? To Terry and Mike, I mean?"

"I sure hope not—and I don't think so. The boys will be all right—they know their way around back home—whomever it is we've replaced is in the same boat we are. They'd think more than twice before rashly committing themselves to trouble. They're probably trying to communicate with the kids—if the kids stuck around that long. I'm wondering more about the Contraption. If they start fooling with it..."

"Then we'd go back?"

"Maybe. Maybe not. I think though that they'd leave it alone, on the theory that whoever invented it knows its use, knows how to handle it safely. They'd be wrong, but I think that's how they'd figure it. I don't think any one'll dare touch it, simply out of sheer fear of what might happen next."

"I'm scared, Doug. Awful scared."

"I guess that makes two of us. Somehow we've got to dig up the parts for another Contraption. And then—" He let the sentence drift into silence.

"And then, Doug?"

"Well maybe with the exact same set-up—same everything, I could do it again. I don't know. But if they so much as try to turn the other one off, try to change anything, we'll lose this point of reference in space-time for good."

SLOWLY, Dot nodded understanding. "The parts," she said then. "Can we find the things you need?"

"I'll give it the old college try, sweetheart."

"How long—"

He shrugged. "A few days maybe. Depends."

They were silent for a moment, looking through the wide window, watching the beautiful vehicles as they slid silently past, re-examining what they could see of the colorful world beyond the rolling lawn. Doug felt an aching in his jaws, a tightness through his lips. God, it was so silly—standing there, trying to explain, when he didn't even know what had happened, where they were or—or when they were. He'd been after travelling light to bring back pictures of the past— every home should have one. Nuts. The future—no, it wasn't supposed to be that way. Unless you accepted past, present and future as the components of one great unit, and progression from one to the other nothing more than illusion, like the illusion of movement given by the hundreds of still frames on a film-strip. If time was like such a film-strip, and you found a way to jump forward along it, bypassing the frames that were in immediate succession—

But then what about the possibility-probability pattern theory, in which time was supposed to exist as an infinite number of possibility and probability paths, intersecting, paralleling, diverging, splitting with each new decision, each new action—Lord it was getting insane.

"Hell I'm all mixed up," he said. Dot put her arm through his. He nodded toward what was beyond the window. "We might as well have a look for ourselves. If anybody says anything to us we'll suddenly see something interesting in the other direction. Game?"

"I—I guess so…"

"Damn, I wish I had a cigarette!"

They went to the front door, swung it open.

THE streets were long and incredibly wide and straight, bearing their traffic smoothly and with hardly a hint of the inevitable jamming that was so familiar. The sidewalks were immaculately kept, yet surprisingly free of pedestrians; a few passed, bowed slightly and smiled, continued on.

"Polite bunch," Doug murmured. "They bow like good Republicans…"

"And all smiling—as if they didn't have a worry in the world."

"Democrats, then!" They laughed, and for a moment the anxiety was gone, and the street could have been any fine street in the world from which they'd come.

"We'd better try to find the center of town," Doug said then. "We've got to do a lot more than ogle if we want to locate the stuff we're after. Sshh…"

This time two women passed. They smiled, bowed, went on.

"Maybe you're the mayor of this town or something—at least an alderman."

"They wouldn't smile, honey! Anyway, there are three things we'd better figure. How to get money, how to get food, how to get the equipment. Any ideas?"

"We should've searched the house for a wallet or something. Or maybe these people don't believe in money—maybe they use a different system altogether."

"It's possible, of course, and—good night!" Doug was staring suddenly upward. There had been a low rumbling sound, which within seconds had ascended the decibel scale to a throbbing roar. A great, tapering thing of silvery metal with no hint of wing-surfaces was bolting skyward, and Doug knew somehow that the sky was not its limit. The roar and scream of suddenly-split atmosphere subsided, and in moments, the vertically-climbing craft was out of sight. "They've done it here, Dot! I'd bet the bottom dollar I don't have that we've seen our first space-liner!"

"Could I have been right, Doug? The future, I mean?"

"I don't know, Dot… I don't know."

There were towering buildings less than a half-mile from them of a simplicity and beauty that left no time for talk. The city was suddenly before them—a sparkling thing, unmarred by eye-stumbling bits and pieces—a flawless, symmetrical sweep toward the heavens that momentarily stupefied credulity. Traffic ramps soared from street-level in gently curving ribbons above spacious quiet parks; sound was muffled to near-inaudibility, and the illusion of a great fairy kingdom was unmarred by the confusion of advertising posters, marquees, store front lettering, or the raucous stampede of elbowing mobs...

"I wonder how they illuminate at night," Doug was saying. "I wonder what they—my God, Dot, look up—all over. Where is it?"

Far above, the sky seemed gradually to darken into an ever-deepening shadow of blackness. But the sun—She couldn't find the sun!

"It's a different planet, Doug!"

"And the city—it *is* lit! There must be a sun but it's down—it's night, and they've found a way to illuminate an entire city as though daylight were perpetual!"

And that was when it caught their eye. It was a small store and she could see neatly-tiered rows of groceries inside—fruits and vegetables were easily recognizable even the street's width from them. But it was the little rack outside the store—the one that held the newspapers.

Almost at a run they crossed the street, and Doug fought down the urge to reach out and grab one of the editions.

The front pages of the newspapers were easily readable. Because, they were printed in excellent English.

The date beneath the masthead of one was April 17, 1958. The paper was the Washington Post.

CHAPTER THREE

IT was light. Terry had been watching the darkness fade for about ten minutes, fascinated, because the diffused glow grew as though from nowhere, and he could not find the sun. At first he'd felt sort of scared, but nothing happened, so he'd kept watching, trying to find it.

He was still in bed. It was when he became aware that it wasn't his own bed that he sat up straight, wondering, trying to remember. He was in a long, narrow place, and there were a lot of beds—bunks, like his own, lining each side, end to end. Across from him somebody else was sitting up. All the others were still asleep.

"Hey!" Terry called.

"Hey yourself! Who're you?" the other boy said.

"Terry Blair. What in the heck is this place? What's your name?" He had a funny feeling in his stomach, and he was hot and sweaty. He wanted to hear the other boy's voice again.

"Quit your kiddin'—Terry Blair's my brother!"

"What're you talking about, anyway?" Terry said, wondering if the other boy was trying to pick a fight. "I'm Terry Blair all right, and I know *my* brother when I see him! He's Mike Blair, and he don't look anything like you."

"Say who are you anyhow? Somebody tell you my name or something? You aren't awful funny."

"Neither are you, tryin' to imitate the way Mike talks."

There were stirrings in some of the other beds, and somebody mumbled "Pipe down!" Terry tried to be quiet getting out of the bunk. He stood up, felt a little light-headed, and walked over to the other's bed. He sat at its foot. The light feeling—and it seemed to be all over him now—wouldn't go away.

"Come on, don't be wise. What is this place?"

"Don't be wise yourself! How should I know? Maybe it's a hospital. I must've got sick down cellar or something when Dad turned on the Contraption—"

"All that funny blue light," Terry said. "But how—"

Then they looked at each other. Hard.

"What d'you know about the blue light?" Mike asked.

"How d'you know about Dad and the Contraption?" Terry countered. "You spying from someplace?" Terry was on his feet and had both small fists clenched. "You get up out of there!"

"Wait up…maybe it put us to sleep, so this is all a dream, like. Nobody looks the same in dreams."

"You're crazy. They don't sound alike, and you're trying to sound like Mike…"

"You sound like Terry, too. You could all right in a dream, just like you know the same things. I'll tell you the first two numbers in the address of our house. If you can give me the last two, then we will know. And if you can't smart guy—"

"You don't even know the street we live on."

"It's Delaware, so how do you like that? And here's the first two numbers—2, 6—"

"8, 1—"

"What'd I tell you? It sure is a dream. You're Terry all right I guess and I'm me—Mike—but in a dream everybody always looks funny you got black hair, all straight and cut short."

"You too. But guess you're Mike though, as long as it's a dream. Only I feel pretty real."

"Sure, me too. Sometimes dreams are like that. Just like for real."

"Well I hope we don't get into a nightmare. They make me sweat awful."

"I'm all sweaty now—so're you. It's sure hot around here. Where in heck d'you suppose we are, anyway?"

"You don't think Dad's thing killed us, and—and we're—"

"Naw—they wouldn't have beds or anything. Anyhow, Dad told us all about that once. There's no such place. It's got something to do with state of mind, whatever that is."

"Well we've been kinda bad every now and then just the same."

"Dad says that hasn't got anything to do with it, don't you remember? Nobody keeps books on you, like a report card, or anything. It's up to you, and you know how you feel about it inside. That's what he said, and I believe Dad. Dad's smart, Terry."

"Wish he was here too."

"Grown-ups got dreams of their own to worry about. You're not scared, are you?"

"Who me? Heck, no. Hey, have a look at the funny clothes hanging up at the side of our beds. Like riding pants, with wide black belts. Look, some belts got three little silver things in each side. And have a look at the boots! Hey, feel this one—light as anything."

"Who ever heard of blue riding pants? Besides you don't know how to ride a horse any more than I do."

"Bet I could though. Boy—"

"Hey, have a look out this window. You can see all over. This must be the same kind of place all the other long ones are."

THE buildings were long and narrow with rounded, Quonset-type roofs. They were built end to end in long, dull-blue rows, and the grass that grew between them was of an exactly matching shade, tall, and lush. At precise intervals, the rows of buildings were interrupted by uncurbed streets of hard-packed, dull black dirt, and at the end of the widest was a field-like expanse trimmed to a perfect circle. The massive, glittering building in its center was immense. Varicolored banners flew from a trio of spires rising antenna-like from a single point atop the highest, oddly flat-topped turret. In the geometric center of the squat structure's otherwise unbroken curving front was a balcony, molded deftly into the severe sweeping architectural lines of which it was an integral, although predominating part. Beyond were rolling hills, and close above them, a foggy, blue-white sky.

Already waves of heat were beginning to shimmer from the triple turrets of the gold-hued colossus in the center of the great circle and the banners above them were being whipped by stiff gusts that seemed to blow from several directions at once. Once or twice, there were flashes of lightning that split the low rolling bottom of the sky, but there were no gathering storm clouds, nor was there rain.

"Gosh," Terry said. "It sure is funny grass—"

A high, shrill sound suddenly pierced the stillness, and at its signal, youngsters, no older than themselves were stumbling from their narrow cots, yawning, standing.

"They're putting on their pants and boots. We better—" Mike was saying. Wide-eyed, they watched the others, carefully imitated them. There were no shirts to cover the young, sweating torsos and dressing was simple. Just the crisply-cut breeches, the light snug-fitting boots, and the black belts.

"You guys been assigned to a quadrant yet?"

Mike looked up. He was a taller boy, and looked a little older than the rest. He wore a gold star in his belt, and there were still-red scars across his chest and across one shoulder.

"I guess not," Mike said. "What's that? Quadrant, I mean?"

"How long have you been here, anyway? Thought you two came a couple of weeks ago. On the *Mikol VI.*"

The twins looked at each other, then back to the tall, blonde boy.

"What's your name?" Terry asked.

"I'm Jon Tayne. Son of Quadrate Larsen Tayne. Your father's a general officer just like mine—that's why we can talk together out here. Otherwise we couldn't—part of the training, you know. Teaches you the undesirability of class-consciousness. I've been here two years—they tossed me back. Insufficient conditioning. But it doesn't matter to me—maybe you'll get as big a kick out of it as I do. I like it here. Not many do, though."

"It's sure different," Mike said, "but we haven't been here any two weeks, I don't think. Anyway it hasn't seemed like that long, has it

Terry?"

"Golly, I—"

"Terry? Thought you two were Kurt and Ronal Blair? Washington, western hemisphere north?"

"We live in Washington, that's for sure," Terry said. "But I'm—"

"Hey I know, Terry. It's all like we said, and here that's us. You can be Kurt. I'm Ronal. But don't get mixed up."

"Your father's Senior Quadrate Douglas Blair, isn't he?" the tall boy said.

"He's the Douglas Blair part, anyway," Mike said. "Makes I guess over thirteen thousand dollars a year, too."

"Say, you sure you're all right? I didn't think you were hit very hard in practice yesterday, but you talk as if you were. Thirteen grand is just about enough to buy a loaf of bread. Your father makes what mine does and what every other adult does—thirty billion dollars a year. Then after he contributes his dutiful share to the Prelatinate, he has a billion dollars left. Didn't you know that?"

"Gosh no. Not exactly, I mean."

"What's Prelatinate?" Terry asked.

"What's—listen, fellows—any one of us, even a Quadrate's son, can be turned into the Director for saying a thing like that, even as a joke. Better watch it. If there's one thing you learn here, it's praise and respect for your government. They're pretty rough on sacrilege, I should think your father would have told you. My training was started when I was four, but you sound almost as though you haven't had any yet."

"I don't even remember when I was four," Mike said

"That doesn't matter. When an adult tells you something—"

The tall boy was interrupted then by a second sounding of the shrill signal, and at once, he hurried to the end of the building. The others fell in behind him in a column of threes. Mike and Terry took positions at the end of the column.

"Where are we going?"

"Breakfast, I hope!" Terry said. The tall boy pressed a stud in the wall, and the front door rolled back. Then he turned his head and bellowed "Section, tench-*hut*! Forward *march*!" And he sounded as though he enjoyed it.

They marched out, and, to Terry's gratification, it was to a huge, diamond-shaped building in which they found breakfast waiting.

IT was during the rest period after the half-hour session of calisthenics that the *Mikol VII* landed. Terry and Mike had been laying prostrate on the thickly matted, damp blue grass, a little out of breath but strangely enough, little more fatigued than had they just finished a short inning of sandlot baseball. They both had been watching the milky-blue sky, and had chosen a place to rest somewhat apart from the others. There were hundreds and hundreds of the others in formations of their own, Terry had noticed, and all together he could only guess at how many there were. There was one adult in charge of all of them, but they had not seen him closely yet nor heard his voice.

Before the first sounds of thunder, Mike had been puzzling a lot of things at once.

"Did you ever jump so high before?"

"It really wasn't awful high. Higher, though I guess than ever before. Felt kind of funny, huh?"

"Sure did. Is it hard for you to walk?"

"We never played soldier much—you know how Dad felt about that. The other guys are pretty good at keeping the same step. We'll catch on, though."

"I didn't mean that. I didn't feel—well, heavy enough, sort of. I kinda bounce when I try to walk."

"Me too, but all dreams are funny. I suppose in a dream you could jump clear over the buildings back there if you wanted to. Boy, wait'll we tell Dad about dreaming we're in a military school. He'll have a fit!"

"He sure will. Remember that time we asked him about it? I guess even Mom was surprised at how he flew up that way. He said if he hadn't thought he could teach us himself how to grow up good without putting us in uniforms to do it he'd never have had us. But it's kind of fun though. So far—"

That was when they heard the thundering sound almost directly above them, but it was like no thunder they had ever heard before. There was a sudden swirling of the thick sky above them, and they jumped up, rooted, watching.

The *Mikol VII* burst suddenly through the heavy clouds, its stern belching flame and rolling volumes of sound. The heavy air about them vibrated as they watched.

It looked like a huge, shining artillery shell, dropping groundward as though held in the grip of some great, invisible hand that slowed it, held it in perfect balance as it descended wrong-end first, directly above the circular place at the end of the long, broad street.

"Like a big V-2 going the wrong way!" Mike said.

"It's a space ship, that's what it is!" Terry yelled. "Comin' in to land. Just like in the movie we saw, Mike. Just like."

"Look, it's almost down—c'mon up on this little hill here you can see 'em driving big trucks or something out to meet it. What do you suppose it's got?"

"Wonder where it's from? Mars, I bet."

"Hi! Pretty sight, isn't it?" It was the tall boy who led their section. He had his thumbs hooked in his belt just behind where the gold stars were.

"Sure is," Terry said, eyes glued to the towering craft, which had just settled perfectly to the ground.

"It's the *Mikol VII*, and it's the last shipment before the games. Guess there'll be another ten thousand or so guys, and then we can start getting all our equipment issued. They don't give us our stuff until everybody's here. That's to make it so that we all have an absolutely equal amount of training. Watch—they're starting to come out now. Just the way you guys did when you came."

MIKE and Terry weren't listening. They watched as a great opening suddenly appeared near the ship's blunt stern, to which an inclined ramp was being towed by a tiny surface vehicle. Then they started coming out, five abreast, in seemingly unending numbers.

"They're still wearing civvies," the tall boy said. "They'll get their game issue tonight, though, and their equipment, along with us. Trucks drop it off at each barracks, and then it's given out by each section leader. I guess there must be tons of the stuff."

"Where they going now?"

As the youngsters poured from the *Mikol VII* they were grouped into formations by adults who had come from the huge, golden building.

"Why, to their barracks, just like everybody else does. They ate before they landed, and their barracks assignments were made at headquarters on Earth before they even took off."

"On Earth?"

"Sure, didn't you know that? Believe me, it has to be efficient. The Quadrates and their staffs work all year at headquarters getting things lined up for the games. They don't show up here until the day things start. The Director's here, but you only see him once, at the opening ceremonies. As far as the games are concerned, he ranks everybody—except the Prelate-General, of course. He signs the orders that split us up into our quadrants."

"Hey, Jon…"

"You better call me lance-sergeant out here. Somebody could get the wrong idea."

"Sure, sarge! Is that what the gold star means?"

"Uh huh. You get 'em if you volunteer. Like I did, before I was ten. Sets a good example, you know."

"Gee. Is everybody here our age?"

"Nobody can be more than a month over ten. That's the law. That is except for volunteers, who are younger, and those who get tossed back for insufficient conditioning and have to stay for the games all over again, like me. I was twelve a couple months ago. I like it though."

"But say, what'd you mean about Earth?"

"Well, that's where all the plans and everything are made before you even leave. You didn't think all that stuff was done here on Venus, did you?"

AS Jon had said, the trucks came with the loads of equipment for each barracks that night after supper. They were large, long trucks and Terry wondered why they didn't make the awful racket that trucks always made. There wasn't the stink of burned Diesel fuel. The huge vehicle just rolled up outside soundlessly, and Terry watched for the driver to get out. None did. He tried to look into the front of the vehicle, but it was too dark to see what was on the other side of the long narrow windows.

"Nothing in there," Jon said. "Those are just for maintenance inspection. It'd be a mess if the robot control ever went out of whack, believe me. Better start help unloading."

The unloading took less than fifteen minutes, and then the truck moved on to the next barracks. The rude, wooden crates were heavy, but not large. There were three for each of the hundred bunks.

When the last was placed at the foot of Jon's bunk, he stood on the largest one and told them what to do.

"I'll distribute a chisel to each of you," he said, "and as you open each box, place its contents on your bunk, so that it can be inspected for fitness before use.

"You'll open the smallest box first. In it you'll find your helmet and polishing kit. Keep the helmet shined at all times—if anybody's isn't it's ten demerits. Fifty, as you've all been told, and you get your records marked 'insufficient conditioning'. Your helmets may look heavy—on Earth they'd weigh about five pounds, but here they're just a little less than four. You'll get used to them.

"In the second box—the flat one—you'll find all your personal maintenance equipment. You should have a whetstone, extra leather thongs, a set of files, and a small can of oil. They're to be kept in the condition, which you find them, and will be worn at all times on the shoulder equipment sling, which is in the third box.

"In the third box—the long, flat one, are your most important pieces of equipment. I'll show you how they attach to your arm belt. Needless to say, they must he kept thoroughly polished—and sharpened—at all times. Now I'll give out the chisels, and you can open the boxes."

They did. Terry and Mike helped each other when they got their chisels. They followed Jon's directions perfectly. First the helmet and the polishing kit. Then the whetstone, extra leather thongs, the set of files, the can of oil, and the shoulder equipment sling.

Then the eight-inch dagger, the two-foot spiked mace, and the double-edged broadsword.

CHAPTER FOUR

THE price of the paper was $3,000.

"Doug—do we dare—"

"No. We've only got a second or so, as though we were just interested passersby, looking at the headlines. Got to be careful."

PRELATINATE OKs MORE FUNDS FOR SCHOOLS the eight-column streamer read. Doug scanned the lead quickly.

"Washington, April, 17—(WP)—Prelate General Wendel announced through his press headquarters here tonight that both houses of the Prelatinate have unanimously voted to grant the request of the Council of Education, 27th Department, for seven trillion dollars in additional funds for school building. The funds will be used for the replacement of 34 outmoded buildings in the Department, the newest of which, it was said, is more than 12 years old. The Council's original request for five trillion dollars was increased by the Prelatinate to seven trillion in recognition of—"

Good Lord, he thought, *good Lord...*

City Cabinet Praises Mayor On Budget Expansion...

Area Industries Vote Shorter Work Week...

Liberals, Conservatives In Accord On Labor Issue...

S-Council Reports Second Arrest In Four Years...

Veteran Civic Leader Admits Wisdom Of Youth Group's Plan...

"Doug—oh Doug, none of this can be real..."

"We'd better go back to the house. And take it easy, lady..." He managed to grin a little.

No one passed them on the walk back, but Dot clung close to him as they walked, as though the mature years since college had never been, as though simple happiness were again all that mattered.

The mature years...

Doug wondered. Somewhere, he had always known, there was the place between resigned acceptance of things as they were and perpetual refusal to recognize a condition for what it was. Somewhere, happiness was a simple, honest thing, uncomplicated by the devious machinations of sadistic, moral codes that would make a struggle of that right. Somewhere there was meaning to action, and the hypocrite was at last fallen from the mocking pedestal of lip-service righteousness.

Somewhere, perhaps long ago, a man had said, "I question" even as, at the same time, another had said, "I condemn" and another had said, "I follow". Thus far, had they traveled the same road, but here, the road was forked. One was a wide path. One an aimless twisting thing that had no destination. The other, narrow, and ever narrower as it progressed. And there would be other forks, other paths, that split and re-split as they tracked the infinite reaches of time itself...

He remembered the first thing he'd learned in his first plunge into space-mechanics research. *Space cannot exist without time; time cannot exist without space. Space-time, then, is the fabric of the Universe.*

So the threads were real. As real as the fact that one day in his life, he had decided to study law rather than to continue as a physicist. There had suddenly been a new split in the thread, and he chose, and had become an attorney, and then a man of politics.

What had Carl said? *"...you'd've made that try for the moon a success last month instead of another near-miss..."*

And how many other might-have-beens could there be?

We conceive of Time, as it is integral with the structure of Space, an infinite... The second thing he had learned.

And therefore—therefore each thread of might-have-been, unto itself, *was.*

Somewhere, there was a Congressman named Douglas Blair. Somewhere, there was an astrophysicist, an artist, a sculptor, a writer, a cab driver, a general, a sailor, a doctor, a thief, perhaps even a corpse named Douglas Blair...

"I know," he said to the woman at his side then. "Dorothy, I think I know."

They entered the beautiful house set far back from a wide, beautiful highway on a lush, beautiful lawn.

And he tried to explain, until he thought she understood.

He was tired, then. She located food in the house, and he found money in a wallet in which the identification card said simply Douglas Blair, Senior Quadrate of Games.

But everything was changed. Not just himself and Dorothy. A whole world. All on another thread, that had started back somewhere, much further back. Through history, there had been so many ifs...

In a little while she lay beside him, and they slept.

THEY had intended to begin the search for materials to build another contraption, but before he was fully dressed, from somewhere, there was a soft tinkling sound. It was repeated, signal-like, from a far corner of the room. It came from what could only have been an extremely simplified, compact version of the telephone, installed integrally with the ample arm of a lounging chair.

"Shall I?" he hesitated.

"Be careful..."

Doug lifted the slender receiver. "Blair," he said.

"Quadrate Blair, sorry, sir, that the liberty was taken to disturb you at your home. However, because of the urgency of this morning's conference at your offices, it was considered wise to remind you of the time it is planned to convene, as per Instruction 43-A. May you be expected at 1100 hours, sir?"

He dared not hesitate.

"Yes, yes of course." The voice he answered was a woman's.

"Will you wish the 'copter as usual, sir?"

"Why—yes of course, as usual. Thank you..." He hung up quickly. Dot was looking at him with the question held at her lips.

"I'm expected at some sort of high-powered pow-wow in—" he glanced at a delicate clock inset in the chair's opposite arm, "—less than a half-hour. They're sending a 'copter for me. God knows what will happen if I don't show up."

And, he observed to himself, only God knew what would happen when he did.

CHAPTER FIVE

WHEN the 'copter swished to a feather-like landing on the wide expanse of the front lawn, Doug was ready. He had dressed himself in one of the dozen uniforms he had found arrayed in neat order in a full-length bedroom closet. He fastened the cape at his throat, wished suddenly that there was some way he could take Dot with him.

Suddenly she was in his arms, and Doug could feel her tremble.

"Don't worry, honey," Doug said. He opened the door. "So far it looks pretty civilized—hell, they couldn't be any worse than the quaint little tribe of cut-throats back home! Matter of fact, if I thought for a minute anyone here'd believe me—"

"Better not, Doug."

"Not a chance. I'm still one of Our Crowd—I don't trust anybody! And don't you— Stay put right here 'til I'm back, understand?"

He kissed her, then walked across the lawn to the idling helicopter.

It was empty.

He got inside, then saw the red button with the one word RE-TURN under it. He punched it.

Effortlessly, the robot controlled craft lifted, wafted him in seconds high above the city. Its rise stopped at what he judged was about 1,000 feet, then proceeded on a course of its own.

"Wonderful, these dreamers," he muttered, and became engrossed in study of the fabulous city below him.

There was no capitol dome, nor could he find the Washington monument. But there was still the Potomac, and there were the cherry blossoms.

Then the city became little more than a rolling pattern of line and color to him, and the thoughts began coming quickly, intensely. An excuse for the difference in his voice—did people here have colds? The uniform—suppose something were wrong...and his own mannerisms—how closely would he resemble, under the close scrutiny of the few there that must know him well, the man whom he'd replaced—the other Douglas Blair, who must at this instant be facing the same problem in a world as alien to him as this was to Congressman Douglas Blair? The woman on the phone had said, "Your offices"—his meeting, then, and they'd ask questions.

He'd been a fool. He'd never carry it off in a million years! They were smart—even a half-intelligent person of his own world could spot the eternal phony trying to bluff for what just wasn't there, even in the guy who'd learned how from the right books. Hell, he'd be as transparent as manners at a pink tea.

HE wondered about the other Douglas Blair, and how the trap felt that had snapped on him. About the kids—what about his kids? Terry was a smart boy and he'd know the Contraption had been responsible for what had happened. Would he try to get hold of Carl or somebody? If a bunch of technicians or even scientists got to the Contraption, touched anything... There would be no knowing about that until they tried to get back. Either the reference frame would be the same or, if someone had tampered, it would be completely altered, and Dot and himself would go from one time thread to the next, *ad infinitum*, with finding their own again as probable as finding a specific grain of sand in the Sahara.

The other Douglas Blair. And of course, his wife. He knew what they looked like—she would have Dot's slenderness, her face, eyes, and hair... No one would know. And the man would look like himself. Suppose even the kids didn't know? Doug wondered if they'd fool the kids... And then—then what? No one would know, but that was a joke. They wouldn't believe it if his alter-ego got to a microphone and broadcast it. People only believed in gossip, in rumor, in the miracles of wishful thinking. They never believed in facts. They accepted them, but they were not convinced. Newspapers would publish accounts of dolls that wept, but carefully steered clear of the scientific phenomenon if it were not between governmental quotation marks. It was true of course—mystery, properly interpreted, could not hurt. A fact defied interpretation; in the final analysis, it must be taken or left. And when it was a fact strange to the beliefs of men, it was left for as long a period as curiosity would permit. And then, of course, misunderstood.

He wondered how the other Douglas Blair would manage, and what, upon realizing that his was the superior intelligence and knowledge, he would do with it...

The 'copter had begun to lose altitude and the flat expanse of a large roof below was its destination. Its edges were lined with other 'copters, hangars, servicing equipment, men. While he watched a pilotless ship gently rose into a flight pattern above the roof toward which he descended. Another was descending toward it even as he was, from slightly above and from the east.

And then there were little cold, stabbing fingers of panic inside him, squeezing, twisting his vitals.

Relax, mister.

Now it was no longer a pleasantly fantastic detached stage setting, with red exit lights glowing reassuringly somewhere off in the shadows of reality. Quite painfully, he felt the chiding slap of reality across his face.

And it hurt.

Forget about the Contraption, forget about the smart guys, and their smart little world—their little dung-heaps of stupidity and moral cannibalism you've had the colossal luck to escape...

Can't do it? That's right—the kids, of course...

Sure, but old Mother Nature takes care of that, doesn't she? When your kids are lying dead on some foreign battlefield you can have more... That's why life's cheap, old man... Nature doesn't care—she'll keep supplying and supplying as long as there are fools enough to flood the market. And you have your woman, if it's kids you want...

It's a clean slate... Pick up the chalk—

But you couldn't name them Mike and Terry, dammit, you couldn't!

The 'copter's landing gear touched.

Its blades were still slowing as the two uniformed men appeared beside it, opened the small door. Doug climbed out, and the two stood at attention, each right palm open and raised. He understood. The universal gesture for peace—a salute. An odd gesture to replace the mock-shielding of the eyes against the glitter of a nobleman's shiny battle armor!

He returned it, and they fell in at his side to escort him across the landing roof to an opening entrance, cloaks swirling gently behind them in the bright morning sunlight.

HE entered the chamber still flanked by the orderlies. There were nine men and a woman about the circumference of the long, elliptical conference table, and they stood as though brought erect by a common puppet-string as he came through the wide door.

The vacant chair was at the far end of the table. Silently, he was escorted to it, seated. The others bowed with but a hint of movement toward him, then seated themselves. The orderlies withdrew, and the softly curved walls seemed to grow in upon themselves as the wide doorway through which he had come soundlessly disappeared.

Here they were, then. Ten people, whom he did not know, called to conference for the discussion of some supposedly vital situation of which he had not the slightest inkling. And he had apparently called it, so the talking was up to him.

It would mean discovery before he had said ten words.

As they sat, his eyes swept from one to the next in unhesitating succession.

The woman, next to him, was clothed as Dot had been. He had seen many less attractive. Of the men, three obviously outranked the remaining six, who would have looked, were it not for the too-serious set of their faces, like college athletes. Their three superiors, he judged, were nearer his own age. The markings at the collars of their blue cloaks were identical with his own, with the exception that they were executed in red rather than in white. Four identical insignia— four identical commands then.

The term Quadrate was at once self-explanatory. Somewhere, there were four great armies...

And he, apparently, held power of decision over them all. What colossal thing surged one way or the other at his order? And—who or what, in turn, ordered him?

Now they were seated, waiting.

You should've run, you should've run... What'd you think it was, just a dream with the label "Impossible" stuck on it? How long did you think you could deny the reality of what you knew was real? How deep do you have to get into a mess before you're convinced you don't come equipped with a guardian angel, a $64 miracle that'll just take you over and bail you out when the going gets rough enough? Charms and such went out with the Dark Ages, mister... Or didn't anybody ever tell you?

"...Gentlemen, you of course know why you're here..." *That's the idea! After all, you learned the old double-talk technique a long time ago—Congressman.* "Therefore perhaps it will be best to reverse the usual question and answer procedure; I shall hear your questions and opinions on the matter first, then present my own. Proceed..."

The girl was writing.

The others seemed to be swallowing it.

"Quadrate Blair," the tallest of the three said abruptly. "Frankly, we were hoping you might lay the matter open in this way! I don't intend to speak for Quadrate Tayne and Quadrate Klauss, but I think they have felt the same as I. Is it to be our understanding that we are to receive no OP for this year's games? I for one would be the first to grant that our overall system, developed since the days of the Sahara as it has been, is well perfected, as nearly without flaw as is possible to make it. Yet the burden of detail is always with us. It is the small details, after all, each built on each, that have brought us to the high level we've achieved. There has always been room for correction, for experiment, for change. Therefore I, and I think here I may speak for the others, am puzzled that, with the first phase of the games but a week hence, we have received nothing—and there were details of last year's Operational Procedure that I know Quadrate Klauss as well as myself felt should have been further examined in the field. The boys themselves keep developing new techniques—one tells the other, a brother, a friend—and we must make it our business to keep abreast of them, or we'll find ourselves in the midst of a confusion that could conceivably assail the very psychological foundations upon which our civilization is built!"

THE one called Klauss rose then. He had a more soldierly carriage than the first man, but he was not as tall. His tone was more conservative, yet of a more subtle firmness. And Doug listened. It was the only way in which he might gain some hint, some shadow of an idea of what these impossible men were talking about.

"Would you answer one question, sir?" the Quadrate named Klauss said. "Is the Director's word on this thing final? I ask this since if there is still the possibility of discussing further any or all of the procedure amendments proposed in our check lists..."

The words meant nothing. So far so good, but it was just stalling—he'd succeeded in gaining time, but when they were finished, they'd expect some sort of decision, and then a follow-through.

Dammit, he was balled up! Somehow maybe he could fake long enough to get the materials, build the Contraption and get out. A tele-radio machine he had examined in the house while Dot slept might provide some of the needed material, but not the vital stuff. He would order that from a government supply office as soon as he returned to the house. His rank should be sufficient to get him what he needed without questions being asked. The Earth he knew with all its clatter of empty heads, its life-long familiarity—Terry and Mike were there. Or this world of seeming intelligence, efficiency, forthright honesty of conviction? Was there a choice?

The girl beside him moved in her chair. Recording secretary, of course. She would know. Everything—

How many times have you dreamed of a world like this? Don't be a fool...

"—and I therefore submit, sir, that unless final decision has been made by the Director, we further discuss the expedited drafting of the new OP for this year, based on the details enumerated in our checklists."

The third one rose, the one referred to as Tayne.

There was something in the look of the man that brought Doug at once on guard. Wide face and shoulders, sharp, small features that gave his face a curious look of flatness, small eyes. The eyes bored in as though they could see through Doug's body and into his brain, examine it, and find it an imposter.

"I think the Senior Quadrate will agree," he said, "that each time the games are conducted, it must be according to a plan which is as closely fool-proof as is possible to make it. I think he will agree that personal feelings have no place in the formulation of such plans—or their lack of formulation."

All eyes were suddenly on Doug, and he knew that here was a challenge—that here was something the others had wished to say, but had considered the risk too great.

"Continue," he said.

"I ask, in the interests of the Council, what the Senior Quadrate's real reason is for having delayed the revised OP for so protracted a length of time. I am not in position to demand an answer, but I point out that I ask the question as an alternative to filing a formal charge of outright profligacy in office!"

THE sharp intakes of breath about the table were his cue. Even the girl hesitated the space of a second in her transcription. Suddenly, the thing was obvious. And Doug knew he could cope with it—he had, so many times before!

This lad, he thought, *wants to be the next Senior Quadrate!*

"It seems," he said, "the Quadrate has forgotten that the Council table is not intended as a political arena. He will be seated."

Tayne reddened. But he did not sit.

"The Director be praised but it's time we got to the bottom of this! Is it not true, Quadrate Blair, that the OP is being delayed so that whole sections may be entirely revised—in order to conform to your personal beliefs concerning what you term efficiency of equipment, on which we hear you expound so often? I suggest sir that you are grossly overstepping your authority! I doubt seriously that our checklists have even been consulted! The Senior Quadrate would accuse me of seeking his position—I'm aware of that—but I ask him point-blank of his own ambitions toward the Directorate!"

There was but an instant of silence; the Council was stunned. Doug felt cold little drops of sweat rolling down the undersides of his arms. What now? Was he supposed to shoot the man on the spot? Fire him, what? He turned to the girl.

"You will make extra copies of the Quadrate's remarks for the—the Director's personal file. Forward them to his headquarters as soon following adjournment of this session as is possible." She nodded. He was still doing it right. But luck wasn't a consistent thing. "Until the Director clarifies the status of Quadrate Tayne, pending his review of this report of his insubordinate charges and my own recommendations for the severest penalty the law allows for such insubordination, we will consider the conference adjourned, gentlemen…"

They stood at once, bowed, and flanked by their junior officers filed silently out.

Doug remained seated. The secretary was gathering her equipment. He dared ask her—what?

She startled him when she spoke.

"I'll get the transcription coded and prepared for A priority transmission on the first open Venus channel. But if I may

say so, sir—not that he certainly hasn't deserved it ever since his brother got him appointed—it's too bad you could not have found some other way—I've always marvelled at the methods you've been able to devise to cope with him in the past. This was—but pardon me, I'm entirely out of place."

"No, no it's all right. His brother?"

"Why—yes of course, Gundar Tayne. The Director."

CHAPTER SIX

HE had thought like a child to have believed he could have done more than bluff. He had thought like a child to have taken the impossible gamble at all. Already he had committed a fatal error, and he knew that were it not for his physical appearance the farce would not have lasted ten seconds.

Nonsense! Was not a high stake worth the toss of any dice? Perhaps he was slightly mad, but he had *not* thought like a child. Slightly mad, mad enough to suppose that to win happiness there must be courage, and with the courage, success, somehow.

He could feel the solidity of the corridor floor beneath his feet as he followed her toward the panel at its end upon which the words Office of the Senior Quadrate stood boldly, with the insignia of the office inscribed beneath them.

Fatal error be damned!

He would satisfy Tayne! As soon as the panel of the large, private office slid shut behind them, he would countermand his order to the secretary and have her scrap the section of her records which was so much more damning to himself than it could ever be to Tayne. There would be some other way…

Yes, it was politics. But it was the only weapon he knew, and for the moment he would have to wield it more skillfully than he ever had in his life.

And idly, he wondered what they would do if he failed. If, somehow they saw through the disguise of his body…

He knew what they would do. They would make him build a new Contraption, make him go. And the Contraption they would make him build—there was of course too great a chance that he and Dorothy would miss their own point in time, become hopelessly lost…

And wouldn't it be sheer idiocy to risk that?

THE office was a miniature of the council chamber. It was elliptical, furnished with two desks of smooth, soft-finished metal molded to fit the general configurations of the chamber itself, and planned for both business-like efficiency and personal comfort. The nameplate on the larger desk bore his insignia and said Douglas J. Blair; that on the smaller said Miss Jane Landis.

He seated himself.

"Miss Landis, about that report to the Director. Perhaps—perhaps as you suggested, it was in, shall we say, bad taste. Better file it. Future reference."

"Why Doug—what on Earth's the matter?" She put the recording device on her desk, walked over to his. There was a look of concern on her face that he didn't understand. What had he said wrong now? Whatever it was, there was no hint of suspicion in her look, only a vague puzzlement.

Young, and pretty. A trap, perhaps—no, they hadn't tumbled yet. Perhaps just Nature's own trap and that was all. Funny, Doug thought, very funny. There were rules. Sometimes you were supposed to be thankful to Nature, worship her, hold her in awe—and other times, you were supposed to completely deny that she existed, and vilify her if she had done too good a job. She had done a good job on Miss Landis.

"Why, nothing. It is simply that—"

"But why the 'Miss' Landis? Did I do something wrong? And the way you just went over and sat down…"

"Sorry…sorry, Jane." He smiled. "It's Tayne. I think I handled him rather badly."

"Don't worry so, Doug! I've never seen such a little thing get under your skin. Everyone knows he never got properly conditioned, even the Director himself. He's a good games officer, and that's that. He's always trying to draw someone into a state of anger, and you told me yourself just yesterday that you're his special target just for the job. It's a good thing you didn't blow up in there. What came over you—giving an order like that, I mean?"

"I—let's say I was confused for the moment."

"As long as he's the only headquarters man like that there's nothing to keep you so upset, Doug. Now come on—"

She was behind the desk, a slender hand on the back of his chair.

"Not—no not now Jane. Anyway you should appreciate my—"

"Your position…yes…But Lisa's not the jealous sort Doug, you know that. Your wife's always been willing to share you with others…"

"I—yes I know that of course…" *Good Lord…*

He hadn't even thought of it, hadn't been ready. The entire setup of conventions would of course have so many differences—what was simple bad taste in his time-phase might be accepted as a matter of course here. And vice-versa perhaps—how was he to know? And he would have to know.

"Doug…"

He said nothing, and she withdrew a little.

"Doug I'm sorry about getting out of line when I said what I did about the way you handled Tayne, if that's what it is…I know my business and I know yours…"

He remained silent, and she left his side of the desk.

He tried to think, tried to remember the early days in the courtroom. And he must say something quickly—

"No—no honestly I'm glad you said it. After all, how long have we known each other, Jane?"

"Ever since—ever since your election to the Quadrature almost ten years ago."

"Yes—it's a long time, isn't it? Tell me, had you ever known anything about me before then?"

"Why, only your name, your accomplishments. Your work for the great cause of politics and government as a journalist, I read a lot of your work. I thought there was never a man more devoted to his party since the formation of the Prelatinate itself. You were a great man then just as you are now, Doug—and you're third in worship only to the Prelate General himself."

"Worship…you mean public admiration, respect…"

"Doug, how can you say such a thing? It's like—well, as if they'd said years ago that they—that they admired or respected their God!"

He felt the muscles in his jaw slacken, caught them.

"There's been a lot of progress since that era, of course. A lot of hard, exhausting work…" He was careful, lest any of his question-marks show. At any moment he could imagine her whirling upon him, shrieking "Imposter!"

But she was taking the bait.

"It seems impossible that there could ever have been a way of life without the Prelatinate, the Quadrature. Impossible even that there was once such a thing as war. How terrible it must have been—no conditioning, the constant killing of valuable adults..."

HE let her words sink into his memory, pushed them, crammed them into it, then tried to make them follow through.

"Ironic, isn't it, that without such bestiality there might never have been a world as we know it now. I sometimes wonder how often they thought about the future—if they thought about it as we do today. You know, Jane, I think about the future a lot. Remember what we were talking about just the other day—a week or so ago, wasn't it?"

And he waited, tensed. Too far, perhaps—

"Doug—Doug you mustn't talk, about that any more! The S-Council would have both of us in a minute if they ever heard us. The boys in white have sterilized people for less than talking about the desirability of inter-political marriages. But God, how I wish I'd been brought up a Liberal! Lisa wouldn't have had a chance!"

"I suppose it would've made the children a problem..."

"An understatement if I ever heard one! Your twin sons—I bet they're good solid Liberals by now! Do they—do they ever question, Doug? I've often wondered about kids, brought up in the family party from the time they're old enough to say 'Prelatinate'. Have Kurt and Ronal ever—do they ever show a streak of heresy—you know what I mean... I should think kids'd rebel, tryout some ideas of their own."

"Well, did you ever, when you were a child?"

"No—no I guess not. I see what you mean. If you come out with a really good question, there's always an answer for you right out of the Constitutional Commandments."

"And of course no one dares challenge them!"

"Doug!"

"Oh, don't misunderstand, Jane." Almost, that time. He could feel the sweat start under his arms again. Dammit what an Organization. They worshipped government, they were scrupulously careful to keep a perfect check-and-balance on political spheres of influence, they had such well-oiled machinery that even war was impossible.

"Don't worry, I don't."

"I just meant that sometimes it really makes me realize what a wonderful balance we've achieved. Education, population."

"No form of birth control could ever have solved the problems of overcrowding and starvation and war as well as the games you should know! Without work like yours, Doug, just think what the whole world could be like! There'd be the problem of enforcing the birth control laws again, knowing that every time they were violated the threat of unbalance would grow a little more."

The games again. What kind of magic, what kind of panacea were they? He thought of the teeming, overcrowded millions in Europe, Asia—World War I, World War II, Korea, the Puerto Rican revolution in 1955. New York and her East Side slums, Chicago, and—whatever it was he headed, it solved these things.

"Guess I'd better get back to the big job," he said then. "—Or Tayne'll be your new boss! And then—"

"Doug what a perfectly awful thing to say! You've got to stop worrying. Sometimes you're hardly yourself—honestly, if I didn't know you better I'd think you'd lost the old self-confidence, the old strut! Your voice even sounds kind of different. You've got to relax, mister."

"When I get things taken care of, maybe then... And I think—I think I can give them something they can't say no to if I go over every detail once more—a whole re-study." He watched her face closely, nerves taut for the first tell-tale sign that he'd fallen on his face. But she nodded.

"Probably help. Shall I bring in the whole file for last year? Checklists, film-strips, the works?

"Yes," he said. "Yes. That's what I want—the works."

NEATLY lettered on the file-tab of the heavy folder she brought were the words WAR GAMES, 1957, and he did not understand.

War Games, and she had said there was no war...

Suddenly, he was afraid. Afraid to reach inside the folder, afraid to find what would tell him that for some fearful reason she had lied, that this beautiful, sparkling world was nothing but a lie...

He read the file-tab again. WAR GAMES, 1957, it said. No—no he did not understand.

He drew out the four thick volumes of bound records, the square can containing the film strips, the thin sheaf of check-lists.

And he opened the personal record titled *Senior Quadrate's Report. May 1, 1957-May 7, 1957· Blair.*

And simply, directly, it began on the first page.

Subject: War Games, 1957: Notes.

Location: Venus, northern mass, west: N Lat. 38° 24' to N Lat. 37°12'—E Long. 41°6' to E. Long 39°12'.

Force: 1,231,693.

Age range: Reg. 10 yrs. 1 mo. to 10 yrs, 4 mos. Av. 10 yrs. 2% mos.

Mortality: 483,912.

Wounded In Action (Retrieved): 202,516.

Balance: Minus 200 M; plus 173 WIA.

Remarks: Within forgiveness margin.

Conditioning: 3 % held over.

Personal observation: Full month training period completed by entire quadrant. For male children of the 10-year age level, exceptionally excellent military discipline this year. From what I witnessed of the quadrants under Tayne, Klauss and Vladkow, they have experienced the same good results. Despite use of outmoded weapons, combat exceptionally vigorous, well executed and effective. This was especially true in final phase, with all quadrants meeting on common front, northern mass (See map, Final Phase,) at which time 692,511 were committed. Full day rest allowed all quadrants during transfer from southwestern mass of quadrants 2 and 4.

Klauss is to be especially commended for this thoroughness in psychologically preparing his quadrant. Each of its members seemed completely convinced that battle was necessary to survival; I assume Klauss' extraordinary success may be laid to a great extent on his expert use of the propaganda techniques so successful in the World War.

Tayne is also to be commended, as is Vladkow, for having trained his quadrant to an admirably high degree of technical proficiency with both broadsword and mace. (See Recommendations, Final Report.)

Removal of dead done with somewhat lower expedience than usual in all quadrants, due, however to the increased vigor on numerous occasions to…

Doug shut his eyes.

No. No, none of this was so. None of it…

"Jane!"

"Yes, Doug. Something—"

"I want to see the strips—now, if possible."

"Hit on something already?"

"The strips I said! NOW!"

"Of course—right away, Doug." She pressed a stud in a panel flush with the desktop. He knew he had startled her.

But he had to see. If he could see, he'd understand. The words had made no sense at all, they were gibberish, crazy and he didn't know what they meant.

HE held his muscles rigid as he waited for the orderly she had summoned to prepare the recessed projector, inset wall-screen. *Hurry, damn you, hurry!*

"Verbal commentary desired, sir?"

"Oh—yes, yes of course."

"All ready then, sir."

"Go ahead then, go on."

The suffused lighting of the chamber suddenly dimmed, and Jane rose from her desk.

"I'll be in the eightieth level records library, sir, if I'm needed."

"I don't—well if you wish, Miss Landis." She left. Because she knew—yes, of course she'd known what was coming. And she had left—

In full color, the pictures flashed on the screen.

He watched, only subconsciously aware of the intermittent voice describing, evaluating, analyzing. He sat and watched as though there were not a mobile muscle in his sweating body.

Ten-year-old children, somewhere beneath a fantastic milk-white sky, painting an impossible blue plain with the red of their own blood...

The broadswords rose and fell with a savagery unknown to any but the ancient Turk, Mongol, Spartan. They glinted strangely in a daylight where there was no sun, and the piked maces swung in circles of red horror as they tore, smashed, at young, half-naked bodies...

They swarmed across the wide, flat expanses of bush, blue grass, and the cries that issued from their throats as they charged like hunger-crazed beasts into the sword-points of their opponents were mercifully deleted; the maddened distortion of the features on their white, young faces was enough.

The voice explained, pointed out, reconciled pre-calculated plans with facts as they transpired.

The masses of mangled young flesh surged now forward now back, to either side; swelled, bunched, drove, fell writhing...

He saw a head fall, a running body split in two down the back.

"That's all, that's *all!*"

There was bitter stuff in his throat and he fought to keep the violent sickness bottled inside him.

"Yes, yes sir."

No no no no no!

THE illumination had returned fully when Tayne walked in, saluted loosely. He carried something in his right hand.

"Yes?"

"There's been an alteration in our rosters— Old Man himself, I had nothing to do with it. Here."

Senses still numbed, he took the thin plastisheets. He tried to get the words to make sense. Subject, transfer, quadrant 3 to quadrant 1, attention, Quadrates concerned.

"Apparently the Director thought it would be better this way. For myself, I don't see that it could make any actual difference."

What was the man saying? What did—there it was. Ronal Blair, Kurt Blair: quadrant 3, Blair, to quadrant 1, Tayne. By Command: Gundar Tayne, Director...

His thoughts spun dizzily. *Mike, Terry—no, those were not the names. The other Blair's sons...*

This time, thank God, the other Blair's sons...

CHAPTER SEVEN

"I AM apparently a relatively high official in the government. It is called a Congressman. Although there are many others of equal and superior rank, I am well liked. I have a strong political following."

"Was there any suspicion?"

"None at all. I had the good fortune, almost immediately upon discovering my role in this civilization, to gain access to a number of speech recordings our host had made. His voice is very little different than mine, and of course within about thirty minutes I had mastered his tone, his inflection, and his manner of speech. We shall have little or no difficulty."

They were seated in the living room of the house; in its den, two young boys were diligently working at the task their father had set them. The books were opened in an orderly array on the wide, polished floor. One read excerpts from the texts as the other quickly gained mastery of a portable typewriter, transcribed as his brother read aloud.

"Father was correct in his reasoning...take this...*with the desertion by Germany of the League of Nations, the stage for World War II was set. Failure of the Weimar Republic...*"

Their sheaf of notes had grown measurably in thickness since the first fact had been written on the first page the night before. The boy had written it slowly as he had begun mastery of the awkward writing machine—1. *Washington defeats Cornwallis at Yorktown, Oct. 19, 1781...*

In the living room, the woman was listening to her husband.

"By their standards, we would seem as improbable in our psychological reactions, our reasoning and our way of life as they seem under-developed and generally inferior in intelligence to our eyes. When you're among them, Lisa, you will have to guard against the self-assurance, which to them could be easily interpreted as lack of emotion. Under any but the most intimate circumstances, we might appear to them as some sort of thinking machinery devoid of what they term 'character' and 'personality'. Other than that, you should have little trouble. If you should err through some lack of detailed knowledge, you will find it amazingly easy to cover up." He toyed with a cigarette in a momentary attempt to deduce its function. He broke it in two, examined the tobacco grains as she spoke. Her voice was quiet, almost as though consciously held in check by some secret restraint.

"From your description, these people can be dealt with more or less at the mental level of a child of eight, then..."

"A child of about 13, on their standards. Not in individual cases, however—you will have to judge quickly for yourself. There are many who approach us in mental agility. I believe, from what I've been able to discover during the last few hours, that our host was one of those. There are few others of his rank, however, who are his equal."

"That would account for the apparatus." And then in a different voice and quite suddenly she said, "Dare we not use it, Douglas, and—"

"And what? Lisa, sometimes I think I don't understand you at all. You seem frightened, I think. Are you frightened?"

"No. No, Douglas."

"That's better. At any rate, we will do best to leave his apparatus absolutely unmolested. Here, apparently, science is not a restricted thing, in the sense that the individual is not limited by law in its study and practice. Technological secrets of the government are of course carefully guarded, and periodically divulged to the public in vague or distorted form. However, the individual may be a free agent in science to the limit of his wealth, interest and intellectual ability. That is why our host was able to complete a project similar to that upon which Zercheq was at work when he was apprehended. Although even my technical training at Quadrature Academy excluded detailed study of space-time mechanics just as it did nuclear fission, I'm quite positive that our host has constructed a successful Chronospan, as Zercheq called it. If we tamper with it, his chances of returning here and ours of returning to our phase in time are reduced to absolute zero. As it is, he will be faced with the task of building another to effect his return—and unless he is a clever man indeed, his chances are of course exceedingly slim, Zercheq was only half-finished when the S-Council apprehended him."

"We are the—innocent victims of a trap, then."

"It need not be a trap, precisely, my dear. There is a slim chance that we may return—but that must of course remain in his hands. Quite probably, he may fail. Therefore, we must go about the process of adapting ourselves, and in any measure possible, alter and adapt this civilization to our own methods and standards."

"Please, Douglas—"

"Yes?"

SHE looked away from him for a moment, then back, but with her eyes lowered.

"I suppose changing them," she said softly, "would be a—a challenge to you, Douglas." Then her eyes came up, looked full into his. "Please, let us use his device. Let us go back. I—It is that I—I *am* afraid, Douglas," she said.

"Afraid?" His tone was that of a man speaking half in doubt, half in impatience. "I still fail to understand you, Lisa. A moment ago you said—"

"Then forgive me," she interjected with a nervous suddenness. "It is—let us say it is the shock."

"If so it shall wear off. But you may be assured, Lisa, there is nothing to fear. These people are at least a century behind us, generally speaking. Sociologically, they are where we were before the formation of the Prelatinate—purely a case of arrested development dating from antiquity. Technologically they are very little behind us— perhaps only decades, I am not as yet familiar with the manifold details of which the causes are comprised, but the effects in themselves are starkly obvious. There are wars, for one thing. They are the end effect of all the other contributory effects. I am in a position to inaugurate the proper political maneuvers to eliminate this end effect—and I shall. The problem of changing these people should be quite simple, and because of their terrible desperation, it should take astonishingly little time. They are slow-moving when it comes to governmental function for the direct benefit of the individual, but in their present state—as I say, almost unbelievably confused and hazardous—I am quite sure that they can be relied on to favor any possible solution to the curtailment of crisis after crisis."

"You mean—you mean the games, don't you, Douglas?"

"Why of course! What else would I mean?"

"They have space travel, I suppose—"

"No—no, oddly, they're highly skeptical of it—it's still relegated to colorful pamphlets for amusement purposes and to a few rather well done pieces of fiction with all too limited circulation. But of course, when the time comes, the Sahara will serve well enough—that is where we started. Ordinarily, it would take years with people such as these to convince them to adopt our game system. I shall work through their weak spots—their fear, their desperation, their willingness to follow beliefs unfounded in fact. Perhaps even within months... Lisa, you're not listening!"

"Yes. Yes I am, Douglas."

"I see. You think that because they're rank amateurs in the philosophy of political mechanics, I will meet insurmountable stumbling blocks. It is true they are quite backward in economic theory, and of course that has its manifestation throughout government as well as the governed. But fortunately, their motives are transparent to anyone except themselves—that will help at least in gaining a toehold. Before I begin, I want a few hours careful study of the notes the boys are compiling. They've been industrious, I hope and not too taken with all this."

She did not answer him.

"You are to be highly credited, my dear," he said. He knew her mood would pass. It had, before... "They are fine sons. I shall see to it, as long as we must remain in this time-phase, that the only arms they shall ever carry will be in the war games, which I feel confident I can inaugurate. They're in the den? After you, my dear..."

He did not notice the sudden tightening of the little lines at the edges of her mouth.

FOR several days, it was little more than a game of watchful waiting. There had been committee meetings, sub-committee meetings, and each had been more tense in the complexion of its discussions than the one preceding it. These men, he found, were little, desperate men, and had but only recently come to realize it.

The notes Ronal and Kurt had compiled for him were extensive and accurate. Fundamentally, he understood the background of cause and effect underlying the tensions, and had realized at once that these men had become mired so deeply in the swale of political intrigue that they had at last come to the point where they would gladly grab at the nearest straw to extricate themselves. But they had run out of straws. They had begun running out in the early 1950's; each had broken pitifully since the Korea fiasco, and now they had been used up. He listened, for his opportunity could come at any moment—and it must be precisely the right moment.

"Gentlemen," one of them began in the soft drawl of the south, "I am in favor of the President's proposal for two main reasons and two alone: firstly, it is an indirect solution to the thorny problem of Civil Rights. Secondly, we simply must have the arms. No one could have foretold that Soviet Russia would have succeeded as she did in ultimately out-producing us. Therefore we are caught by surprise, and simply must have the funds, gentlemen. I wish to go definitely on record as favoring the 50 percent tax on individual income..."

"Impossible! I think the Congressman forgets the inherent strength in the will of the people! I tell you they've had all they will take. Especially in your own state, Congressman—they will become slaves in a far more severe sense of the word than they ever were before the Civil W—pardon me the War Between the States."

"As I pointed out, Congressman, the President's proposal will solve the thorny Civil Rights problem. And at any rate, the people of which you so respectfully speak, Congressman, seem to have learned that politics is after all a matter for the professional politicians. I think we both realize that whether or not they feel, as you say, that they have had all they can take, they will do little about it. When, in recent years, have they, may I ask? I suggest, therefore..."

Several of the conferees looked in Blair's direction, as though, expecting him to do something. But the time was not yet. And when it came, he must be careful—even in their desperation, they would not accept it whole-hog.

"—and I b'lieve it is obvious that by working gradually, as we have in the past, we should not have any of the trouble the Congressman from New York suggests. Each year, we have simply added a little more, and promised it would be the last time. Until now, even at 30 percent we are in a position to continue almost indefinitely. One thing the people do fear, gentlemen, is war. We have been skillful, and let us not mince words about it. They have been thoroughly frightened!"

Of course that was it. Gradually, with accompanying promises... The fear had been made a direct thing, and the tangled, subtle causes beneath had become psychologically, if not actually, inaccessible.

All of the causes, of course, he might never learn. But the general effects were obvious, so it was on them and with them alone that he must build his case.

IT was now a matter of discerning how many of these men were genuinely concerned with bettering the situation, how many were tenaciously satisfied with the status quo, and how many were intent on using the situation to better their own interests. All were desperate men. Only their goals were different.

In time of course he would be able to do away with most of them. They would in all probability fail to fit in a world organized about the psychological concept on which the games were built. The people themselves, however, if what the southern Congressman had said were true, would fit perfectly.

And inwardly, he smiled. It was almost a simple thing, because it was obvious that what the man had said was at least true to a degree. Their economic set-up was proof of it. Millions and millions of pieces of green paper, in which they had implicit faith despite the facts which they knew to be true—that far less than half of their paper currency was validly backed by the standard metal on which it was based. There was not that much ore in the planet's entire crust!

But they *believed* that the system worked, and that was all that was necessary.

Just as the people of his own time-phase believed that a child could actually be conditioned for life against violence, after sustaining the temporary psychological shock caused by a week's subjugation to the bloody horror of wanton slaughter. It was understood that such severe psychological shock during the early years of mental development was sufficient to condition each new generation for life against any future acts of violence as adults, and it was believed because it seemed to work. And because it seemed to work, it was believed *in*. Each surviving youth grew into adulthood as convinced as his neighbor that the conditioning of the games was lifelong, that the psychological scar they left was permanent, and would therefore render impossible any form of violent conflict.

The belief, scientifically questionable as it might be, was never challenged, because there was always the fact to face that there was, after all, no war.

There was none primarily because the games simply solved the main cause of it. Carefully controlled mortality rates on the battlefields kept the population where it belonged, prevented the ultimate over-crowding which was directly and indirectly responsible at 90 percent of the causes of any armed conflict. The few who were sufficiently timorous to probe the philosophy upon which the system was based were at once amazed at its simplicity: it consisted simply of a logical premise that the killing of a required number of immature children was self-evidently worth the saving of millions of valuable adults. It was a matter of necessary sacrifice.

Yes, the people of this time-phase would fit into the plan well. Not because they were intelligent, but because they had a natural tendency as followers, and because their limited imaginations held them in a mentally astigmatic state, too concerned with the status quo to ask questions concerning the future until it was too late.

Blair smiled, this time openly. Tayne could have the directorship back there! Here there was no Tayne. Here was a world for the asking, upon which he would at last be the object of primary, not tertiary, worship by a planet! He could take the shapeless clay—could cultivate it, could forge it in time into a great, brilliant civilization—and it would be his, all his. What greater monument to the genius of a man...

IT was a week later when the time came. The Congressman from the south had been on a brief inspection of a hydrogen bomb site following a test detonation. The pink flush had subsequently vanished from his jowls and in its place was the color of ash. His brain had been mightily disturbed; he had been forced to the painful recourse of thought, and that had disturbed it even further.

Two other Congressmen were getting away with intelligent debate, because the Congressman from the south was at last quite silent.

"...And I contend that our armed forces have not at all times been informing us truthfully, especially regarding the need for vast land armies, when it is obvious that they have become obsolete. It is my opinion that their maintenance is used simply as a tool, gentlemen—a tool to gouge extra taxes from the public, thereby enforcing their increased dependence for survival on the government itself."

"You mean, Congressman, to say that the Army lies?"

"Like a rug, Congressman!"

There was a murmur throughout the group, short, whispered exchanges.

"You can substantiate this claim?"

"Do I really have to, Congressman?"

A gavel rapped quickly. Blair had slipped for the moment into the comfort of relaxation; by the Prelatinate, it was *amusing*!

Then the debate continued, and he was at last convinced that these men were genuinely afraid that the war from which no amount of influence or money could buy their safety was imminent. The third war in their history, which would genuinely be fought to win. The others had been their American Revolution, and their Civil War.

Then, "Congressman Blair. You've had little to say for the last few days. Perhaps this subcommittee could profit by an opinion from you..."

The chance had come.

He rose. "I have a plan," he said, "that may seem fantastic to you. I have waited until most of the routine arguments were heard, so that this thing would not be any more confused and bogged down in senseless debate than necessary. I am prepared to answer all questions directed to me regarding it, but I am finished at the first sign of the usual harangue."

HE watched their faces. They were suddenly intense, and there was a new alertness in them. It was true, then—they did respect him; he had a good following.

"It is quite evident that our enemy has taken the advantage by surprise. The nuclear weapons on both sides have kept us deadlocked for about seven nervous, uncomfortable, difficult years. And the deadlock is now on the verge of finally being broken, and to his advantage. He is now capable of out-producing us—his dealings with unscrupulous American businessmen have finally borne fruit, and he has sprung his surprise. His nuclear weapons outnumber ours five to one and he is in the driver's seat whether we care to deny it or not. And we are stuck with twenty million men under arms in the field—rifles and hand-grenades, lumbering tanks and a few other ridiculous toys. An organization so tremendous that it trips itself and falls flat on its face at every attempted move.

"But you gentlemen are painfully aware of all this, as are the high-ranking, tradition-bound military leaders who are still denying it. What you may not be aware of is that we may equalize our position if we are quick to act—we may counter-surprise, counter-shock, if we do not delay.

"I therefore ask your support, gentlemen, when I introduce my bill to immediately lower the present minimum draft age from seventeen to thirteen years."

The gavel clattered for order. Many had risen to their feet.

"Your questions, one at a time, gentlemen."

"Very well. The chair recognizes the Congressman from New Jersey."

"May I submit, Congressman Blair, that your plan is crazy? You yourself admitted that manpower alone is woefully insufficient to cope with this situation."

"It is, as such. In the form of surprise—and believe me, it would surprise the enemy ten times the degree to which it has obviously shocked this group here—it would prove of great value, in that it would reflect a murderously frightening desperation. It would, of course, have to be simultaneously accompanied by an immediate step-up in production of nuclear weapons. All other types would immediately be dropped. Factory shifts would in all instances immediately become full-day, full-week."

"The Congressman from California."

"And you mean to imply that our enemy would actually stand in fear of a thirteen-year-old?"

"Human mass has nothing to do with age, Congressman."

"The Congressman from Ohio."

"What you suggest, Congressman, is inhuman, unbearably horrible—you suggest that we support you in a bill to draft *children*!"

"To make my point more clear, perhaps I should ask some questions of my own. First, am I to understand that this group was at any time in *opposition* to Universal Military Training? And—second, is the youth of seventeen a grown man?

"Or shall I ask the question this way—where would you rather place these youngsters—in a position to possibly solve our dilemma, or in cities that cannot possibly be adequately defended, and have them marked for certain death along with the rest of us in them?

"You say my proposal is unbearably inhuman. You are right. War is. It makes little difference how you draft its plans.

"Are there any further questions?"

There were none.

"Well, I will call for a confidence vote with the chair's permission."

"Permission granted."

The Congressman from the south was very white. And very silent.

CHAPTER EIGHT

DOT'S face was tense as she watched him. Doug held the delicate phone device to his ear with pressure that made his flesh white around it. He was oblivious to the wonder-like comforts of the beautiful home now, cursing it subconsciously as though it had been built for the sole purpose of trapping him, imprisoning him here.

The high-pitched signal in the receiver repeated evenly and he forced himself to wait. His fingers drummed an uneven tattoo on the low table, vibrated the dismantled parts of the tele-radio set that he'd examined earlier. The open pages of the catalogue from the Science Council library trembled in his left hand.

"Electrosupply, Federal Service Division," the voice said suddenly.

"Hail, this is Senior Quadrate Blair again."

"Hail, sir. Is there something unsatisfactory? The equipment you ordered should have arrived at your home—"

"It has, it is satisfactory. However I find that I neglected to request a high speed bl—correction, high-kempage power

pack." He tried to steady the pages. The closely printed alphabetized lines kept running together.

"High-kempage power pack? Your reference, sir?"

"Reference?" The veins on his throat stood out, but his voice was not a sudden bellow from indignation. "You forget my position! How soon may I expect the unit?"

"As soon as possible, sir."

He hung up. "Damn," he said. "Damn it to hell anyway!"

"Doug, can I do anything?"

"No, honey, no. We've just got to sweat it out until that pack gets here. It'll be all right." He forced a smile, sank to a chair, put his head in his hands. She knelt beside him, "The film-strips, that you saw—they must have been—horrible."

He looked up. "Horrible isn't the word. God, what people. And at first they seemed so— What a cold-blooded, ruthless—"

"Easy, mister." She came closer to him and he felt himself relax slowly at the warmth of her touch.

"What a system... I guess I read over those reports a dozen times. They know there is no possible way to tell how long such an awful mental shock will stay—even in the impressionable mind of a half-grown child. Yet they accept it as a full-blown conditioning process—they *believe* in it! They *believe* in everything around here—they worship the government, the Prelate General, the Director—even me! And because there's no war and hasn't been since the first Prelatinate, they keep right on believing that from the day you fight in the games—if you survive—til the day you die, you're thoroughly conditioned against physical violence—" He let the sentence taper off into silence.

"Just rest awhile, darling," she murmured.

He smiled. "Thanks, Dot. But I've got to get that mess downstairs cleaned up. I'll be all right."

The equipment—the neat sorted rows of resistors, condensers, vacuum tubes and the rest of it glittered on the long, wide expanse of the workbench he'd installed. At one end was a half-completed framework, and at the other—was the blackened ruin of what had been a transformer.

The burnt-out unit had cooled, but the stench of overheated oil and melted insulation still hung in the air trapped in the blue haze of smoke.

"Can any of the rest be assembled in the meantime, Doug? I'll help…"

HE busied himself with the blackened junk. "It could, but it's not worth the chance. It's got to be so damn perfect. I've got to know exactly what I'm going to be able to get out of the pack. Got to have at least 1,000 Volts—or should I say Kemps—anyway. Damn the DC…"

He hadn't found out about the utility power in the house until he'd blown up the transformer. It was a little thing, direct current rather than alternating current, but it meant time, and there wasn't much time. He knew there'd be no chance of his getting through the games undetected, even if he found a way somehow to stomach such a horror.

There was a gentle chiming sound.

"The front door, Doug!"

"Guess I really threw a scare into 'em! You go up first, I'll douse the lights."

There were two of them, and their uniforms were white. Their helicopter idled on the front lawn. They saluted.

"Quadrate Blair, if you'll accompany us please."

They stood there, their faces impassive, their tones matter-of-fact as though they had asked him to pass the salt.

"Accompany you? I understood that you were going to deliver—"

"S-Council, Department of Security, sir. You appreciate our position. We have our orders. The Prelatinate-Attorney suggests an interview immediately, sir. If you will accompany us, please."

"You may tell the—the Prelatinate-Attorney that I'm quite busy, but that I shall be glad to make an appointment for him later tomorrow."

They stood there. There was a questioning look on Dot's face, and he had no answer for it. Somehow, they'd gotten onto something. Jane. No. Tayne again—

"We are sorry, sir."

"I'm afraid I fail to understand. You make it sound actually as though I'm to have no choice in the matter. Who issued your orders?"

"Office of the Director, sir. And actually, sir, you have no choice. If you will please accompany us."

They stood, immobile, waiting. There were only two of them. But he knew that in minutes there could be two hundred.

He went with them.

HE judged the pneumatic elevator tube had descended at least 20 levels below the surface before it came to a softly whispering halt on a resilient cushion of compressed air. They left the tube and the same miracle of lighting that kept the city in eternal daylight was gently suffused through the entire length of the wide, silent corridors.

They did not walk far. Doug forced his mind into what order he could. If this were some adventure fantasy from the pages of fiction there would somehow be an escape, some thing he could suddenly do and the tables would be turned. But it was not. It was fantastic, but it was as real as the day the first atomic bomb was dropped.

The sliding panel admitted them to a round, low-ceilinged room similar in most respects to his own office, even to the intertelecon screen inset in the curving wall to the left of the large metal desk. The man behind the desk was thin-faced and slight, but there was an intelligence behind the high forehead that seemed to put a snap in his wide-spaced eyes as well as in his voice. But it was the eyes that made Doug's nerves feel that they must break like an overdrawn violin string at any moment; the voice was smooth, controlled.

The orderlies saluted and were dismissed. The panel slid closed.

"Sorry to have to call you down here like this, Doug. But damn it, it's my job, and besides that you've done something this time for which there'd be hell to pay if the PG ever found out and you know it as well as I do."

He gestured Doug to a chair. The Prelatinate-Attorney's tone was relaxed, but Doug wondered how it might have sounded to a man of lesser rank than himself.

One thing was certain; it was time to go back into the act. "I suppose this all is leading up to threats of the S-Council—"

"Doug, when the DO buzzed me and said they'd been notified by Electrosupply that you'd refused to give a reference for a piece of equipment you ordered, there was nothing else for me to do but to get you down here on the spot. You can imagine where I'd be if I didn't."

"It was Tayne I suppose."

There was a quick flick of the attorney's eyes, but his face didn't change. "Personalities don't matter, Doug."

Doug waited for it. Behind the nonchalance, the employer-to-faithful-but-errant-employee tone, there was something of hard spring steel, coiled, waiting to be sprung.

"I'm not sure I like your tone," Doug bluffed. "I have some degree of position you know—"

"Yes, I know—you seldom let anybody forget it. I understand you've even reminded the Director on occasion…"

Doug shrugged. "Suppose we get down to it. Just what is there this time that has the DO so upset?"

THE Attorney stiffened visibly. "What *is* there? You mean you don't realize that you've come about as close as anyone can come to committing a capital heresy? Did you actually suppose you could order a thing like that without a triple-endorsed Science Council reference? You know as well as I do how strict the law is about possession of restricted equipment of any kind by anyone except members of the Science Council itself. Even the Director has to go through channels! Where d'you think we'd be, anyway, if just anybody and everybody could read any books, tinker with any kind of paraphernalia they wanted to? Damn it, man, if every Tom, Dick and Harry went fooling around with the knowledge that wasn't food for them the whole damn planet would be in the S-chambers!"

"What do you mean, restricted—?"

"And we can't have any exceptions! Except, that is, for the special training such as picked men as yourself received at the Quadrature Academy. But when it comes to personal possession of restricted stuff, without the required reference, you might just as well be caught with a copy of Freud in your library!"

The pack. That had to be what he meant—he'd been phoning for the pack, and they'd asked for a reference… Somehow, he had to— the catalogue! *The closely printed lines that got tangled up because he couldn't hold it steady!*

"You're accusing me of ordering restricted—"

"Now look, Doug. You'd better tell me—I don't want it on the record that I had to use Right of Office to get an answer. You ordered a high-kempage power-pack. Now what for?"

"High-kempage power pack? You can't be serious!"

"I've warned you, Doug."

"Warn and be damned! You sit there and repeatedly accuse me of ordering restricted equipment—without reference, and you haven't even got your facts straight! Did Electrosupply tell you that?"

A peculiar look was on the Attorney's face.

"DO said so."

"Well you could've saved us a good hour's time if you'd have called me to see what I had to say first before dragging me over here as if I were a common criminal! I think an apology will be in order!" *If only Barnum had been right!* "What I ordered, just in the event you're as interested as you say you are, was a high-speed blower-rack!"

"A—what?"

Reel him in!

"A high-speed blower-rack. So happens I'm having trouble with the electronic units of my vento-conditioner at home, and I'm doing the work myself more or less as a project in avocational therapy—"

"Now it is you who can't be serious. How great a fool do you think—"

"Damn it, whose word are you going to take in this?" Doug stood up. "Some Electrosupply technician's, who can't hear any better than you can reason, or mine?"

There was a second's silence.

"All right, Doug. You're a fool, you know. You are, and so am I... It was a high-speed blower-rack. I'll make sure it's set straight."

"Well, thank you."

"Just be careful, Doug."

"That's good advice—don't wear it out!"

He turned quickly, made his exit before the panel had widened halfway.

CHAPTER NINE

THE ugly, black building stood out like a shapeless smudge of soot against the milk-white sky, but it was by sheer accident that Terry and Mike discovered it, built as it was at the water's edge where the high blue grass had been neither trampled nor trimmed, and at a distance further from the training areas than they had ever ventured.

"We'd better go back, Terry. We'll get in trouble." Mike's young body glistened with perspiration as he stood on the knoll with his brother, eyes still fastened to the low black structure as he spoke. His equipment belt was heavy and he tugged again at it to change the distribution of its weight. The broadsword swung loosely at his left side, not quite counterbalancing the mace, which hung by its thong to his right.

"They said there were a couple of hours before the next class, didn't they? The guy in the sharp uniform said we could amuse ourselves any way we wanted."

"Sure, but this isn't the way the others are doing it. They all went out and started practicing with the swords again. We oughtta."

"You rather do that than go exploring?"

Mike touched the half-healed flesh-wound on his right shoulder. He remembered how the short, dark-haired kid had laughed when it had started to bleed, and then how mad he got when he found he couldn't use the sword well enough to cut him back.

"I'd like to get that guy."

"Don't be a dope. It's only a dream—you didn't really get hurt. Come on let's see what that place is. Nobody's around…"

"Maybe it is only a dream, but he made me mad. Boy I'll cut his ears off if I—"

"Aw, come on."

They had barely started down the opposite side of the knoll when Jon Tayne's voice hailed them.

"Hey, you two! Where d'you think you're going, anyway?" They waited for him. There was a cross look on his face which Mike immediately resented.

"Over there." He pointed toward the black building. "What's it to you?"

"Nothing to me, but it'll be double duty to you if you don't get back to the recreation area right away."

"There's a lot of time yet. He said we could amuse ourselves, didn't he?"

"That doesn't mean walking around wherever you please. It means just what it says—giving your weapons a workout. I was called away from a good match just to come and find you two. Come on."

They turned, fell in at either side of him.

"We didn't mean anything wrong," Terry said.

"They'll let it go this time because you're new, and because you are who you are. But you guys had better be more careful. That's restricted back there."

"What's that? Restricted?"

"You should know that!"

"What is it?"

"Your father never told you anything, did he?"

"Sure—course he did. Lots of things. But there's no way he'd know what that place is."

JON stopped in mid-stride. "No way he'd know? You crazy?"

"Who's crazy?" Terry clenched his fists, stuck his chin out.

"Look here—you want a fight or something?" Jon's hand went to the hilt of his sword. Terry unhooked his mace. Mike had his sword half free of its wide scabbard.

Jon let his arms drop to his sides.

"Come on, wise guy, who's crazy?" Terry glared at him.

"You know what'll happen to you if you do anything to a section leader?"

"We didn't ask to be here," Mike said. "And we didn't ask to be pushed around, either, or told where we could go and couldn't go. Or be called crazy, either. The whole thing is dumb."

"After the games, if you're still alive, I'll report you for that," Jon said.

"Still alive? Who you kidding? You talk like there was going to be a war. Grown-ups do that, kids don't."

"What do you think you're being trained to use your weapons for?"

"That's easy," Terry said. "So we'll know how to use 'em when we're grown ups. It's called UMT or something."

"You guys *are* cr—ah, don't be funny. The games start in three days, then you'll know if you're in a war or not. And frankly, I hope you both end up back there." He turned, started walking.

Terry and Mike let their hands fall from their weapons, followed after him.

"Nobody's being funny," Mike said. "Suppose we do end up back in that place? So what?"

"Listen the hero," Jon said. "You planning on taking on the whole First Quadrant single-handed or something? They sure don't bring you back to life back there, if that's what you think. They just make you a little deader."

"Deader?"

"Well I'd rather be buried if I get killed than burned into a little pile of ashes and sent home in a jar. And that's what they do. There's not enough land on Venus to bury everybody every year, and they sure aren't going to go to the trouble of hauling a bunch of corpses out into the ocean just to dump 'em. Not when they can burn 'em up, anyway, right here."

141

"Burn 'em up?" Mike said, feeling funny in his stomach. "Alive?"

"Not often, I guess. Only when there's a mistake and they don't notice it in time. Or if there haven't been enough guys killed to make the year's quota. Then they take unconscious ones. That's what my father told me once, anyway."

"Suppose—suppose you're just hurt bad? Do they—"

"Not if they've made the quota. If you end up hurt they take you to the other landmass—there's a big hospital there. I've never seen it, but my father says it's the biggest single building ever made."

"How long are you kept there?"

"Until you're recovered, of course. The longest case on their records was my cousin's. He got a broken neck when he was hit in the face by a mace, and lost both eyes. They repaired the cut nerves, gave him two new eyes, and fixed his neck in about a month. They can do anything, so you don't have to worry. I got a broken back myself last year—I was out walking in two weeks."

THE recreation area was almost in view. Already they were able to hear the clash of metal on metal, as though a great tangled mass of scythes was being shaken by some huge, clumsy hand, which could not break them apart.

"Jon..."

The section leader was quickening his pace. "Yes?"

"How in heck do they know about the quota? How do they know if they should pick you up if you're hurt, or just leave you there?"

"The tab ships take care of it. There's a whole fleet of 'em, and they cover each area where there's fighting. They tabulate everything that happens with things called telescanners, and they keep in constant communication with the Quadrate's ship. Any time during the fighting, they know if they're ahead of the quota rate or behind it in their own area. And all the time, the Quadrates are comparing the figures they get from the tab ships with each other so they can keep a running record of the quota rate for all four quadrants. As long as the rate's right, or high, the medical ships keep landing and picking up the wounded, and flying 'em back. When the tabulations show the rate's lagging, the medical ships take it easy until they get the word to get to work again."

"They wouldn't have so much work to do if we could use guns instead of these things," Terry said. "I think guns would be more fun, don't you?"

"That's what your father thinks, isn't it?"

"Gosh, no, he doesn't—"

"My father says that killing at a distance isn't much good, because you never get into close contact. And if you can't see what happens when you actually kill somebody, you can't get conditioned very well. You'd get bored just sitting around with a gun. And even in the short time of a week—"

"Is that how long it lasts?"

"Usually about that. But even then with guns, you'd get used to it. With swords it's different. You don't get used to that in a week. You still feel pretty shaky when it's all over, believe me…"

"Were you scared, Jon?"

"You shouldn't be scared," he said. "All you have to remember is what they keep telling you—the others will kill you if you don't kill them. Always remember that. Then it gets to be sort of a—well, like a game, to see who's strongest, who can use a sword the best…"

"Yeah," Mike said. "Wait'll I get that guy!" His fingers brushed lightly against the half-healed wound again.

Jon laughed. "Sore at somebody already?"

"I'll cut his ears off!"

"You're getting the idea all right! Just be sure you don't go breaking any more rules—you can't kill anybody until the games begin, you know."

"I'll show him!" Mike said. "How long do we have yet to practice? Now, I mean?"

"Half an hour, maybe. I'll see you later. I'll forget about reporting you this time—but don't go for any more walks!" He left them, and they walked into the recreation area with the others.

Mike found the boy who had laughed. And he found that it was as Jon had said. There wasn't any reason to feel afraid. The sword wasn't as heavy in his hands as it had been at first, and it was more thrilling to use than just fists…

The other boy was grinning, and it was easy to get mad enough to want to cut his head off. Both hands on the long haft of his weapon, Mike swung harder, more surely than the first times he handled the sword. He could parry, now—and cut. Like *that*!

The boy staggered back. The side of his head was bleeding profusely, and the blood spurted through his fingers as he pressed them to the gaping place where his ear had been.

"Rules! Rules!"

Mike lowered his sword. That was right, the rules. He couldn't kill now... So he tried to laugh. At first he had to force the sound from his throat, but suddenly he found it coming easily, clear, and loud.

The boy left the field toward the medical tents.

And Mike found another with whom to practice. It was what Jon had said, a great game—a great, crashing adventure!

He swung the sword and wondered if the dream would ever have to end.

CHAPTER TEN

DOUG worked silently. His eyes stung, and he wasted a moment to rub them again, because he must see, must see so precisely, so exactly. The worktable was almost bare of the equipment he had ordered. The new Contraption had devoured it into its fantastic vitals as fast as his taut hands and flagging memory were able to feed. Yet it was useless work—the gleaming thing he had built would never so much as fry an egg.

Yet he worked as though the power-pack were resting on the table among the scraps of wire, bits and pieces that were left, as though somehow it would be there when he needed it, and then they could go, could escape, and then forget... The two shiny terminals glared at him dully like two tiny eyes, each telling him that he was such a fool to hope that they could ever be anything else than bare. They glared at him, told him that he was finished now, finished, but with the end impossibly far away.

He let the tools drop amid the bits and pieces. The Contraption was a cold, dead thing, a mockery without its great surging electric heart. A mockery, a precisely assembled heap of shiny junk.

He was near exhaustion as he looked at the two empty terminals. The anger in him had burned out and became a cold leaden thing. He no longer cared about the ridiculous beliefs, the regulations, the laws that prohibited him from obtaining the thing he needed to free himself—no longer cursed himself, for it was not he who was to blame.

He went upstairs to where Dot slept, and wondered if this was how it felt to be a thousand years old. Finally tired, finally fed-up, finally weary of being a fool.

He watched her as she slept, watched the gentle rise and fall of her breasts, let his eyes wander over the soft symmetry of her body, and asked himself why men were so dutiful in creating their clanking idiocies about life and about death when all that such diligence accomplished was eternal blasphemy of the pure and simple. The beautiful they defiled, then disguised the ruin they left with a cloak labeled Duty, and went forth armed with the rotten wood of what they called Law to build a dingy world more to their liking than the garden that had been given them for nothing…

It was not fair, no it was not fair, but he was tired at last. Too tired to look now for another time-track, to throw the Contraption wildly out of focus and careen through a thousand tracks, a million, and look for a place where a man and a woman could be simply that and nothing either more nor less. For in all infinity there was no such place, and the running would be worth less than the wasted breath it took.

With Dot, one last time, then.

She stirred. Her eyes opened, and she smiled.

"Doug? Did you finish it, Doug?"

"Yes. Yes, I finished it, as far as it ever will be finished."

She dropped her eyes. "We can keep trying." They met his. "We will keep trying, Doug. We've got to—for Terry and Mike…"

He said nothing. He sat heavily on the bed, his features grim.

He took off his shirt and dropped, exhausted, beside her.

HE awoke with the idea, "Dot! Dot I think I've found it!" He was instantly on his feet, trying to jam the sleep back from the center of his brain, trying to make sure it was no leftover figment from a nightmare, a wild dream. He heard her footsteps coming almost at a run.

"What is it? You sound as if you've found a pre-Truman dollar under the bed—"

"I don't know—it may be as half-baked as the kind that came later—worth even less, perhaps, but it's worth a try. They say desperate situations call for desperate action…"

"Take it easy, now. You aren't the blood and thunder type, exactly!" There was a note of cautious anticipation in her voice, but there was hope in it, and it was enough.

"Tomorrow—or more exactly, some sixteen hours from now, we are scheduled to take off for Venus headquarters to begin the games…"

"Yes, I know," she said quietly.

"Well that's it, don't you see? I'll go of course—I'll go but not all the way!"

"Doug I won't let you—anymore than you'd let me try to seduce the Prelate General into giving us the thing!"

"And I'll bet you could, too!" He laughed, and it was a real laugh for the first time in what seemed all his life. "But I'm afraid the Prelate General is going to be denied that dainty bit of intrigue, my darling. Don't you see? Space ships—they've got to have a method of communication! High-frequency radio—high-voltage stuff! Ten to one I'd find a power-pack aboard!"

"No, Doug, no…"

"It's a chance, Dot, and it's a good one. I'll be the ranking officer aboard of course—I shouldn't have too much trouble in pirating the thing—I'll make them rip the pack out for me, then I'll order them to bring me back. Then it'll just be a race against time."

He stood there, staring at the delicate tracery of a latticework wall, not seeing it. But he heard the fear in Dot's voice.

"A space ship, Doug… Why you'd—you'd die."

He laughed. "I'm sure the other Quadrates don't plan on dying, not for awhile yet, anyway. And I know it'll work, if I'm careful. And I've been careful so far." He looked at her, and the fear had not left her eyes. "You mustn't be afraid, Dot," he said then. "There's less to fear this way, because this way there's at least a chance. Don't you see the beauty of it—right up to the last moment, everything will appear to be as it should—and then before there's even any suspicion I'll take over—probably be almost back to Earth before they even know anything's gone haywire."

"Won't they be able to radio back from the other ships, I mean, when they realize things aren't as they should be—that the ship you are in isn't tagging along in the formation? They'll just be waiting for you when you land, Doug."

"They'll want to be waiting, sure—but they won't know where, not until I'm down, and safely out, headed here."

Dot didn't say anything then. It was such a storybook plan, such a crazy thing that it would never work; she knew it would never work.

"Doug, Doug…"

He held her close to him.

"Dot," he said, "we have two choices I think. We can be mature, we can be logical, we can make a tragedy out of a desperate situation and die martyrs to conservative thinking. Or we can keep grabbing at straws until we are sunk or end up ingloriously alive. Which way?"

She looked up at him, tears in her eyes. "I guess a knock-down drag-out thriller, mister… But Doug—I'm scared."

He stood still, apart from the other three as they talked in low, casual tones, waiting for the space-tower signal to board their ships. An early morning breeze tugged gently at his blue cloak, and he had to shield his eyes with his gauntlets as he looked at the four slender columns of glittering metal that tapered to needle points high above him. A quarter their diameter and height they might have been simple V-2 rockets on some strange desert proving-ground. At the same time they were the fantastic silver darts that he remembered from the pages of colored Sunday supplements which had foretold the coming of flight through Space. Yet the feeling of everyday security that they tore away was replaced with a vigorous thing inside him that was of firmer stuff than awe, more challenging than fear, more exciting than adventure. And suddenly, sailing ships were the toys of children, and oceans were spilled tea in a saucer.

They were a strange people, Doug thought. A horrible people, perhaps, a people whom he wanted desperately to escape. Yet a people who had learned that the sky and the Earth were not enough, nor were ever meant to be.

A green light flashed. The three Quadrates ended their conversation, boarded waiting surface vehicles and started toward their ships.

A car with a pennant bearing the insignia of a Senior Quadrate flying from atop its sleek passenger enclosure drove up beside Doug.

"Your transportation, sir."

He returned the salute. "Thank you, no. I shall walk," he said.

It was a short walk—less than two hundred yards, but he did not want it all to happen too quickly.

His steps were measured in slow, deliberate cadence as he crossed the plaza toward the great craft on which his insignia was emblazoned.

At length he was swallowed up inside it, and at a flashing blue signal, the four great ships thundered for the stars, and left Earth a little thing behind them.

PART TWO

CHAPTER ELEVEN

ACCELERATION had left Doug at the brink of unconsciousness despite the hammock in which they'd secured him, but gradually the roar in his ears subsided and the words took shape, as though they were being spoken from the bottom of an empty well.

"...SQ check one...speed five-three thousand one two oh, acceleration two point one, steady...trajectory minus two point oh five seconds at eight thousand two hundred, three hundred, four, five, compensate please...plus point oh three seconds at nine thousand, seven, eight, nine, compensate please...SQ at stand-by, over."

"Three-dimensional plot-check, sir. Reconciled, and steady as she blasts..."

"SQ to control, SQ check one, trajectory secure. Out."

He fumbled with the wide straps across his chest and hips, and his arms were awkward as though he had lost at least half of his coordination. He could taste blood at the corners of his mouth, but it was already caking to his flesh.

"Old Man had a tough time this trip, sir..."

"Yes. When they're desk passengers for six months running and then try to get aboard a space-deck they find it isn't as easy as when they wore an ack harness every day. The price of being eager, sergeant."

"Yes, sir. He ought to be coming out of it soon."

"We'll be locked tight on the curve when he does. Off a half-second and he'll holler like a Conservative—especially after final compensation. How close did we come to the C-limit this time, anyway?"

"Had almost a minute to spare, sir."

"Nicely done, sergea—I think I hear him trying to get the deck under him. Better get over to the trackers."

The words Doug heard still weren't making sense, but he was on his feet and had his balance. He had slid oddly down to the metal deck from the bulkhead on which the hammock was built, and he had the peculiar feeling that up was no longer up, nor down exactly where it was supposed to be. His body did not feel as though it were all of lead as he'd half-expected, although it didn't feel its usual hundred and sixty pounds, either.

He was still focusing his eyes when they saw the weird blur of color on the bulkhead above the crewman's head. Teleview screen of course—and the middle blur—Earth.

In moments he was able to see it plainly as it receded—a tan and blue mass dotted with white, shadowed to the shape of a football, hanging in what seemed direct contradiction to all the laws of physics in a great, black void.

For minutes he stood without moving, oblivious to the immaculately polished masterpiece of engineering which surrounded him.

As a video-image, what he saw could have been nothing more than a cleverly done stage prop, an ingenious painting by some futuristic artist. But the realization that it was real held him fascinated. Of all the human emotions, here was one that could only flounder helplessly for expression, for it had no precedent for comparison. The awe and the strangely-placid fear were intermingled with a sense of brute power; the sudden loneliness and strange humility were woven inextricably with an irrepressible consciousness of godliness, of unbounded omnipotence. And Doug knew that the first airmen had but touched a tiny edge of the sky, for here was the sky in her entirety—the infinite woman, at once belonging to man, yet an unending mystery to him, and granting of her uncountable secrets but slowly, enticingly, stubbornly.

As he watched, the tan-and-blue shape shrank gradually as though Space were tauntingly erasing it from existence.

THE interior of the compartment in which he stood had been designed with the same simplicity of line as had the ship itself, and with so smooth a compactness that it seemed to occupy more of the ship's long interior than a bare third. The two crewmen had evidently not seen him as yet; they stood with their backs to him, their eyes intent on the long, curving banks of dials that ran the gamut of geometrical shapes. Oddly, their hands hung idle at their sides. Doug wondered if they constituted the entire crew, and if they did not, how many more of them there were.

He would let them speak first. He walked over to a panel of dials, gave them a studied scrutiny. The officer turned immediately.

"A blast thirteen minutes, sir, at fourteen thousand miles. I believe you'll find our track with zero variation. C-limit was passed four minutes ago. Glad to have you aboard again, sir."

Doug returned the salute, nodded his head in acknowledgement of information he had no way of understanding.

"Communications effective?"

"Why—yes sir. Sergeant, prepare space-radio for message—"

"No, no." Doug waved the sergeant back to his post. "Just—checking, captain. How long since the last overhaul of your unit?"

"Why, at the prescribed overhaul date for the entire ship, sir. I believe about four months ago, sir."

"Don't you know, captain?"

"Four months ago, sir."

"I see. If I may inspect the unit, captain."

"Sergeant! Prepare communications for inspection!"

He had no way of knowing how unorthodox his procedure was, only that while aboard the ship, at least, his rank was the final law, and that they would never land on Venus. Yet, these were intelligent men, of the same high caliber as those Earth-bound in the headquarters units. He must be cautious.

Within minutes, the complex communications assembly had been bared, and its circuits were half-mystery to him. Yet the fundamentals would be the same, as they had been with the equipment he had ordered to build the second Contraption. Only the shapes, the sizes, the juxtapositions different.

"Your transmission power supply, captain—"

"The power-pack, sir?" Inadvertently, the officer glanced at the unit and Doug followed the glance. Smaller, more compact than the best he'd seen in his own time, yet obviously evolved on identical principles. But now he had to carry the farce out, had to wring some of the freshman stuff from his memory.

"Sergeant—" He gestured toward the unit as he removed his gauntlets. "What is the v-Kempage on the plates of the final amplifier?"

"Eleven hundred Kemps at 300 milliamperes, sir."

"Very well. Suppose you give me the final power supply nomenclature!"

"Yes, sir. Genemotor, type A-26-F modified. Two hundred fifty Kemp input, eleven hundred Kemp output, at three hundred milliamperes. Two filter condensers, type L-73 new departure, one filter choke, L-12, one bleeder resistor—"

"That's enough, sergeant. Captain, upon perfunctory inspection at least, your communications unit seems to be in excellent condition. However, I suggest that after this you commit each successive overhaul date to memory."

"Yes, sir."

SO far, so good, Doug thought. Yet it was a thing of mocking irony. He was actually perfecting the act so well that one day the risk of impersonation would vanish entirely—yet now, now he must use it to its utmost to carry through a desperate plan to escape, rather than to stay. Worse, it was even a double irony, for had he sought escape at first rather than a lifetime of imposture in this next-door world, they would have helped him. Of course there were the games—he might never have learned enough in so short a time to have gone undetected through them. It was a strangely reassuring thought; it eliminated choice. But at the same time it heightened his desperation. There was only one mark at which to aim but it was a bull's-eye with no margin for error.

The captain was speaking to him.

"...care to check the flight-pattern coordinates? Sergeant Zukar here is quite justifiably proud, I think, of his ability to delay terminal compensation until the last fraction of a minute before C-limit is reached..."

"No—no thank you, captain, I am quite satisfied. I would like, however, a routine check of the remaining crew."

"Remaining crew, sir?" The captain's face was suddenly a mask of perplexity, and his features were again taut. "I'm afraid I fail to understand, sir. Unless there were last-minute orders which I failed to receive assigning two additional—"

He had discovered what he wanted, but he had been awkward...

"Yes, yes of course, captain. The orders for Tayne's ship. For some reason I—"

"Of course, sir."

Not a natural, but he'd made the point. But he couldn't let the dice get cold now. Only the two of them aboard; that made it simpler. And the sergeant had said the power-pack used 250 Kemp input, the same as the wall current at the house. Usable, then, and he had to get it back...

He walked slowly over to a bulkhead seat, sat down.

He groped uncertainly for the brief-tube he'd brought, let it fall with a clatter to the deck.

The captain was scooping it up in a trice, and Doug twisted the muscles of his face into a grimace of discomfort.

"Sir—sir, is there something wrong?"

"I—no. I don't think so, captain. Nervous strain, I'm afraid. I—" Another grimace.

"Sergeant! Three neuro tablets at once—"

"No, no—" Doug said. "Like poison to me." He doubled over. "Captain…"

"Yes sir, what can I get—"

"Nothing, I'm afraid… Back to Earth as quickly as possible—"

"Back to Earth, sir? But that's impossible! We're at least thirty minutes past C-limit, sir…the trajectory's locked. We must continue, of course."

"Must—must *continue*?"

"Why, yes of course, sir."

Doug straightened his body, but kept his arms locked around his middle, kept the grimace on his face and feigned shortness of breath.

"Of course *what*, captain?"

A LOOK of comprehension came suddenly to the captain's face. He straightened, stood again at attention, "According to Constitutional Commandments Four, Part 3, Subsection 12 as amended July 9, 1949, part A: 'All space craft shall be robot-controlled and shall fly predetermined trajectories, save

(1) when bearing members of the Science Council and/or their certified representatives, to whom manual operation and navigation at will is singularly permissible, or

(2) when insurmountable emergency shall occur. All other craft shall be launched on the predetermined trajectory as hereinbefore stipulated, and shall be compensated to their true course by remote control from Earth for so long as radio impulses between ship and Earth shall be for all practical purposes instantaneous. Beyond this limit, to be hereinafter described as Compensation Limit, where after distance shall create a time-lag of communications and corresponding control impulses so as to make further remote control an impracticability the ship shall continue on the trajectory as last corrected under control of its own self-directing, or autobot, units.

These units will be constructed so as to be inaccessible to all passengers, including instrument and communications technicians.' "

For a moment Doug said nothing, let the captain remain at attention, struggling to regain his breath and composure. The man had thought the feigned sickness was simply a device to get him off guard so that his alertness might be tried with some disguised test of his knowledge of regulations. Of course that was it...unthinkable that any officer, any rank, should give such an order as he had given for actual execution.

Funny, how the twists saved you when there was no longer any point in being saved. He was trapped here—trapped, and on Venus the trap would tighten and finally close when Tayne found some opening in his guard and plunged through it.

"Well done, captain. As you were. Your qualifications seem quite adequate. See to it that they are continually maintained."

"Yes, sir."

With what nonchalance he could muster, Doug dropped the sickness act as though it had been a trick the captain might have expected, and opened the brief-tube. He would have to memorize every word of its contents, every direction on the plastic sheets it contained. If he wanted to see his own home again—for that matter, if he ever wanted to see Dot again, he would have to run a bluff that would, he mused, even amaze the United States Bureau of Internal Revenue.

And that, he knew, would be damn near impossible.

CHAPTER TWELVE

AFTER Doug had gone, Dot tried to make herself forget why he had gone, where he was going. She wanted the old conviction to come back; she wanted to be smugly sure again that it was impossible for him to fly to another planet, and that what he had said was just a great joke.

She twisted a dial on the luxurious radio console, sat for a moment beside it and wished that she could as easily twist fact away from belief, so that the awful fear would go. Yet blindness to fact was no answer to fear of it.

It seemed long ago that space flight had been something for light dinner-table conversation, something for fanciful conjecture in an idle moment, something to discuss politely when the over-imaginative person became serious with his day-after-tomorrow talk.

But now suddenly it was none of those things. Now suddenly it was a thing of life or death to her; it was real, and she was afraid. The science-fiction stories she had leafed through in an idle moment—what had their writers said? What had they, in their irrepressible way, so logically theorized about the balance of life in the impossibly deep reaches of Space—about the precocious ships that men would some day build when they were at last free of their age-old fear of infinity?

The soft music from the radio had stopped, and the newscaster's voice disturbed her reverie.

"...this afternoon, the Prelatinate announced eight new amend-ments to the Constitutional Commandments, making the total for the day so far a slightly-under-average twelve. This afternoon's amendments deal specifically with Commandment Ninety-three, Sec-tion 189, Chapter 914, paragraph 382, sub-rovision 2103-K. The first stipulates..."

She tried to find another program of music, but the daily amendment announcements were everywhere. With a fleeting smile she remembered what Doug had said—that at last the commercial had met its match as an instrument for ruining radio listening. Yet logical enough, for here the dollar was secondary, and Government was God.

She turned the console off, and again the house was quiet, and the chill mantle of worry drew closer about her brain, grew steadily into a stifling strait-jacket of helpless fear. Lord, there was nothing she could *do...*

Then of a sudden her pulse was racing as the large helicopter land-ed at the side of the house. She looked out the window.

But it was not Doug. The word ELECTROSUPPLY was stenciled in large letters above the craft's opening freight-door, and she watched as a dolly was lowered from it. There were four men, and they were unloading a large crate. It went on the dolly, and then the dolly with its load was being pushed by the four to the side of the house.

The door-signal sounded.

"Yes?"

"Madame Blair, would you please sign for the shipment?"

"Yes, of course. But what is it that I—"

"Sorry, Madame. Only the Order Division knows the nature of the consignment—policy, you know. There, that'll do it. Thank you."

HE left with her permission to leave the crate in the cellar and after a few minutes the 'copter and its efficient crew was gone.

She knew intuitively that it was the equipment he needed so desperately—ironically enough it must be that. She had to fight back the impulse to rush to the cellar and rip the crate open. For if in some way she should slip, do something wrong, damage what was inside...

Quite suddenly her thoughts were marshaled from their uninhibited adventuring and became sharp hard-edged instruments. Even the tiniest error now could mean the difference between winning and losing, and it was still not too late to win.

A message to him through his office, but it must be contrived somehow so that they could not suspect that she was telling him he must return immediately. She could simply say something like "as per your instructions, am informing you of arrival of the last item for which you phoned. Am sure it is exactly what you wanted. Good luck, Lisa." That should work—

But the telecall signal sounded before she could pick the slender unit from its cradle.

"Yes?"

"Madame Blair?" It was a woman's voice.

"Why yes, speaking."

"This is Madame—Doe. We missed you at the culture lecture yesterday afternoon my dear, and just wanted to make sure that everything was—all right, you know."

"The lecture—oh, yes of course. Why I'm sorry—"

"But everything is—all right? You're not ill?"

"Oh, no. It just must have been one of my usual oversights," Dot bluffed. And she knew there was something she was missing in the woman's voice. Something...

"Oversights?"

"Why, yes—I'm afraid so. Dreadfully sorry. But of course I'll try not to forget next time."

"But Madame Blair—" and then suddenly the tone changed. "Yes, I know how it is—we all have those days, don't we? Well, there's something you really should know, so don't forget our next little get-together, will you?" An enchanting little giggle was attached, but there had been no giggle in the first three words.

"No, I won't forget," Dot said.

"'Til next time, then. Goodbye."

Dot hung up, and the room seemed suddenly to have become cold. Intuition was one thing—she wouldn't be a woman if she didn't trust that. But imagination was of course quite another. It had been simply an unexpected half-minute phone-call. Short, almost too short, if she were any judge of the ladies' society type. Nonsense...

She sat down. And the chair was cold.

Nerves, girl, that's all. Like the night you saw the man in the shadows outside the house and Doug wasn't home from the banquet yet, and it turned out to be the neighborhood cop waiting for his beat relief...

She had to forget it, get the message to Doug. What would she say, now? "As per your instructions—"

But Madame Blair—!

Damn! This was ridiculous—pure imagination—since when was a culture society a thing to get goose-pimples over? That was all it was of course. Just the knowledge of the crate downstairs...God the house was quiet.

She reached for the phone.

And again, the door-signal chimed.

She half-walked, half-ran to answer it; tripped, caught herself. It chimed again.

Then somehow she had the door open, and there were four men in white uniforms standing before it.

"Madame Blair, if you will please come with us."

"No, I'm sorry—I can't. Why, what are you here for?"

"You received a telecall several minutes ago, did you not, Madame?" He phrased it as a question, but she knew that it was a statement.

"Why, yes I did. A social call—"

"We know that it was not, Madame Blair. If you will accompany us please." They stood there, unmoving.

"I—I don't understand. My culture society, if it is important for some reason that you know..."

"Precisely. We've known for some time about the society, Madame. We are sorry that we have at length linked you with it. Now if you will accompany us please."

There was no choice. She did not want to think of what might happen if she ran.

CHAPTER THIRTEEN

"INSIDE Venus compensation limit, sir. They've taken over. Inversion in three minutes; jet-down at NMHQ in twelve. Secondary check please, sergeant."

Space had been monotonous. After the first thrill of watching Earth grow smaller and smaller until it was nothing more than another planet in the heavens, after the realization that the studded blackness to each side was real, and not some gigantic planetarium show, the trip had been a seemingly motionless thing, like high flight in a light plane at less than cruising speed. They had licked the problem of weightlessness by an artificial gravity set-up, which functioned, as far as he was able to find out from the captain, on a complex system of gyroscopes—but not even they furnished so much as a tremor to the deck plates, and he might as well have been planted firmly on Earth for all the sensation there was of movement. Even when inversion began, the gyro system automatically compensated for its inertia effects, and he would have been unaware of it had it not been for the series of oral checks between sergeant and captain, captain and the base on Venus.

Then suddenly, the second planet loomed large and white—it blotted out the blackness, and then there was no more blackness, and the telescreen seemed to be swimming in pea-soup fog.

"Six minutes, sir."

The syrupy whiteness seemed limitless and for a moment Doug felt little pangs of panic, of fear that they must be falling into a great pit to which there was no bottom, only the eternity of the falling itself. Then suddenly it was above them like a diffuse, infinite ceiling, receding quickly at first, then more slowly, more slowly...

There was a gentle pressure beneath his feet. The gyros had compensated to their limit and had automatically cut out, and true gravity and inertia once more were settling their grip about the sleek ship.

"Switch the screen aft, captain."

"As she blasts, sir."

Blue. Great, incredible expanses of blue in every shade of color, every intensity of pastel, forced to the bending curve of a horizon that seemed like some great arching bulwark against the heavy, stifling whiteness that was the sky. For moments he was not able to distinguish land from ocean, but then he discerned it as the midnight blue, near-black mass that undulated slowly, in long, even swells—and it was the vari-shaded, lighter area, smaller in size than the state of Connecticut—that was the northern land mass. And it was toward that which they descended. Their formation had already split and far to starboard, he saw two long darts of silver pair off to land on the planet's southwestern mass.

He drew the cloak about his shoulders, secured the decorative dress sword at his waist.

Down. As silently as had been the long drift through Space, save for the nearly inaudible rumble of the great engine as it had checked in for deceleration. The descent was so perfectly controlled that if there was the heavy whine of atmosphere about their hull from too-great downward speed, he could not hear it. Down.

He drew on the gauntlets.

There was a gentle jar.

THEIR escort formed at once midway between his ship and Tayne's. They marched abreast, flanked by echelons of cadre officers and Quadrature Academy cadets. They marched silently toward a great, shining building that commanded the entire edge of the landing plaza. Its size alone made Doug catch his breath, yet it was dwarfed by a frozen human sea of tan-bodied pygmies, amassed before it in wave after spreading wave of superbly formed divisions. To realize at once that they were not formations of some stunted denizens of the planet, but children of Earth not yet eleven years old, was almost impossible for him although he had known, had seen the terrifying figures... But here were the statistics, immobile, at rigid attention, not in black and white, but in the hue of living flesh, with red blood still coursing through them. Here were what tomorrow would be the numbers—small still things, cold, impersonal, and dead. Here was the stability factor of a people, which had forged a device for peace. Here was the monument to their stupidity, the warrant for their ultimate place in infamy.

They faced the building in a long arc at the far edge of the plaza, an arc that Doug judged over a mile in length, easily 300 yards in depth. In it were the children of two full quadrants, his and Tayne's—perhaps a half-million—and the number would be matched on the southwestern mass, where Klauss and Vladkow had landed later, the survivors of their commands would be shipped here, and there would be the last battle. It had been planned that way for key psychological reasons.

After the first taste of battle, then the indeterminate time of waiting... And suddenly the waiting would cease, the sea-going troops at last would land, and swarm from their swift ships, clanging in droves to the attack. And the small, still dead things would mount again. Until margin was reached. Then they would stop.

Midway the length of the arc, where it was cleft by a distance of about a quarter-mile, the escort halted. It faced left. Doug and Tayne followed suit. The escort fell back to each side, once again forming the impressive flying wedge with the two Quadrates at its point. Then, facing the fantastically pretentious edifice looming silently before them, the great assemblage waited, the mute silence broken only by the rustling sound of a half-million sword-sheaths as they swung gently in the warm gentle breeze.

Gradually, then, the sound grew. A rumble like far-off thunder was above them, and it mounted slowly to a vibrant roar. The milk-white sky suddenly swirled as if in indecision, then was ripped asunder, and torn tendrils of it groped to fill the gaping rent in it as a great, silver shape plunged through, descended on a seething pillar of flame.

It landed atop the building itself. It was like a towering, silver spire there, as though to become an integral fixture to transform the sprawling Colossus from administrative nerve-center to the temple of empire. Doug's own ship beside it would have been as a sloop to a battleship. He knew that in a moment the main port of the flagship would open, and through it would be escorted the Prelate General himself.

A half-million pairs of ears were tuned sharply to hear the voice of their God. And when it had thrown them into conflict here, the mighty ship would rise and vanish as it had come, to bear its high priest to the southwest, where the lesson would be read for the second, and final time.

DOUG tensed, knowing as he did from sleepless study what was to come. Suddenly, from well-concealed amplifiers through which the Prelate General's voice would soon sound, there were the first thunderous strains of The Battle Hymn To Peace. Doug whirled, faced Tayne.

"Quadrants to salute!"

Tayne pivoted.

"Division leaders, give your divisions present arms!"

A hundred cadets about-faced in turn, bawled in unison *"Regimental sachems, give your regiments present arms!"*

And the command was passed in swelling unison from regiment to battalion, battalion to company, and the timing had been perfect. As the surging hymn of hysteria struck its climaxing strain, a cacophony of two thousand young voices swelled hysterically above it—"...PRE-SENT—*ARMS!*"

There was a piercing shriek of sound as 500,000 broadswords whipped from their scabbards, glittered like the teeth of some Hell-spawned, pulsating monster as they flashed in salute.

And Doug sickened. For he had seen it before, and only the sound had been different. There had been the resounding slap of taut rifle-slings against the wood of polished stocks...

The terrible music ended on a measure of rolling drums, and the command was relayed for order arms. There was the crash of a half-million blades slammed home in their scabbards as one, and then the silence fell as though some great impenetrable curtain had fallen.

The Prelatinate General, borne in a highly-polished sedan chair of lightweight metal on the shoulders of the colorfully-uniformed members of the Inner Prelatinate, appeared in the pocket-like balcony which was dwarfed only by the immensity of the building itself. Visible only as a jewel-encrusted shadow behind the transparent metal enclosure in which he was ensconced, he began his speech. The two quadrants stood again as statues.

"Once again, for the glory of the highest order of life and with the blessing of the Prelatinate Saints, we unite to do battle for the salvation of Man. May our mission be one of success."

A great rolling murmur of sound swelled from the throats of the half-million, subsided... The word was undistinguishable, but Doug knew what it was. They had said *"Amen."*

"Our sacred duty to the One World, to the Universal State is before us, and handed down to us by the will of the people as they worship in their countless community senates, we shall discharge it without fear, and for the love of our way of life. Sobeit.

"It behooves us all, as children of a mighty government, to believe without contest in the inviolate concepts upon which our all-powerful way of living and thought is built. There have been those who were unbelievers; there have been those who would profess to debase government and political philosophy to the level of mere intellectual function and enterprise of policy, yet even those were heard to admit before paying the terrible price for their heresies that, because their beliefs were different, they must have of course been wrong.

"For those of us who aspire and pray that we may one day hold a seat in the great Quorum of the Perfectly Governed, let there be no doubt, let there be no threat to the mightiness of the glorious order which we foster...

"As it is to be found in the immortal words of the Constitutional Commandments, and I read from Four Chapter 18, Book of Sections, Section 932: *There shall be great honor to those who give of their blood that the One World shall live, and great reverence for the glorious memories of those who give of their lives that the One World shall not perish.'* Sobeit."

Once again the rolling murmur of a half-million voices. "Amen..."

"It is then to you that I command, go forth, and perform the duties of your great faith; go forth, for the dead shall inherit the living!"

And as at a signal, the air was, rent with a deafening surge of voices strained to their topmost in a savage cheer.

SLOWLY then, it subsided, and the Prelatinate General raised his left hand as though in half-salute, half-benediction. And again, there was silence, and the living things that were statues had lost their shape and form, and had become row upon row of symmetrically-hewn markers dotting a large graveyard on Sunday afternoon in July.

"And now, let us join minds as we listen to the ancient tongue voicing the Prelatinate's Creed which has taught us to believe..."

And the sounds were strange, their meaning neither having been taught nor studied for the century and a half that English had been decreed by law as the universal tongue. Doug knew that only he, of all the half-million, understood the sounds. With difficulty at first, then with increasing facility, he translated the Latin. The Latin which the others heard and obeyed. And which they had never, nor ever would understand.

"...believe in the purchase of everlasting peace with the blood of the young; in eternal adherence to the regime of the Prelatinate because it is the sole existing concept in which to adhere; in sacrifice of thought upon the omnipotent altar of Belief to Government Almighty, and in the everlasting spirit of the Founders, to whom we daily pray for the strength to forever remain unchanged, unchangeable, despite the temptations of knowledge, progress, and human feeling: Sobeit. I believe in the infinite divinity of the two parties, and in the concept of truth as they shall dictate, rather than as it may seem to exist through exercise of mere reason; in the…"

The sing-song tones droned with heavy monotony through the hidden speakers, as though weaving some hypnotic spell to insure the captivity of the young myrmidons upon whose ears they fell, unintelligible, but Law.

The sea of young heads was bowed and a million eyes were focused unmoving on the ground, for to view the heavens and to think upon their unbounded freedom, with which they sought to lure the mind away from the patterns which had been decreed for it, would be tantamount to heresy.

And then suddenly the drone had ceased. There was movement in the balcony. Two of the Inner Prelatinate, cloaks swaying heavily with the weight of the precious metals with which they were gaudily embroidered, took posts as though sentinels at each side of the Prelate General's shoulder-borne sedan. The naked broadswords in their hands swung upward slowly until their lips touched directly above it. And the Latin came again, in low, swift cadences.

"…*You who are about to die, go forth*…"

And as the words were intoned, the broadswords were brought level, were swung slowly, in wide, horizontal half-arcs above the high-held heads of the regimented multitude.

"*God*…" Doug thought. "*God! A blessing!*"

Then the ceremony was over, and the strains of the hymn again burst forth, and Doug caught himself almost too late. He whirled.

"Troops pass in review!"

Tayne returned the salute, relayed the order until within seconds it was a surging, shrieking thing, the more frightening for it's perfect unison. *Hysteria*, Doug thought, *by the numbers!*

He knew the plan. The ranks that formed the long arc of formations would face right, and then, at simultaneous commands, would step off to the beat of the terrible hymn, preserving the curvature of the arc so that the actual line of march would be a perfect circle nearly a mile and a half at its inner diameter, with the great building as its precise center. And the ranks would be kept in perfect dress as they fanned out in 300 yard-lengths, and the cover of each endless column would be of such precision that at a command, the inner columns of each quadrate would march to the rear, and the spectacle would be one of four immense, counter-marching arcs. As they met at the opposite pole of the great diameter, the perfection of their circle would be proven.

He took his station near the edge of the inner circumference. Tayne took his, nearly a half-mile to Doug's rear. The cadre officers and Quadrature Academy cadets took posts of command at equally spaced intervals for the entire length of the arc, marching to them along invisible radii as the thousands of young section and squad leaders shrilled their commands.

DOUG drew his sword then, held it high over his head, then swept it in flashing salute to the ground. And together, he and Tayne gave the first order.

"Troops march forward!"

The cadremen and cadets repeated it.

"*For-ward*—"

And like an echo bounding its way into infinity, the word magnified into an undistinguishable roar.

"*MARCH!*"

The throbbing hymn was again at its climax, and the volume of sound was so great about him that the tiny shrill note, which his ear had singled out for the briefest instant, could only have been in his subconscious. Yet for a split-second, it had been by itself, for it had been out of timing with the rest. And it had been near him.

He would listen again, when the counter-march command was given. Impossible, of course. Unthinkable, unthinkable...

It seemed suddenly that the two-hour long march about the 5-mile mean circumference would take two days. The display was ridiculous and time-consuming, but he was thankful for it even as he cursed it. For he must hear the sound again. Yet if he heard it, then the spectacle must never end.

Slowly, slowly, at a measured, tireless step the Prelate General's Review marched in indefatigable tribute.

And at length, at the halfway mark, Doug raised his sword for the command, whipped it downward.

"Inner columns march to the rear!"

The relay began.

"Inner columns as assigned, to the rear—"

And the last words were magnified to the proportion of thunder, but his ears heard it only as a faraway thing. And again he heard the near-by command, again a split-second off.

"*MARCH!*"

This time it was unmistakable. A recently designed section or squad-leader, of course, who had not yet mastered the timing of commands to perfection. Nearby. He looked desperately into the files of marching boys at his side, now muddled as the centermost columns marched to the rear. The command would not have been re-layed to the outside columns, since they were continuing their march forward. Then he must quickly search the reverse column as it shuttled its obscured way to the rear.

But of course not! He would not recognize a face, even as—as his had gone unrecognized! But the voice he had heard it three times, three split seconds! And somehow it was, it was Terry's voice! In there somewhere—Terry, Terry and Mike! Swords and maces swinging rhythmically at their sides.

CHAPTER FOURTEEN

CARL GRAYSON lit a cigarette, Senior Quadrate Blair watched him closely as he went over the last of his notes. The man was obviously disturbed, but only about the interview itself. There had not been an instant's suspicion; Blair was certain of it. The greatest danger was over. It had been a danger ever-present with first meetings but with each, it had become progressively easier with which to cope, yet with the man Grayson, there had been unexpected pitfalls. These strange people indulged in a peculiar relationship called friendship, he had discovered—in essence it was a psychological thing, a thing from which to derive a satisfying personal pleasure. In actuality, it had become a rather distorted relationship, forged as it had been into a many-ratcheted tool. Between the Congressman and Grayson, however, the relationship was genuine and—the subtle thing, which he had missed until it had been almost too late—of a partial nature. The thing called friendship was a thing of varying degree. And Grayson was a "best" friend. He had almost missed that. It was so different to stabilize things here…

"Doug, I want to get this straight for sure, and then I think I'll have the works. What do you mean by 'new sources of military manpower yet waiting to be tapped'? You mean simply the next UMT draft in July don't you—all the new 17-year-olds?"

"For broadcast—immediate broadcast, Carl, I shall explain the phrase by simply saying, uh—a new program of draft-age analysis and evaluation is soon expected to be under study by the Blair Defense Preparedness Committee…"

"Yes, but—Doug that's just a mess of words. It doesn't tell beans about…Oh. I get it—OK." He pushed the hat further back on his head, made a marginal clarification. It was comfortable in the small office, but there was perspiration on Grayson's wide forehead.

"You don't sound too satisfied, Carl."

"Who, me? Hell, I'm satisfied. I keep getting the exclusives, so I can't holler, I just thought somehow you'd never get around to using that method, that's all, Doug. If you want to tell 'em, you can—and I guess you always have. But I suppose if you don't want to, but want 'em to think you have, it's as legitimate as ever to just confuse 'em. Get me. Philosopher." He completed the marginal note. "Now let's see…OK, OK, OK."

"Carl, how busy are you this afternoon?"

"Not, especially. Got to get this ready for my seven o'clock stint tonight and knock out the rest of next Monday's column, and then there's some of the routine junk but that can wait. Why?"

"I think I need your personal reaction to—well, to be frank about it, to a new angle the committee's got in its sights on this UMT business. I want to know what you think the radio—and the press, of course—will do with it."

"I guess I better put the pencil away?"

"Afraid so. But you'll get it first when the time comes. And perhaps you can help me decide when that should be, too."

"Shoot. All ears and no memory." He folded the uneven sheets of newsprint, crammed them in an inner pocket.

"The story I've just given you, Carl, is a lot more important than it looks. At first glance it's just Sunday feature stuff—that's the way you'll play it in your column, and you'll probably just give it a tag-end spot on your program. And that's the way I want it played. But—it is important. I think you could call it a sort of—of a cornerstone story."

"Thinking of a series, you mean? Hell, Doug, you've got the next elec—"

"Not as a series, that's the point. Not so direct. More like a good propag—public relations campaign I mean. The development will be gradual, and not too regular—that part of it I'm going to leave up to you to some extent, I think—until it automatically becomes the top news."

"Don't get it, Doug. I've told you before what's page one and what isn't. This thing you've just given me hasn't any big names in it, anything about money, taxes, or things to make anybody good and sick at heart. This is just—well, just opinion. Thoughtful analysis. The thoughtful stuff never makes the front pages, you know that."

THE Quadrate smiled. "Precisely. I feel it should be pretty casually introduced. But don't worry—I won't ruin its news value. I think you'll agree with me when I'm ready for the top spot on your broadcast and for the front pages, I'll have something that will—how do you put it?—make people suddenly sick. Point is, I want them to be unconsciously thinking along the right lines first, so that when they get through being sick and stop to think about it, it will make sense."

He was careful. It was difficult to maintain the curious bantering way of speech these people continually employed. An end-product, of course, of their emotional degeneration, and therefore as difficult to perfectly imitate as a provincial misuse of the language. But it was not as difficult as at first.

"Sure Doug—what you're talking about is done all the time, every day of the week. That part's easy enough—too damn easy. But—you keep saying 'it'. 'It' will make sense. What are you gunning at?"

"Suppose I give you an example. The final development of that statement you weren't clear on. 'New sources of military manpower yet waiting to be tapped.' What it will mean, when the time comes, is the UMT drafting of children ten years old. Thirteen at first."

"*The what?*" The man Grayson looked almost ludicrous. His mouth hung foolishly open, and there was no sound coming from it.

"I'm afraid you not only heard correctly, Carl, but that I had better tell you that if you're thinking of sending for the booby-wagon for me, you'll have to send for about thirty others for the rest of the committee. Next week, the Blair Defense Preparedness Committee will introduce a bill for unlimited lowering of the draft age, for either war or peacetime use. Within a month after its passage—and I can guarantee you that it will be passed—the committee will give you what you'll need for your first big story on it. It will urge, and then it will demand that all male youths from the present draft age of 17 down to the age of thirteen be immediately registered for selective service."

"Good Lord, Doug—"

"The committee is strong, Carl. It is strong because I knew how to pick it. I did not pick it, I assure you, on the basis of intelligence or learning or capability. I picked it in terms of personal political and financial influence and in terms of my capability in persuading its members to my way of thinking. That was not too difficult—they're all band-wagon men.

"But to the point. On the heels of the new Blair Law's invocation, the committee will again make a demand—registration of all youngsters down to and including the age of ten years."

"Doug for God's sake—"

"Sit down, Carl!"

"Sure…"

"I'm quite sane. Worried?"

"Hell yes I'm worried."

"Take it easy. They thought a man called Litvinov was deranged once—around 1913 I think it was, when he predicted World War One, and the fall of the House of Czars."

"BUT you can't be serious about this—this kid business. Why my God if I think you've been—overworking, let's say, what d'you think the reaction of the man in the street'll be?"

"That, Carl, hasn't mattered for quite some time. You know it, and I know it. He's already swallowed UMT itself, don't forget."

"But—hell, the Blair Committee isn't the only bunch of politicians around here. And they—"

"I told you, Carl, my committee is strong, I picked it that way. Others can yell all they want. But no amount of yelling—even by the most widely heard commentators and widely-published columnists—has ever really accomplished much when a particularly strong political faction has decided how things are going to be. It's the things that make you sick that have always made the front pages, remember?"

"I—you're crazy, Doug. Crazy as a 1951 tax program. You've gotten bitter about things in the past, sometimes a little cynical. Hell, who doesn't. But you've always been the one man the people knew they could count on—and your fellow-workers, I can even add. If you try to come out with a thing like this—"

"A moment. Just a minute, Carl. I want to ask an easy one. It is really easy. How long before the next world war breaks out?"

"Easy, what d'you mean, easy? Tomorrow, next month, next year maybe. Maybe not until 1960. Nobody knows that—"

"I still say, easy. There's certainty it will be at least by 1960, and probably sooner. That's terrifyingly close enough, isn't it, when you're speaking in terms of the inevitable?"

"I see."

"The world is a pretty desperate place right now, wouldn't you say? Worse even than five or six years ago."

"Desperate, desperate—yes of course it's desperate. And you—you're going to make something of it, is that it? Doug, you're not being very original. I never thought—I never honestly thought the day would come when I'd hear you—"

"Give me a chance, Carl."

"If I do I don't think I'll ever broadcast another word of what you have to say."

"I'll take that chance. But first I'd better clear some things up. First of all, I'll tell you how much I've explained to the committee. I've pointed out to them that there is but one way open—and one way only—of offsetting the Soviets' superiority in arms production, and that's to shock the living daylights out of them. Shock them so that they'll be convinced we're—we're a nation gone mad, perhaps. As you think I've gone mad, this moment. But—what stomach would any foreign enemy have for fighting a madman, armed to the teeth with atomic weapons? They say a lunatic with a gun is a great deal more deadly than a sane man similarly armed.

"So—we shall shock them, Carl. We shall, perhaps before the year is out, not only double our own production regardless of cost, but register every kid in the country down to the ten-year age level. And have a gun ready for each one, too. As I explained to the committee, it won't be even their tremendous numbers that will be frightening. It will be the seemingly crazed desperation of the country that would consider calling them to arms that would throw the scare. And then, of course, we'll take advantage of the scare. We'll produce A-weapons as we never have before. Hell, every parent in the nation will be breaking his back at a defense plant—not just for the ridiculously high wages that a riveter gets, but to insure the safety of their kids' skins."

"Doug, you're either really nuts or—or—"

"So much the committee knows, as of now. And, I've sold it to them. I sold it to them by simply asking them which was less desirable, my plan, or the end of civilization in a few short years. And, by asking them what other solution they had."

"Any straw—any straw at all." The reporter was not speaking to be heard, but Blair heard him.

"You've hit it precisely, Carl. It's come finally to that. Any straw at all."

FOR a few moments there was silence in the small office, and Carl Grayson just sat, staring at the floor. At length he put a fresh cigarette between his lips, lit it, and smoked automatically. It was half consumed before Doug said, "Now, I want to discuss the rest of the plan with you. The part I've not broached to the committee as yet."

"The—rest? Doug what are you talking about?"

"The rest of it. You see, sooner or later the initial shock is going to wear off, Carl. Then, perhaps if we're lucky, we'll be evenly matched in armament and personnel under arms, but that will be all. A balance of peace is no good. You convince no one that peace is desired. You simply convince them that for awhile, there's no way they dare break it. But again, sooner or later, the dare is taken and then—"

"I want to go, Doug."

"Not yet. I want you to hear me out. And, I'm going to ask a rather special favor, Carl. Judge the plans on the merits of its logic alone. For the moment, imagine you have no emotion."

"I can, but it won't do any good. Afraid I have emotion, Douglas."

"I see. Tell me, if it is so valuable a thing as to be allowed to cloud your reasoning, why would you instantly throw it away if something called patriotic duty were suddenly thrust upon you?"

"It would shake me up a little of course—"

"Yes, but you'd chuck it. You'd perform the duty."

"All right. I don't know the tricks of debate, you do. Go ahead I'm listening."

"I'll begin this way. If, we'll say, an infantry captain realized that by sacrificing the lives of three of his men and possibly his own, he could save the lives of his entire company, what would he do, if he were what is termed a 'good' officer?"

"Why, if that were his only alternative—"

"I assure you, it would be, for the purposes of my analogy."

"He'd—he'd save the company. That's happened."

"Even to men with emotions."

"Why—yes of course. Damn you Doug—"

"Even when one of the three to be sacrificed might be a kid who was still in high school when he enlisted—"

"Yes. Yes I guess so."

"Now remember what you've just told me, and switch to this... What, actually, is the basis for armed conflict between nations? Generally speaking, with the long view of history?"

"I—I suppose covetousness. Materially translated that would mean just plain wanting the grain fields, the ore mines, the sea ports, the wealth someone else has and that you no longer have, doesn't it? Land, then. Hitler called it *Lebensraum*. One outfit thinks another is stepping on its toes over this chunk of real estate or that. Etcetera, ad nauseum, ad politics."

"Good. And what's the real root of this material covetousness do you think?"

"Grass is always greener, I guess."

"That is motive enough for the small-scale wars, yes. But I'm speaking of the kind nations fight in desperation, not merely for the sake of warring."

"Then, well—they run out of what they've got. Want more. Is that the answer you want?"

"Almost. What makes them run out, Carl?"

"Not enough stuff to take care of their population, not enough work to supply the money to buy what little there is to buy. Too many people, not enough resources to keep 'em happy."

"Now, essentially, you have it. Now, if you'll remember those two things—the captain's sacrifice and *Mr.* Hitler's fight for *Lebensraum*—we'll switch again. If I owed you a dollar, Carl, and gave you a bill, you'd accept it. What would it be worth?"

"Why, about—let's see—"

"No, I mean in terms of the metal backing it."

"Well—actually, it could be worthless. But as long as I don't think it is—"

"CORRECT. As long as you, and everybody else of course, has faith in it, it is of value, and is working currency. Now one more thing. Did you ever have anything really bad happen to you when you were a youngster—say about ten years old, Carl?"

"I don't get this, Doug. You're way over me—"

"No, answer me. I want you to think of something unpleasant that happened—"

"Don't have to think. I still get goose-pimples when I hear a near-by train whistle. Almost got killed once when my father's car got stalled on a railroad crossing. Sort of a—I guess they call it con-ditioning. Pretty strong with me, I guess."

"Yes. Now—we'll put the four things together, Carl. First of all, according to my plan, the world must somehow be given implicit faith in a method for the elimination of warfare. A method in which they will so strongly believe that, although the supposed reason for such belief may be scientifically quite fallacious, they will practice it nonetheless. To do this, they must be shown a method which, by one means or another, actually works. And, that is possible. There is such a method, based on the sacrifice of the few for the ultimate preservation of the many..."

"Go on. So far you've brought in the dollar-bill idea; the business about conditioning, the captain and his company... What method?"

"Taking the drafted ten-year-olds—first of just this nation, then of the entire world—placing them once each year in four divisions in the Sahara desert, and setting them at one another with manual weapons."

Carl turned white. He sat, unmoving, silent.

"The accepted theory will be that the horror of death by arms will create so deep a mental scar on the young plastic minds that in adulthood they will never again be able to kill. In actuality, the theory is in many respects fallacious, granted. But it will be accepted, because the practice—the desert fighting—will reduce the basic cause of warfare to flat zero, and there will eventually be no war. How? Through such a plan, many male children of course will die yearly. The number killed will be subject to strict control of course, in exact proportion to annual world birth-rate, and potential multiplication. Such, Carl, that the population of the world will, in terms of future generations as well as those almost immediate, be always stabilized.

Of course, since a period of from twenty to fifty years may be needed for practice of the method before the first tangible stabilization results are shown, the 'conditioning' angle must be heavily stressed, before as well as during the actual desert fighting. Backing by the press will greatly help toward this end—you yourself know how terribly potent it can be—and I'm certain, once the method is explained to them in terms of survival, we will also be able to count on the 'corroboration' of the world's most popular scientists.

"However, as absolutely necessary insurance, an influence infinitely more powerful than those combined will be employed to positively insure unquestioning belief in the validity of the plan, not only before and during the first few years, but for all time!

"I have, therefore, already taken steps to bring it into play. I have already issued invitations to one hundred of the world's highest ranking ecclesiastical leaders for a conference here next week. By then, the committee should be rolling with quite a bit of momentum. As we said, these are desperate times…"

CARL remained silent. His question was in his eyes, but he would not give it speech. But Blair saw it.

"The clergy? Their assistance will be essential. I just told you why, didn't I? You see, once they realize that they can materially contribute to lasting peace, I am sure they will cooperate. If necessary, they—all of them—would consent to a merger of church and state. History bears me out."

"The mer—"

"Naturally. How else can I make *sure* the people are made to believe implicitly in the plan until they can at least see its tangible results? And how better to maintain that belief? Government and politics and all they imply are already worshipped more than God, Carl! So let's put it on a paying basis!"

"And you think—you actually think you'll get the support of the world's clergy in this revolting scheme—"

"I told you that history bears me out, Carl. For instance—from the fourth to the fourteenth centuries, one of the world's most powerful sects was heavily involved in temporal government—because, it said, of necessity to preserve itself. And surely you must remember the cooperation of the church with Constantine and Charlemagne when their empires were in danger of disintegrating, when unity was so sorely needed, and they knew there was but one that could help them? Often the church—the sect to which I referred before—actually took over the powers of government during Charlemagne's rule—not, perhaps, because it wanted involvement in those things which were Caesar's—but because it realized the grave perils which would face it if whole empires were to break apart, and their peoples reduced to pagan savagery as a result.

"I think you see my point. And—I imagine the simile about the captain and his platoon will also be appealing, don't you? The idea of sacrifice that others might live...?"

"You—you son of a bitch!"

"I'm sorry you said that, Carl. Because the plan will work, you know. From telling it to you, I see that its shock-value is valid. From seeing your final reaction, I realize that you are inwardly as sure as I that it will succeed. It is actually all I wanted, to get your immediate reaction."

"Doug, I'm going. But there's just one thing I want to ask you before I smear you from here to damnation. Just what, Congressman, is *your* cut in this?"

"None. I have not once mentioned money."

"You're a madman, Blair."

"When you've convinced yourself of that, Carl, you may try to smear me if you wish. But first—*first, convince yourself!*"

CHAPTER FIFTEEN

As Doug marched, he thought. There was less than an hour yet of marching to complete the great circle, to devise a plan.

Two boys in five hundred thousand. An impersonation now demanding so complex a knowledge of the situation of which it was the center that to carry it to successful conclusion would be impossible. Even a moment's belief otherwise was rank stupidity. Escape? Yes, by himself somehow, perhaps he could escape in one of the two sleek ships even now being serviced on the plaza; that had been the basis for his original plan. But the plan was junk now. Junk, unless he could find Terry and Mike first. Two boys, in a half-million!

Aircraft were being rolled out on the plaza. The immense aircraft in which he and Tayne would fly as they directed the maneuvers of their quadrants, and the aircraft of the tabulation and evacuation specialists. They were huge, and there were fully a hundred of them. But for all their size and number, they offered no hope. It was like being in a nightmare wherein one had to run for his life, but the ground beneath was a sucking, miring bog.

His reason hinted temptingly that the voice he had heard might well not have been that of his son. How many voices were there in all creation that were precise echoes of each other? Thousands? Millions, even. But among them, there was of course the *one*. And he must know. He had to know.

The Contraption. Again, what had it done? It had transmitted himself and Dot into their physical counterparts on a parallel time--track. If the blue glow of the contraption had touched Terry and Mike, then they too would have been transmitted. But because they had not appeared in the cellar when the transmission was complete, he and Dot had assumed that they had been just outside the Contraption's limited range.

That was it, of course—the cellar. That was what had thrown them off, confused their logic. Through some quirk of coincidence, the other Blair, Senior Quadrate Blair and his wife had been in their cellar at the time of the switch. Had they been anywhere else— anywhere else at all, even just upstairs, the mistake in logic would not have been made. And if Madame Blair had no sons, Terry and Mike would not have been transmitted at all. But Quadrate and Madame Blair had had sons. Two, ten years old. He remembered when Tayne had told him of their transfer from his quadrant to Tayne's own... Ordered by Gundar Tayne, Director. He remembered. He remembered how thankful he had been that they had not been his. But now—now, fantastically, they were. Because when the switch happened, Ronal and Kurt Blair had not been in the cellar. They had been on Venus.

But it was too much, the coincidences—the marriage of two counterparts; their children, same sex, same age.

And then he remembered what he had told Grayson so terribly long ago. *There's a million possible results when you go fooling around with the structure of the universe, Carl...*

THOUSANDS of voices in the universe that were exact echoes of each other. But Terry and Mike were here, and there was no doubting that. And in Tayne's quadrate, the one beside which he was even now marching. Oh, he was doing well with his thinking! He had narrowed the field down to a trifling two hundred fifty thousand!

And he knew that by any direct means that would not arouse Tayne's too-willing suspicion, it was as far down as he would narrow it.

Indirect, then…Somehow, through Tayne himself, perhaps. Tayne had his boys. Tayne's brother had seen to that, with of course no reason given. Pressure—simple pressure. Doug wondered if the pressure was supposed to break him. He wondered what Tayne's reaction would be—and his brother's—if it did not. Easy enough to guess. If his sons' deaths at Tayne's careful arrangement were not enough to break him, shatter him, make him throw down his office, then the corpses of Kurt and Ronal—Terry and Mike—would somehow end up on the battle area occupied by his quadrant, far enough behind the front lines of fighting to convince any martial court that he had violated the Director's order, had obviously at the last moment brought his sons back within his own quadrant, where they might be in some measure protected.

That was how it would be. If the pressure was not enough, then a simple frame. A simple matter of good timing. Yet if the timing should, by some miracle, go wrong…

If the timing went wrong! God there it was!

Suddenly, the blood was pounding through his body, throbbing in the large veins at his throat. Five minutes more and this thing would end. Three hundred seconds, four hundred strides. Then the final salute as the Prelate General left as he had come. And then thirty minutes for deployment, and the games on the northern mass would begin.

But before those thirty minutes started… It must be done just as the Prelate General's ship disappeared into the white syrup of the sky. It must be done just before the order to break ranks to prepare for combat deployment.

And then of course it would be a gamble at best. But it was a chance, where before there had been no chance at all.

FIVE hundred thousand swords flashed in final salute as the Prelate General's glittering ship leapt skyward, trailing a satisfactorily impressive wake of flame and thunder as it ascended into invisibility. And the sprawling headquarters building was at once denuded of its steeple. The Director had taken his place in the balcony. Divinity had withdrawn, entrusting its mission at length to the obedient officer of its lay hosts.

The swords were sheathed. And in a moment, the Director of the games would signal dismissal.

Now!

Suddenly, Doug was striding from his post at the point of the flying wedge, the thin flanks of which still joined the two quadrants, heading unerringly for a point directly before the balcony itself. And as suddenly he stopped, stiffly raised his open palm in salute. His cloak fluttered in the warm breeze.

"Your Very Grand Excellence! Senior Quadrate Blair wishes to report a suspected breach of command!" And he held his breath, but not intentionally, for suddenly breath would not come.

His salute was returned. And the field behind him was again still as though carved from stone.

"Report, Quadrate!"

He mustered all the wavering strength in his body, for each word must be crisp, clear, strong and flowing with confidence.

"Your Very Grand Excellence, it has come to this officer's attention that there exists the possibility of failure to execute a quadrant reassignment as prescribed in your command of June 3, in which Ronal Blair and Kurt Blair, identification numbers 28532 and 28533, were ordered transferred from the quadrant which I command to that of Quadrate Tayne. In order that such a failure be rectified at once if, in actuality, it has transpired, I request permission to order an immediate inspection of the units concerned!"

His muscles were rigid and his throat felt like so much wadded sandpaper. Everything hinged on what happened now. Everything.

"In the interests of military efficiency and discipline, your unprecedented request must be granted, Quadrate Blair. I will expect, however, a full report in writing concerning the basis of your suspicion of such failure at your earliest convenience. Order the inspection; you may have ten minutes!"

"At once, sir!"

He saluted, about-faced, and strode, the single animate figure in a great open amphitheater of statues, toward the Post Tayne held behind his own. And as he walked the foreboding silence was suddenly shattered by the roar of starting aircraft engines. The tabulation and evacuation planes, readying for warm-up flights, last-minute terrain checks. There was so little time. And the Director's flat, superbly confident tone had been enough to tell him that only a naive fool could hope to win. In it there had been no trace of surprise, no trace of suspicion, no trace of hesitation. It could mean that he was already beaten. Or, there was the thread-slim chance that it meant the Director had seen no threat in the request to the subtle plan against him. For, regardless of the inspection's outcome, the sons of Quadrate Blair would end up where they belonged, under Quadrate Tayne. And so the plan would thence go forward.

But for the record, the Director had demanded a report!

A report, Doug knew, which one way or the other, he would never write.

Somewhere behind him a flight of tab planes thundered into the air.

And then suddenly, he was facing Tayne, and it was time to play out the gamble to the end.

"Quadrate Tayne, in order to satisfy the Director and myself that the transfer of my sons to your quadrant has been effected as ordered by the Director's command dated June 3, you will order forward for inspection the unit within your quadrant to which they were assigned."

"Yes, sir."

Tayne pivoted.

"Divisions Six and Eighteen, forward—march!" Again, the familiar relay of command. Then the two great masses surged forward, one behind the other, leaving the two behind them still in formation. "Six by the left flank, march!" Six had cleared the quadrant formation, moved off as commanded to the left. "Eighteen by the right flank, march!" And Eighteen did the same. "Divisions, halt! Six, right, face! Eighteen, left, face!" And as quickly as Tayne's commands were relayed, the way was methodically cleared for the rear rank division he called next. There were perhaps seven minutes left... "Division Thirty forward, march!"

AND it came forward, and Doug realized at once that in this formation, this Division Thirty, were his sons, if they were anywhere among the five hundred thousand at all.

"Division, halt!" A second flight of evac ships roared over them, and Tayne waited. Six minutes... " 'A' Company, First Battalion,

Second Regiment, forward—" This time, the unit Tayne wanted was in the very front, and at once, two hundred boys were separated from a division of over five thousand, as the division itself had been picked from among forty-eight others in a quadrant of a quarter-million.

And then—

"Squad leaders Kurt and Ronal Blair, *front center*!" And from the squads of a rear platoon, two bare-torsoed, helmeted youngsters rushed forward on the double!

They halted three paces from Tayne, saluted. And to Doug, their young faces were completely unrecognizable.

Curiously pinched, worried young faces, drawn taut with the tension of bewilderment and sudden fear.

Tayne pivoted, faced Doug.

"Sir, Kurt and Ronal Blair, as assigned by command! At your orders, sir!"

Doug returned the salute, said nothing. He walked with a careful nonchalance to where the two boys, swords and maces still swinging at their sides, stood at attention. Their arms rose in salute. There was no sign of recognition in their eyes.

He dared linger near them but a moment, the fleeting moment it would take for him to identify his own sons beyond doubt. And again, it would be a matter of timing. For until the right moment, Tayne could hear every word.

"How long have you boys been in your present unit?"

"Since—since June the third I think, sir," Terry's voice. And it was Terry's way of saying words. It was Terry, and it was Mike beside him.

But he remained silent. He waited, and he prayed.

The silence drew into seconds, and it was deadly.

And then suddenly a third flight of evac ships thundered their paean of power as they fought for altitude above him!

And with the prayer still at his lips lest his words be either too loud or drowned altogether, Doug shouted almost in their faces: *"Terry, Mike! It's Dad! The Contraption's done all of this! Watch for me—I'll pick you up off the field!"*

Their eyes were suddenly wide but the roar was already subsiding. He had managed about twenty quick words. He turned to Tayne. And Tayne's sword was not drawn. On his face was the masked look of hatred, but not the unveiled one of sudden comprehension. He had not heard…

"My sons, without doubt, Quadrate, you may order them to fall in, and reform your ranks. You shall receive my apology of record as soon as practicable."

He saluted stiffly and took his post at the apex of the wedge.

Tayne bellowed his commands for the reformation of his quadrant between the fourth and fifth ascending flights of tab and evac planes. And then, once again, there was the fantastic tableau of helmeted statues.

And through the speakers came the Director's command to deploy for combat.

AS their quadrants were marched off to take the field under the ground command of the Junior Quadrates of the headquarters cadre, Doug and Tayne were escorted by an honor guard of cadets to the hangar-sections of the headquarters building where their command planes waited in the dank heat, engines idling. Huge aircraft, powerful, but not built for speed. Propeller-driven instead of jet, and the reason was obvious enough—the great, broad-winged craft had been designed for observation, not pursuit. Although there was no sign of a rotor assembly on either ship, Doug knew that for all their size, they were capable, in the thick atmosphere of Venus, of hovering at very little more than the speed of a slow human run. Every thing planned to the last detail. Every thing, irrevocably woven into the unchangeable fabric of destiny itself.

The last half of what little plan he had remained only partially within the pattern, and after that, it would simply be a race between fugitive and pursuer—fully-committed race between hunter and hunted. Nothing more, he knew, than a desperate attempt at escape where there could be no escape. But at least there would be the brief, red-hot satisfaction of trying—there was always that, when there was nothing else…

It would be simple. As Senior Quadrate, his was the duty of overseeing the campaign not only of his own quadrant, but that of Tayne, Vladkow, Klauss. His was the prerogative of flying his ship over or landing it among any of the troops, wherever they fought. He could land in any quadrant—in Tayne's quadrant. The detailed campaign maps, kept in constant conformation with each phase of the battle as it progressed by picked tabulation personnel, would show him where to land. Wherever he found A Company, First Battalion, Second Regiment, Division Thirty... And if the boys had understood, they would be watching, waiting. And after that, back to the plaza, the ship, with the prayer that its return trajectory was already plotted, its autorobot already reset for the return journey to Earth.

That was where he must break the pattern. That was when the hopeless, foolish race would begin.

And inwardly, Doug smiled an ironic, tight little smile. So funny, so tragically funny. A down-to-earth, practical man like Congressman Douglas Blair, running for his life from a fantasy that could not possibly exist! As the people of Hiroshima had run on the day of the atomic bomb...

Their cloaks started to whip in the slipstreams of the waiting aircraft. Another ten strides and he would have been aboard the plane.

But before he had taken five of them, the speeding surface-vehicle had drawn up beside them and stopped scant feet short of the plane's opening port, Cadremen leapt from it, swords drawn. And behind them came the Director himself.

The formation halted as though it had suddenly struck an invisible wall.

As he walked between his flanks of guards, the hulking Gundar Tayne drew his own sword. And Doug knew what the gesture meant.

"Senior Quadrate Blair, as lawful husband of Madame Lisa Blair, who was taken into custody by the S-Council of Earth at 1300 hours Earth Standard Time today, I hereby place you under official arrest, Guards! Disarm this man."

CHAPTER SIXTEEN

DOUG stood motionless as his dress sword was whipped from its scabbard, snapped across the bent knee of one of the Director's guards, and cast at his feet. A second denuded him of the wide belt and narrow scabbard, which had held it.

"Sir, unless you are able to cite well-founded charges for this outrageous action, I can assure you it will be reported to the Prelate General at once!" Doug bit the words out knowing that as a defensive threat they were hopelessly impotent, but he had to know what they had done to Dot. He had to know that even if they were to kill him within the next second. He sensed Tayne's presence behind him, could all but feel his swordpoint at his back. The cadets, a moment before formed as a guard of honor, were, suddenly in a bristling ring about him as though from some melodrama from the pages of Roman history. Their faces were impassive, their feet widespread, their swords hip-high, and pointed unwaveringly at him.

And the sneer in the Director's voice was only carelessly conceal-ed.

"This is hardly the time for jests, Quadrate. I hardly think I need quote the Commandment subsection setting forth the law concerning the status of husband and wife when either is found guilty of heresy. Your rank permits you to deny your wife's collusion if you wish, but— unfortunately, Madame Blair has been unquestionably linked with one of the pitiful but vicious little underground groups of men and women whose constant and sole aim is not only to abolish the war games, but to accomplish the eventual destruction of our sacred government. She—as well as yourself, I might add—has been under painstaking scrutiny for almost a year. I am informed that a carefully guarded but all too unwise series of telecalls to your home has at last established the necessary link. Ever hear of the Saint Napoleon Culture Society, Quadrate? No? No, of course you haven't! Quadrate Tayne!"

"Yes, your Very Grand Excellence!"

"I'm putting this man in your custody for the trip to Earth. Your orders are to deliver him in person to the S-Council—You'll take off immediately. The games will be under my personal supervision until you return. Any questions?"

"I am to deliver this man in person to the S-Council. No questions, sir."

"Carryon, then." He returned Tayne's salute with a perfunctory dip of his swordpoint, then sheathed the weapon and followed Doug into the waiting vehicle.

TAKE-OFF black-out was but momentary and wore off quickly. Escaping Venus' lesser gravity was noticeably easier, and the fog-shrouded planet still filled the viewscreen when Doug got to his feet. He was half surprised to discover that there were no steel cuffs at his wrists, and that he had not been bound other than by the safety belts to the acceleration hammock. But it was logical enough. A robot-guided ship in Space was quite efficiently escape-proof. It had been an effective trap before, and now it was an equally effective prison. And Tayne, who had already opened trajectory compensation communications with Venus headquarters, was the one who had the sword.

Tayne's back was to him. A sudden leap—

No. With Tayne unconscious or dead, it would make little difference. His presence aboard the ship was apparently only for the satisfaction of protocol. Placed aboard it alone, Doug reasoned, he would have been as well secured a prisoner as had he been accompanied by a guard of one hundred men. It was not Tayne, but the autorobot guiding the ship that was his jailer. Yet, Tayne had not removed his sword...

Doug watched the white mass of Venus as it receded with torturing slowness in the screen, let it half hypnotize him. There was something stirring uneasily somewhere far back in his brain— something, something—but it did not matter. Nothing at all mattered now. The race—the great, hopeless race he had planned for freedom had never even begun!

They had denied him even that satisfaction. Yes, he could attack Tayne, and Tayne would kill him. But that would not be a fight. It would be simply the choice of suicide, at the hands of the man who would derive the most satisfaction from being its prime instrument. The man who already signed the death warrants for Mike and Terry...

And Dot. Dot, after some awful agony would see him again perhaps, but she would see with uncomprehending eyes, hear with unrecognizing ears. If she lived through what they did to her, she would no longer be Dot at all.

Dully, he could hear Tayne's words in a background that was a thousand miles away. *"Reconciled and steady as she blasts. This is QT to Control, C-Limit check—trajectory secure. Out."*

And again, there was something far back in Doug's brain, struggling harder...

Then even as Tayne turned toward him from the dial consoles, it burst into the forefront of his mind like a flare in the darkness. *Twelve hundred Kemps at three hundred milliamperes, sir...Genemotor, type A-26-F modified... Sergeant! The neuro-tablets at once...Commandments Four, Part 3, Subsection 12 as amended...all space craft shall be robot-controlled and shall fly predetermined trajectories, save (1) when bearing members of the Science Council and/or their certified representatives, to whom manual operation and navigation at will is singularly permissible, or (2) when insurmountable emergency shall occur...*

And suddenly, Doug's brain vaulted from the lethargy of hopelessness and it was again at his command, a sharp, poised weapon of battle. *For Tayne knew! Yet he would die before he would tell—unless, somehow...*

"Such confidence, Quadrate Tayne! Admirable! But you would look so much more fit for our role with your sword in your hand, not in your scabbard!"

Tayne reddened. "If it were not for my orders, Blair—"

"Why, such a lack of conditioning, Quadrate! Don't you know killing me is supposed to be so repulsive to you that you couldn't even stomach the thought of it? Tell me, don't I make you sick, Quadrate?"

TAYNE'S hand went to the hilt of his weapon. He half drew it, slammed it back in its scabbard.

"Blair, we have twenty hours aboard this ship together. We can be at each other's throats like children. Or not, as you please."

Doug sat down on the edge of the acceleration hammock. Perhaps it would not be so difficult. Carefully, he entered the role further. He must have just the right kind of smile.

"Ah, but think of all the trouble I can get you in if I make you lose your temper and kill me! And you have got to admit, where I'm going, it doesn't make much difference—to me, I mean."

Tayne turned back to the instrument panel as though to signify that he had suddenly become a deaf man. And Doug kept talking, as though to signify a complete lack of interest in whether Tayne was a deaf man or not.

"As the matter stands, they took my sword away. So you'd never get anywhere with a self-defense alibi. Lord, how they'd make you sweat! By Saint Napoleon's mother I like the thought of that! And, after all, since this is going to be my last flight, I really think I'm entitled to a little amusement."

Silence.

"You know, Quadrate," Doug kept on relentlessly, "I don't imagine you expected even me to act like this, did you? No, of course not. Not very much the officer and gentleman. But that makes us more or less even. You don't know what a gentleman is. You're so stupid you don't even know who the next President of the United States is going to be!—Oh, sorry. I keep forgetting—I don't think I ever told you that I'm not the real Senior Quadrate Blair, and that I'm not from your universe at all, did I, Tayne? Ever hear of the World Series? Oh, there I—"

Tayne turned his head.

"Easy does it! I imagine you must think I've gone mad. Don't blame you. I don't act at all like the Blair you know. Of course if I am mad, you'd better be careful. And if I am from another universe, you'd better be even more careful. As a matter of fact, at the moment, Quadrate, your life may not be worth very much."

Doug rubbed his fingernails on his tunic, inspected their new sheen. Then he looked up at Tayne.

Tayne stood, face mottled, an uneasy little thread of uncertainty deep under the surface of his eyes.

"Very well, just to make it easy for you, *Mr.* Tayne, we shall say I am mad, because that's easy to believe, and I can see you're quite sure of it already. Yet just the same I can outwit you, Quadrate. That is, I think that in the twenty hours of our flight together I can reduce you to a gibbering idiot, far worse off than myself! Why, I may even have you mumbling that you're Saint Napoleon himself! Now wouldn't that be a picture!" Blair slapped, his right hand to his tunic-front.

And Tayne drew his sword.

"If you killed me, Quadrate, you would have no proof of my madness for the others—and I'm sure that our standing enmity would be reasoned as the far more credible motive. Reasonable people, yours. Very. So much so that they're all above making a rather ridiculous harangue like this. Face the S-Council rather stoically, I should imagine. Quietly, as befits their dignity. *Right?*"

Tayne almost jumped clear of the deck.

"By jingo, you're nervous, man! Sweating, too. And twenty more hours. Let's see—what'll we talk about?"

Tayne was tense, immobile, undisguisedly confused.

"I bet you're thinking that if you could get me in a state of—shall we say, unconsciousness, your troubles would be over. But you'd have to get close to me to do that. And we both know that sword of yours is no threat. Besides, I'm a madman. Either mad, or from another universe—ha! —and then I might be able to kill you with a glance! Of course, you can suppose this is all just an act, but even if I told you it was you wouldn't be exactly sure, would you? Would you, now?"

TAYNE sheathed the sword. And slowly, as though he had

reached some desperate decision, he turned to the control panels. But not to the ones at which he'd stood before. He touched one of a row of white studs above which were the words S-C ONLY. And a rectangle of metal hardly more than a foot in length and half as much in width slid back beneath his fingertips, exposing a compact console of control keys.

Or (2) when an insurmountable emergency should occur...

Tayne was pressing buttons, and Doug knew that the trajectory had been broken, and that the ship was free of its autorobot and under Tayne's sole command.

The manual control console. Tayne had had enough! Were he an Earthman as Doug was an Earthman—but he was not! He was a creature of pattern, and there was only the pattern to follow. And an 'insurmountable emergency' had indeed arisen. Flight with a madman who spoke of other universes, and who, by definition of orders, dare not be killed.

Doug, still seated, braced his feet on the hammock's bottom edge, and checked his spring even with his muscles tensed.

For Tayne turned suddenly. And the fear, the confusion were gone!

"Thank you, Quadrate Blair!" he said, "Madman, I am convinced—yet brilliant to the last! I admit, I may not have thought of our personal enmity as a motive for my actions—as a motive, I mean, that would justify them!"

Something turned to ice in Doug's stomach. It was going wrong, somehow.

Tayne drew the sword slowly. "I shall kill you now, you see, you hated me so much that I am afraid your hatred broke its bounds. And you not only attacked me but—but I'm afraid you also attempted to take over manual control of the ship in your madness. And for that of course—"

The sword was descending even as Doug launched his body from the hammock.

They went down then, and the sword clattered from Tayne's grasp. The blade-edge was speckled with red, and there was a searing pain across Doug's back. But his hands were on Tayne's throat, and they were closing.

And then they opened. The whistle of air into Tayne's lungs as he fought for breath and for consciousness told Doug he had only seconds before there was full life in the Quadrate's body again.

But the seconds were enough, for within them, he had the sword's hilt firmly in his own hand. And then he had its tip at the Quadrate's swollen, pulsing throat.

"You damn near threw me off schedule, Grand Imperial Wizard. Come on get up."

Doug felt little rivulets of blood trickle down his spine. The wound still stung, but it was not deep.

Slowly, Tayne rose, the sword-point beneath his chin.

"Don't make me nervous," Doug said. "Sudden moves get me all jittery, and sometimes when I'm jittery I kill stuffed shirts just to ease the tension. Back up. Now around—slow, Noble Grand Knight, or you'll fall down without your head." The sword point traced a thin line of red halfway around Tayne's neck as the man turned. "Now we're going to have some fun—only wish you were a tax-writer and I'd get a bigger kick out of this. Venus, James. And at the first peculiar maneuver—such as maybe cutting out the pseudograv or dumping us on the carpet without enough backblast and your nice uniform will get all gooked up. Blood, you know." He dug the point deeper into Tayne's flesh until some of it was red, the rest white with pain.

And again, there was nothing to do but play the gamble out. How brave, Doug wondered, was a creature of pattern?

VENUS filled the viewscreen, the white sea of the planet sky stretching unruffled beneath them.

"Northern land mass, Tayne. Your Quadrant. Thirtieth Division, Second Regiment, First Battalion, Company 'A'."

Tayne still said nothing. Doug kept the steady pressure on the sword point.

The round, black buttons were arranged like an inverted T. Beneath them were three square, flush-set dials. One was easily recognizable as an artificial horizon-ecliptic indicator. The second, Doug thought, indicated both plus and minus acceleration. And the third, simple velocity and altitude.

Tayne's fingers had not punched the buttons, but had played them almost as though they were, the keys of a musical instrument. The horizontal row was for change of direction to either left or right. The vertical, change in axial thrust, for either upward accelerations or forward, depending upon flight attitude. A slow turn executed by pressing the buttons of desired intensity of power in both horizontal and vertical columns simultaneously, with turn sharpness simply a matter of coordinated button selection.

The top button was for full thrust—full speed in level flight, blast-off from take-off position, or full deceleration in landing attitude. Those below it were for power in progressively lesser amounts. A twist of a fingertip would lock any of the buttons at any degree of power output desired. With practiced co-ordination, simple enough. Yet—what about climb or dip from the horizontal? Or inversion for landing? That was something for which he must wait.

The cut across his back throbbed now, and he dared not brush his hands across his eyes to smear the sweat from them.

And suddenly, Tayne's voice grated, "You had better drop the sword, Blair." There was the tightness of pain in his words, but they were clear. "I refuse to invert the ship. If we are to land, it must be inverted in sixty seconds. If you kill me, you kill yourself, for you do not know how to operate the panel beyond what you have seen—and you have not seen the operation for inversion. If you give me the sword, you will land alive."

"You're out of your head, *Mr.* Tayne! I'm Senior Quadrate Blair, remember? I know how to operate the panel as well or better than you do. Get going!" He dug the tip deeper, and fresh blood started.

But, Tayne's fingers remained immobile.

"Mad or sane, Senior Quadrate Blair or—or something else, if you knew how to use the panel, you would not have taken the risk of forcing me to do it! I would already be dead—"

There was a sudden, empty space in Doug's stomach.

"Thirty seconds, Blair."

The white mass of the sky was scant miles below them. He would need all of the thirty seconds, and there was no time to think—only time to realize that if he were to live, he must kill Tayne. It was like that time so long ago on the beaches of Normandy...

With all his strength he plunged, the sword through Tayne's neck. And his own hands were at the control panel before Tayne's gurgling corpse had slumped to the deck. The life-blood seeped from it far more slowly than the seconds slipped beneath Doug's taut fingers.

Not the buttons, not the dials, for he had seen them. But part of the panel itself—it had to be!

The panel *itself!*

He pressed one side, the other. Nothing. Ten seconds perhaps...

The bottom or the top next. But which? If it moved on a lateral axis—that would be it, for elevation or depression from the horizontal! But to accomplish what would amount to a half-loop...

He pressed the top of the panel. And it gave beneath his touch. In the viewscreen, the white mass, which rushed to envelop, him seemed to shift—

Further down—that was it, all the way around!

Slowly, against an unseen source of pressure, he revolved the panel a half-revolution about its lateral axis. Already he could see its reverse side—on it in the same pattern there was an identical set of control buttons, dials.

In the viewscreen there was a half-second's glimpse of the blackness of Space before the inverted ship tumbled tail-first into the white ocean of the Venus sky.

And again there was the awful sensation of falling through infinity. Desperately, he pushed the top button.

CHAPTER SEVENTEEN

HE locked the top button at full depression and struggled to keep his legs straight beneath him, braced as they were now against a bulkhead which but a few minutes before had been, not a floor, but a wall. The ship's gyro system was no longer functioning as a pseudograv unit, but rather as a vertical stabilizer, and the second dial said four gravities.

The acceleration needle dropped with agonizing slowness. Four gravities, three point seven. The altimeter said one hundred thousand feet, then ninety thousand, eighty, seventy-five.

Three point five gravities. Three point three. Even three at last.

Fifty thousand feet, forty-five, forty-two, forty thousand.

Two point six gravities.

Thirty-five thousand.

Two. One point nine. Point eight, seven, six, five.

Twenty-three thousand.

One gravity.

And the ship was hovering balanced by her gyros, at twenty-one thousand feet above boundless reaches of Venusian sea.

Gingerly, Doug pressed the top of the panel, released the top button.

There was a sickening drop as from somewhere deep inside the ship new sets of engines rumbled automatically to life as her nose came down, her belly-jets belching, breaking the drop on their cushion of power. And again the craft hovered, but now horizontally.

Tayne's corpse tumbled grotesquely off the bulkhead to the deck, made Doug miss his footing, and he fell.

But nothing happened. The panel, without pressure, had returned automatically to zero setting, and the belly-jets held steady.

Swiftly then, cursing himself for his awkwardness, Doug tore at Tayne's cloak, the blood-soaked tunic beneath it. Somewhere he must have it—logically, he must have it.

Something crackled. Doug smeared stinging sweat from his eyes as he bent closer, found the neatly hidden pocket, thrust a hand inside.

It was hard to keep the thin, bound packet of wide plastisheets steady. Clumsily, he flicked to blank pages of Tayne's unused record tablet. In those he had examined at his office the campaign maps had been in the back.

And he found them there. *Estimated deployment, Phase One, First Hour.*

No good...two, perhaps three hours had elapsed. Gamble on Phase Three.

Division Thirty, Second Regiment, First Battalion, 'A' Company. There.

He stood up, locked a deep breath inside him, and placed his fingers on the inverted T of control buttons for a second time.

North was the top of the viewscreen. What shown in it then, must slide from the top down.

His fingertip caressed the bottom-most button. And there was a gentle surge of acceleration, and the screen picture was moving diagonally. First button on the right...

THE picture swung slowly around. And then it was moving from top to bottom of the screen. He pushed the bottom button all the way in, and the velocity needles swung slowly up. A touch on the button above it, and the needle quivered five hundred ten.

And then on the horizon there was suddenly a light blue blur, and he braced himself against the shock of forward, acceleration as he pushed the button all the way in. Its limit was close to two thousand miles per hour, and he locked it there.

Moments later he released it, eased pressure on it as the blue blur shaped itself into the coastline of the northern land mass. Gradually, he depressed the panel a full ninety degrees.

And the hurtling craft swung again on her blazing tail. Doug let the panel return to zero and held the bottom button in. The belly-jets had automatically cut out, and again he hovered, sinking slightly, this time not above the dark blue waste of the Venusian sea, but above the place where fantastic young armies with ten-year-old soldiers were writhing, dying.

The altimeter needle showed five thousand feet, and already he was able to discern the battle-lines of the two quadrants, no longer in close marching formation, but now spread wide to cover an irregular area of more than one hundred square miles. The lines surged first forward then back, as though joined in some Gargantuan tug-of-war—shifted, changed, like a great wounded serpent in its death--throes.

The lines were little more than a hundred yards in depth because deployment for the games provided for no rear echelons—there were only the battle echelons, with their ends defended mightily against encirclement, attack from the rear.

Eventually, Doug knew, the flank defenses of both lines would give way, and the centers of each would rupture, and then, until the hovering tab and evac planes gave the signal that the Phase Three limit had been reached, the battle would wage in a great undulating mass, without formation, without plan, without reason. He had to reach Mike and Terry before then, for once the lines disintegrated into Final Phase—deployment at will—they'd be lost to him for good.

And Phase Three lasted at best for three hours. Final Phase, when it begun, would last as many days.

Somehow, he had to jockey the hovering ship over the area where the map-estimate indicated that Mike and Terry would be fighting. And when he landed, he must somehow halt the carnage momentarily—just long enough for them to see him, to run...

Doug tilted the great ship at an angle of about seventy degrees, compensated it on the main drive and the single bank of bow belly-jets that automatically checked in as the ship left vertical balance. And the terrain below him moved slowly, canted oddly between horizon and sky.

Slowly, toward the area designated on the map—slowly, sinking slightly, so that he could see their faces now, watch as their maces shattered the glittering helmets into junk, smashed into living flesh, as their broadswords glistened red and swung, struck...

MOMENTARILY hypnotized by the horror that screamed below him and by the sickening realization that what he saw was real even though his reason rebelled through force of habit from admission that such reality could exist, Doug watched the tilted battlefield as it stretched but hundreds of feet below him now, watched as a smoothly-oiled, carefully calculated device preserved the peace of a planet.

A small, sweating body was hewn in two.

A helmeted head fell; an arm dropped grotesquely beside it.

A boy's boot was bathed in blood as he kicked viciously at his opponent's chest to withdraw his sword from it.

A brief, two-handed struggle with sword and mace—a sword stroke was parried, the swinging mace was not, and a splintered rib with shreds of flesh still sticking to it clung to the mace-pikes as an adversary fell, the left side of his body gone.

And the dead, still-quivering masses of flesh and bone were trampled as they fell, to be swiftly covered by other still-dying bodies which collapsed, writhing, atop them, to be trampled in their turn...

Doug shuddered uncontrollably. Kids, dying on a battlefield like this!

A pair of helmeted heads suddenly disappeared in a twin red gush from two pairs of sweating shoulders, and a group of twenty boys converged on the spot, fought for almost a minute, and then the heads were covered, and one boy a length dragged himself away, arm limp, helpless. He died while an evac ship was landing. The swinging mace that broke his back had not been necessary. He who wielded it fell also an instant later, his spine severed in a long, diagonal gash. And Doug thought how odd it was that a sword-cleft could look so like the tearing wound, which a flying chunk of shrapnel would gouge.

He was so low now that he had long since lost sight of the lines' ends, had no way of knowing when encirclement at last would begin, when the center of each line would give way, when Final Phase would begin. But it seemed that the fighting had become less orderly, more closely-grouped, more frenzied. Within minutes the Third Phase map would be useless, and in Final Phase, there would be no knowing. No knowing until long after the end.

The altimeter needle said two hundred feet, when, if he had read the map with any degree of accuracy, he was over the area assigned to Tayne's Thirtieth Division. He had the ship straightened and descending when the blue light inset in the communications panel began to blink. He would let it blink. Yet if he answered, at least he would know their intentions...

Bloody young warriors sought desperately to give the great craft room as he descended. Some were incinerated in its back-blast, and Doug murmured a prayer that they had been among the already-dying. He would not let himself think that of all he had seen die, any two could have been Terry and Mike. He refused to let himself think that of the dozen turned to cinders by his descending jets, any two could have been Terry and Mike...

THE blue-red ground came slowly up to meet him. The blue light kept blinking. He increased pressure on the bottom button—hovered, sank, hovered again, sank.

And when the ground was obliterated with the searing flame of his drive tubes, there was a gentle jar, and Doug let the button snap from beneath his finger. He was down, and there was not even time to feel relief.

He tripped over Tayne's body, fell heavily against the communications panel. His fingers fumbled for a switch near the inset microphone. The words blurred... FIELD ADDRESS. RADIOSEND. RADIO-REC. FLEET INTERCOM.

He twisted the knob to RADIO-REC. and the blue light stopped blinking.

"...D to QT, D to QT, over..."

He turned the dial to RADIOSEND.

"This is QT," he said. He switched back, waited.

"Larsen, this is Gundar! What in Napoleon's name are you doing? What did you do with Blair?"

Doug tore a plastisheet leaf from Tayne's note tablet, thrust it over the mike-face.

"I had to kill him."

"*Kill* him? Larsen you fool... You know what they'll say—"

"He tried to get at the manual controls…succeeded in wrecking the autorobot, so I had to use them. And I had to kill him when he tried to take over by force. Give you a—"

"Larsen, something wrong with your communications? You're coming in badly—didn't read your last. Say again please."

"He wrecked the robot control," Doug repeated. His lips were dry across his teeth and it was hard to keep his voice even. "I had to break out the manual. He tried to take them over, too, so I had to kill him. He was like a maniac—you know how he hated me. Must have figured out the whole plan somehow, and went berserk. I'll file a complete report when this is finished. Over." He waited, sweat rolling in icy rivulets the length of his arms. The wound on his back stung, and his muscles were trembling with fatigue.

"What do you mean, when this is finished? Got to be immediate, man! There'll be hell to pay as it is. I was afraid something would go wrong—he was a smarter man than you thought, and I told you as much. Take care of whatever you're checking on down there immediately and then get back to headquarters and draw up a form, 312-L-5. File for my office and the PG's. You should've done that at once. Out."

"Yes, sir, right away. Out."

There was a silent prayer on Doug's lips as he turned the knob to FIELD ADDRESS. It was worth a try…

There was a humming sound. However it functioned, it was ready.

"This is Senior Quadrate Blair. All units within range of this command will cease battle immediately…"

He twisted a control under the viewscreen, kept twisting until its scope had undergone a ninety-degree shift. And then he saw them, waves of them, slowing, stopping, turning to face the ship. Unbelievably, the sound of his voice had somehow been carried for a radius of at least a mile, and thousands of them, their blood mingled with their muddied sweat, were suddenly still, listening. Some fell; untouched, as a last wound belatedly took its toll. But all that could remained standing. There could be no sitting rest, for none knew when the command to resume battle would come, and when it did, it would be death to be sitting.

Within a half minute, a great circle of them was still, battle continuing only at its periphery where his command was either being defended or had gone unheard.

"Attention, troops of Division Thirty, Second Regiment, First Battalion, A Company. If—" and he dared not hesitate, must say it quickly, and then wait, "—Ronal Blair and Kurt Blair are able, they will report to this ship on the double! Terry, Mike—" and there was a sudden catch in his voice that he could not help. Then, *"Come running."*

And he watched the viewscreen, turned the knob slowly to revolve its range, a complete 360 degrees.

Nothing, nothing as he turned slowly.

IN moments Gundar Tayne would contact him again, question him, and he would have no convincing answer. And then it would be too late. He would have the choice of punching the top button and catapulting himself to safety, not knowing even if Mike and Terry still lived somewhere down there, or staying to carry out a gamble that should have been lost a dozen times already.

Suddenly, he saw it. The huge ship of the Director, in a long, circling glide. And the boys were moving again, raising their swords, circling their maces. He had been countermanded—

The blue light was blinking.

Another ten degrees of turn—

There was a terrible clattering at the stern of the ship as though it was being rent apart plate by plate. The screen would not depress that far. He revolved it back. Tayne's ship had landed a scant hundred yards away and a guard had already been flung around it. And men were approaching on the run, strange devices in their hands. Then they stopped, were putting the devices in position on the ground.

The clanging grew louder now.

It would be one of them. One of them with a warning, and if he did not open up, surrender... But the blue light still blinked.

He could have missed them. As he swung the screen, they could have been running in an area yet untouched—the last ten degrees...

The clanging was lessening.

He hauled down the knife-switch marked "STERN PORT."

The clanging ceased.

And then, muffled almost to inaudibility, a wild, far-off yell, *"Shut it, Dad, for the luvva mike, SHUT it!"*

And he jammed the switch home.

There was an awful racket then. An awful, wonderful racket.

Mike, Terry, clambering hell-bent up the spiraling catwalks! Mike, Terry, safe aboard...

A movement in the viewplate stilled the cry that had formed in his throat. The strange devices—there was a bluish-white flash, and the viewscreen was suddenly white with a ball of coruscating brilliance. Short...

Had to blast off—but the kids, not braced on the cat-walks... Still clambering, maybe only halfway up...

Another streak, but no flash. Over. They were bracketing.

The next one, whatever it was, the next one would be a bulls-eye.

With all his voice he bellowed "*HANG ON!*" even as Mike and Terry burst, breathless, into the control room.

His finger hesitated only a moment. And then he jammed the bottom button in and his knees bent, but they held.

And in the corner of his eye he saw the blue-white flash erupt dead-center below.

He eased the button pressure and hovered, out of range.

In a moment Gundar Tayne's craft would be in the air. Then...

"Kids—kids, you O.K.?" He locked the ship in its hover and then he was beside them, scanning their half-naked, bruised bodies in quick glances, then holding them to him with all the strength of both arms.

"Dad?"

"Yes. Me, your old man..."

"We been dodgin' and watchin' for hours. Let's get out of here!"

He held them to him a second longer, then turned to the communications panel, Mike at his left, Terry at his right. "They almost caught us at the door down there... Dad I—I think I killed one..."

"We did as you said, Dad. We watched as much as we could, but most of the time we had to stay on the ground, playing dead..."

The communications dial was still at FIELD ADDRESS.

He looked at it, then looked at the viewscreen. Thousands of them, stilled for so short a moment, now surging, tearing at each other's vitals again. There was a terrible hurt somewhere deep inside him, and he wanted to voice it, to get it out, to tell them somehow.

But they would not understand him if he were to speak for a minute or for an hour. These whom he watched had been lost from the day of their birth.

But, thank Heaven, not the two at his side.

"Get in those hammocks, kids," he said.

They did, and he braced himself against the bulkhead. He was twisting the top button even as he punched it home, and it caught.

The deck rushed up with smashing force.

CHAPTER EIGHTEEN

THE white, sterile room seemed to have closed in upon itself since she had been first brought to it so many hours before, and the heavy desk was now just a great mass of steel, its curved lines no longer distinct, but trailing off somewhere in an incomprehensible geometry of their own. There was movement behind the desk, white, blurry movement that blended with the walls, but the flesh-colored mask that hovered above it did not seem to move at all. Dot's eyes could no longer focus for the fatigue of the tests had sucked the well of her physical energy dry, but she knew the face.

He was Mannix, director of the S-Council, they had told her.

The tests had torn her soul from her, turned it inside out, stripped it naked, examined it beneath their microscopes of unending questions asked in a thousand different ways with a thousand different inflections, connotations... The sterile white rooms, the lights, the darkness...

To hear what she and they had known from the beginning, and what the blurred, unmoving face was telling her now.

"...tests have been evaluated according to Section 679, Sub-section B of Commandment Seventeen, Part E, as amended, and you have been found to be unquestionably sane. It is my duty therefore to interpret the law with a finding of guilty of acts of heresy, as charged in each of the counts cited, committed with the premeditated deliberation of a sound, and therefore fully responsible mind."

Dot no longer felt fear, only a terrible tiredness. It did not matter what Mannix said, nor of course, could it matter what she might say. There was the truth, of course, but it would be doubly incriminating, and would spell disaster for Doug.

She would never see Doug again.

"...entitled, by rank, to denial..."

Or know him if she did.

"...may speak now as privileged, before you are sentenced..."

Never see her Earth, her Terry or her Mike again!

"...and in the absence of remonstrance as privileged..."

Or know that the sun and the stars above the alien planet upon which she would walk were not those under which she had been born...

"...hereby sentence you, Madame Lisa Blair, to loss of privilege to breed offspring through sterilization, and to the complete loss of all ego and all memory therewith connected through psychomutation, which treatment shall immediately follow the first. In the name of the Prelatinate, the Prelate General, and the party hosts, I do so pronounce sentence."

A panel had opened noiselessly behind her.

The blurred face nodded imperceptibly, and arms suddenly were lifting her to her feet, leading her from the white sterile room...

THERE was an empty roaring in his ears as he struggled for consciousness, and he could only half-feel the tugging at his body, half-hear the frightened sound of Terry's voice.

"Dad—dad, you've got to get up, dad!"

Painfully, he made his shaking muscles take over the burden of his weight, forced himself to his feet.

The viewscreen was black save for the receding white disk that was Venus. The acceleration needle quivered at just under two gravities.

"—Dad, everything feels funny. So heavy. For a long time we couldn't even move out of those bed-things."

His head hurt and there was drying blood on the side of his face. His body felt as though it had been flailed by a thousand of the maces, and his back wound was a long, throbbing ache, and it was sticky-wet again.

He tried to force a grin to his face, and even that drew tiny shards of pain.

"Wish I could've gotten to one of those bed-things, Mike! Believe me I never want to hear the expression 'hit the deck' again."

"Well you sure hit it. Anything feel busted?"

"Everything sure does! But I'll be O.K. in a minute." He sat heavily on the edge of a hammock, fought against the tugging urge to sink back into unconsciousness. But when the acceleration needle said one gravity and the gyros took over, he had to get back on his feet.

"Dad! Where the heck are we going?"

"And when you get us there, will you tell us what the contraption did to get us in this place, and make us all—even you—look all different? We thought it was one of those scary dreams until you got us out in front of everybody…and I still ain't so sure…"

Doug still hurt, but the dizziness was going, and there was Terry's question to answer. It was a good question.

"Earth, that's where we're going! Ever hear of it?"

"This is a *real* space-ship, Dad?"

Doug smiled down at him. "It's pretty real," he said.

They watched him in silence as he began his search.

He wasted twenty minutes at it before he was forced to the conclusion that there were no astronomical charts, no star maps. The Science Council would have its own, and the robot didn't need any…

He was glad the boys were with him. Glad, because without them, the cold panic that welled inside might have taken hold. Glad, because with them, he could muster the will it took to keep from telling himself how terribly big and empty infinity was.

Maybe you should've stuck with the MIT degree after all, Carl Grayson had said. And, he had stuck himself with it! But, if the things he had learned to get it had gotten him into this, then they would damn well have to get him out!

Doug ripped the blank plastisheets from Tayne's unused note-book, tossed them to the flat surface of the console. There was an ink-stylus in another pocket of the dead man's tunic.

He pointed to a bulkhead chronometer, "Tell me when an hour's up, boys," he said.

He must have his answers within the hour, for in computing them he would need a constant to represent known navigation error, and the hour would represent it, once he determined its value. And if he should exceed that time, its value would be changed—and the constant, the calculations, worthless.

With the viewscreen, he began his search of space for the bright, blue-white planet that would be Earth. When he found it, he would use twenty minutes of the hour to establish the plane of its ecliptic. Then, if he could remember what the books had said, remember its orbital speed, its orbital arc for the month of August and its resultant distance from the sun. And then of course the same mathematical equivalents for Venus, and subsequent establishment of the necessary relationships. And then interjected in it must be his own speed and relative direction for the space of one hour.

And when he had his dead-reckoning solution, it would still be like shooting ducks—with Earth the biggest duck that a man ever had to bag. And with a slingshot—his stylus—not the finely machined shotgun that would be the slide-rule and calculator, which he didn't have.

He kept turning the screen. In six precious minutes he found it, like a bright new jewel pinned to the white silk scarf of the Milky Way.

Earth.

He reached for the ink-stylus, the blank plastisheets…

THERE was a searing, bright light above her and it sent stabbing tentacles of pain through her head, and they lashed at her flagging brain.

They had lain her prone on a cold, flat surface, and their faces circled her, blurred as Mannix' had been, and infinitely far above her.

There was the murmur of voices, and the bright light was divided and divided again into myriads of white, stabbing lances as it was broken into glittering bits upon the edges of the slender instruments they held.

Let them, let them…

No, scream—scream or something, you idiot!

In a second there would be the hypodermic or the anesthesia and she would not be able to scream—

"You're so—so stupid…" she heard her voice saying, a dimly audible echo off the edges of infinity itself. "Sterilize me. Keep me from breeding. What I want, you fools! They all do, they all do, you know. And you, yourselves, give the answer to it. To our question, how much longer, how many, many more…"

She could not be sure if she spoke waking or dreaming, in the delirium of exhaustion or in the unintelligibility of anesthesia. But she was thinking the words, and she could still feel the motion of her tongue, its fuzzy touch against her teeth.

The glittering instruments were immobile.

"If heresy brings us this—this relief from a fear of forever being only a machine of flesh and blood to produce—to produce as any machine with no value whatever other than to produce until it falls into wreckage—then, then heresy will some day flourish, and you'll all be wrinkled and old, and there will be no young voices."

She let the words bubble from her, not caring, yet somehow caring, somehow fighting with all her being. But it was not a clever ruse, for there was still not strength enough to consciously pit her wits against them. It was something else, this strange fight, something else that stemmed from deep within her.

And now the murmur of voices above her had changed tenor; oddly interrupted by jagged bits of silence.

Done something. What she had said had done something, and they were hearing her. Hearing her, so she must speak louder, must open her eyes wide and let the bright light send the stabbing flashes of pain deep into her brain, whip it stingingly into consciousness.

It hurt, it hurt...

Colored circles, drifting, but it was from the light—and she was thinking now, and in a moment she would be seeing their faces more clearly. Had to talk again...

DOT lurched up on her elbows; felt the curious relaxation of a smile on her lips. "Go ahead! The rest of the women know what you're going to do to me! And pretty soon they'll let you do it to them! If we're no good as an underground to stop you, we'll let you use us to stop yourselves—think that one over before next election!"

From somewhere very near her a voice said "Madame Blair, please. You are interfering with the operation!"

But now the words were coming more easily. Her hands and feet were cold and wet, and her muscles shook, but now she was fighting with the last of the energy in her, she was fighting because she had found the chink in their armor, and she could widen it, could break through!

"Oh, very well—I wouldn't do that! Because I've been looking forward to this for so very long. Just to think, I'll be comfortably dried up, and—it'll be legal! No more fear!"

"You must be silent, Madame Blair."

"Is there some new amendment to the precious Commandments that says I must be silent? The last one I heard was just before I was brought here—Yes, have you heard the latest, gentlemen? An amendment prohibiting the execution of a sentence on an official's wife, until that official is present as a legal witness? But no, I can see you haven't, and hope you get into all kinds of trouble! Chapter— Chapter 580, gentlemen—Book 631, Section 451, Paragraph A, Sub-paragraph 34, Sentence."

And abruptly she let the bitter spurt of words taper into silence, and her eyes were wide. Only one of them was at her side—the rest were suddenly grouped around the one in charge, who was nervously fingering a telecall dial.

Like children! Doug said they were creatures of pattern, and something had suddenly smashed the pattern to smithereens, and they dared do nothing until they had a firm hold on the torn-up ends again. She had got them scared stiff!

This is it, girl! Move!

The last of her strength. A swift, sidewise kick, and she buried the heel of one bare foot into the groin of the man who had stayed to guard her. She had braced her other leg on the edge of the low operating table, and thus anchored, the kick carried all the merciless, impact that was needed. She did not wait to see the quick look of agony that mottled his face and she was off the table and running before he had sunk silently to his knees. The surgical robe was short and did not hamper her legs, and for the first time since she was a little girl, she ran for the sake of pure, uninhibited speed. She had reached the door marked EXIT ONLY before the rest of them realized what she had done, and then they were after her, their howling voices a mixture of disbelief and dismayed anger.

It was a long, wide corridor. The enraged shouts of alarm behind her had already turned it into a thunderously echoing cacophony of pure and terrible noises, and she knew that within moments, around some turn ahead of her there would be more of them, and she would be trapped, and it would be all over.

She would have let the sudden pain in her side double her when, less than a hundred feet ahead of her, more of them did appear; her flagging strength would have let her fall at their feet had she not seen it at the last moment, hardly twenty feet from her—the thing for which she'd been so desperately looking, had not been able to see through the stinging mist that still made things blur uncertainly... Another door. Another door marked SERVICE EXIT at the top.

She ran through it, breath sucking painfully into her lungs, the surgical gown already wet and clinging to her with ice-cold sweat. A long steel ramp, forty feet above the ground, curving in a gentle half-spiral to the broad street below.

She fled the curving length of it, swiftly past other service exits, her flight becoming more of a fall each split-second than a run, for her legs would not keep up. And then her momentum pitched her headlong into the street and she struggled desperately for balance.

She heard them behind her, feet thundering on the ramp, thundering in her ears.

A silver vehicle sped by, missed her, its undertow plucking at the sodden fabric of her garment. Another, and then suddenly the thundering grew louder and there was no more strength left.

The speeding golden-hued vehicle bore down on her, and Dot screamed, fell headlong in its path.

DOUG'S error was wide; but mercifully, he had led his target by too great a distance rather than by too little, and the ecliptic had been right. It would not be a chase, but a meeting. He brought Ship QT into a sharp, angling turn when he was sure, and there was silent thanksgiving at his lips as the moon of Earth rolled slowly far below him. And Earth itself became a pale blue bull's eye, growing perceptibly larger with each minute in the viewscreen.

He did not unlock the top button. He could be already many, many hours too late, but there was no knowing.

Like a great torpedo, the ship hurtled toward its target as though to blast it from Space. In eight minutes it would be midway between Earth and its moon, and in nine, Doug would invert, cutting the difference between crash and controlled landing perilously thin.

"Terry, get the dead man's sword and belt. Mike, help me find some tools—anything that even looks like a wrench."

When two of the nine minutes were gone, Doug had found a tool that would serve. When a portion of the third was gone he had a section of the communications panel naked. When seven of them were gone he had its high-kempage pack loose on its bearers, and when there were but seconds left in the ninth, he had it free, and lashed with torn strips of his cloak to one of the hammocks.

"Hold on, now," he said then. His voice was raw and it hurt to talk. There was a dryness in his mouth that made his words fuzzy and indistinct, and his tongue felt swollen enough to choke him. "I want both of you on that hammock—get that thing between you, strap yourselves down, and then hold onto it for all your life. When we land, get the straps off quickly, and—" he clenched his teeth, had to push the words through them, "—and have your swords ready. I'll take care of the rest; you just follow me. Understand, boys?"

They nodded silently, strapping themselves securely to the hammock.

Three seconds…two, one. Release the top button. Press the panel full around, all the way…there go the bow belly-jets—stern jets topside… Top button, all the way in, twist it—

The Moon swam into the viewscreen, was shrinking fast, too fast. No, slowing a little…

He swung the screen to full stern, and Earth was rushing up, not quite yet filling it.

Speed in thousands per second…sixteen…fifteen point five—fifteen. The needle fell so slowly. Gravs were coming up, one point five—two full. Over two now, and speed falling a little faster.

Earth filled the screen.

And then he took his eyes from the dials, for he knew that whatever they read, he was at the full mercy of the ship itself. The top button was all the way in, and locked. She was giving all she had.

When the grav indicator quivered at four, Doug slumped to the deck, unable to stand. He rolled to his back, winced, and tried to keep his eyes on the grav needle.

THEY blurred, stung in oceans of hot tears. The shrill siren-scream of atmosphere pierced the thick, heavily insulated hull and Doug knew what was coming—heat, unbearable heat.

His short gasps seared his mouth, and his heart was like a gigantic pile driver inside him, struggling to burst its way through his chest.

And then as though it had all been but part of a timed experiment in some weird laboratory, the sensation of being crushed to death began to abate. He could see the grav needle again, and it had already fallen back to two. Speed was now in unit miles per hour, and the figures were dropping from nine hundred.

Doug forced himself to his feet.

"Dad…Dad, are we O.K.? Dad?"

"Maybe," he said.

When the grav needle was steady at One, Doug reduced thrust to hold them hovering at a little more than two hundred thousand feet over the Atlantic, with the coastline of what to him was France almost directly below.

A sickening, quick drop and the horizon-ecliptic indicator showed parallel flight, and Doug could feel the thrust of the belly engines beneath his feet. Then he pressed the bottom button, then the middle, and the Atlantic was rushing beneath them. Carefully, he depressed the next one up. All the way in, he locked it. The velocity figure in unit miles per hour was fifteen thousand.

Eleven minutes later he cut the power again, slowed, brought the ship once more on its stern, and began his descent over Washington.

Within moments they would spot him, would be ready.

It would have to be fast, miles from the central space-port—a suburb, near a highway.

He let her fall fast. Ten thousand. Eight. Four.

He tilted, angled a little north and west, then dropped again.

At five hundred feet he trebled the power, and it was as though a great chute had snapped open above them.

Three hundred feet—the highway perhaps a quarter of a mile distant.

No one down there, but they could be hiding, waiting.

Fifty feet. Had to time it just so, now…

The last ten feet they fell.

CHAPTER NINETEEN

HE estimated that there would be five minutes at the most before the area was flooded with S-men. The rest of the gamble hinged entirely on what they succeeded in doing, or failed to do, within the space of a few hundred heart-beats.

They made the roadside in little more than a minute after leaving the ship. Terry and Mike lay prone in the wide drainage gutter, their swords drawn, their bodies camouflaged by a few handfuls of hastily hacked scrub brush.

Doug stood at the side of the superhighway, the power pack at his feet, his shredded cloak in his hands to wave.

The traffic seemed light for so late in the afternoon. The sun was hot, and he was breathing heavily from the stumbling, desperate run across the small, rutted field. The ship towered above what few trees there were, and it marked them for a target.

A streamlined shape was racing toward him. It seemed to take all the strength he had left to wave the cape, and he wondered if he were waving it at searching S-men…

The vehicle sped by, whipping the cape in its undertow. It was going nearly two hundred miles an hour, and there was no driver inside it. A robot carrier.

Thirty seconds went by before the next one came. It was going slower, and it too was driverless.

Doug glanced at the sky. To the west, high, tiny dots—

It was a full minute before the next one came. With both hands, cloak dropped because it was too heavy, Doug waved, and the vehicle was slowing.

"Ready, boys…" There was a slight rustle behind him as they came to their knees.

The driver stopped his car almost abreast of him, and opened the passenger door.

"What's the trouble? You crack up? While we're riding you can use the autophone—"

Doug moved into the vehicle slowly, then lashed out at the man's head with the smooth, heavy rock that was in his left hand. In his exhaustion he struck only a glancing blow, and there was barely time for a second, but the second connected, and the driver slumped, jammed behind his semicircular steering wheel.

"Mike, Terry—"

In a moment the helicopter would have him spotted, or an S-Council patrol car would be braking beside him.

They hauled the driver out, left him at the roadside. He was not dead, and Doug was curiously thankful for that. He had killed one man already…

He wasted a second for another glance at the sky. Closer now, and it was obvious that they had spotted the ship. He had to get the vehicle in motion somehow. A robot sped by, its air wake rocking them slightly. He had the pack on the seat beside him, and Terry was slamming the door.

No clutch or brake pedal. Only one pedal, and it could only be an accelerator. But pivoted in the middle. There was no sound to the engine, no way to tell if it were running because the only dash instrument was a speed indicator.

He pressed the pedal forward. And they did not move. Backward, then…

It moved. In five seconds the speed needle was climbing past eighty, going smoothly upward.

He wondered if they had been seen.

In a dash mirror he saw Terry and Mike turning their heads up, looking through the curved transparent metal top.

"Must be a hunnerd of 'em—they're starting to land I think!"

"All of them?"

"I guess so—wait! Yeah, he's gonna land, too I guess. I can't see 'em anymore. Gosh, we're sure moving."

"Creepers, a hundred and *eighty*! Hey Dad, where are we going, anyway?"

"To the headquarters hospital building. I think—I think that's where your mother is."

"Is she hurt?"

"I don't know, Mike, I don't know."

He pressed his heel to the floorboard. He was glad for Tayne's sword at his side. Even for the ones the boys carried.

THE sign said City of Washington, District of Columbia, Population 531,423. Speed Limit 55 MPH.

Doug raised his heel, the car slowed. He frowned. No roadblocks, no pursuit! There had been plenty of time since the helicopters had landed—five, six minutes perhaps. They knew where he was going, and were going to let him walk right into it, some neatly conceived trap at the hospital. So they'd be sure to have him alive...alive, to be used as an example!

Savagely, he heeled the pedal down. Let them be waiting—they were fools if they hadn't figured on the swords! Or—or he was a fool, for counting on them.

The car's tires wailed as he rounded the long, curving turn that brought him onto St. Jefferson Way, past the Payne Monument, and within two blocks of the headquarters building hospital wing.

The traffic was thickening, planned of course to make things look as natural as possible—not to arouse his suspicion at the last moment...

"Get those swords ready, kids..."

He heard them scrape from their scabbards.

And without warning the form of a woman darted into his path. He swerved, jammed the pedal forward, and the car rocked sickenly.

And he had seen her face in that one awful second—it was Dot who had fallen in the street behind him!

The boys were at his heels as he leapt from the car. There were white-clad men rushing toward them, and he had Dot's form in his arms as the first of them closed in.

There was the quick blink of sunlight on steel as Mike and Terry swung their weapons.

And as though stunned, the men in white stopped short, suddenly silent, awkwardly poised statues.

Doug knew the spell would last for only seconds. The half-naked boys stood grimly, feet wide apart, sword-hilts grasped in both hands.

Doug, with Dot's limp body in his arms, broke for the car.

"Come on!"

And Terry and Mike were at his heels. The men in white broke their frozen ranks then and swarmed over the small area of street that the two broadswords had commanded for the telling few seconds.

Doug bolted the vehicle into motion. And then they were free.

"What dopes," Mike was saying. "Were they scared! I bet they didn't figure we'd be ready to fight 'em! But who did we—?"

"Boys, see what you can do for your mother. It is your mother, she just looks different, like we do…"

"Mother—"

"Hurry up. She's just fainted, that's all. We didn't hit her."

DOT was conscious when they arrived at the house, and she was managing to speak.

"Are they—"

"The boys, yes Dot. Our boys. Now look, we've got to run for it. I'll carry you, and you hang on to the pack… Mike, Terry—"

"Ready, Dad. Will there be many?"

"I don't know. Maybe none, but if there aren't, it'll only be for a very few minutes. Let's go!"

They ran, and the boys burst through the front door with their swords lunging at emptiness.

"The cellar!"

He heard them clamber down the steel stairs.

"It's O.K. Dad—come on!"

Dot's face was white, and her eyes were open wide. He carried her as gently as he could, but she had never been so terribly heavy in his arms.

It happened at the cellar doorway, at the top of the stairs.

He stumbled, fought for balance, fell to one knee, clutched hard and Dot screamed.

But he held her, and her arms were choking at his neck.

And there was a crashing, clanging noise as the power pack fell from her, caromed from step to step, and lay finally in a shattered ruin on the cellar floor.

CHAPTER TWENTY

SLOWLY, Doug straightened, descended the stairs with Dot's trembling body still in his arms. The boys stood motionless.

There was only the sound of Dot's quiet sobbing, and that of Doug's boots as they struck hollow sounds from the steel stair treads, moved heavily as though fitted to the legs of an awkward robot to scatter the shattered bits of the power pack tubes and crush them as they came underfoot.

Gently, he put her down. The boys knelt at either side of her, Doug himself before her.

"Don't, please don't, Dot," he said.

"Oh, Doug—"

And then she clung to him, and her face was wet against his own, but they were the last of her tears.

"Afraid?"

"No. Scared a little, but just scared. I don't fear them, Doug…they're not worth enough to fear."

Mike and Terry had gone over to where the Contraption was, had pulled off its dust-cover, and stood looking at it as though puzzled, as though wondering why, so suddenly, it had become a worthless thing.

"Nobody's touched it, Dad," Doug heard Mike saying. "I don't think anybody's done anything to it."

Doug didn't answer, for he did not know how to tell them, how to make them know that there was no way.

"I just—just dropped it, Doug…"

He tried to smile, and his face felt old and tired. "We were over-due anyway," he said. "Way overdue. I guess it's against the rules to beat the odds forever."

"I just…just dropped it…"

"Don't, don't my darling. It wasn't you, don't you understand? It wasn't you, or me—the little fight we made just prolonged things for awhile. Sort of like living itself, I guess. The big system, you can let it sweep you along as it will or you can fight it if you're fool enough…"

"Doug! Doug, you don't believe those things!"

He felt the muscles of his face tighten, and he said nothing. No, no he did not believe them, but what difference did that make? It was the ways things were that mattered!

He picked up the broadsword Terry had let fall.

"How long—how long will it be, Doug?"

Her voice was calm; there was even a faint flush of color in her face again.

"I don't know," he said. "For awhile at least, this might seem the least logical place."

"Dad, what's in this big box? Hey, Dad!"

HE stood up, turned toward them. The kids—so full of life and the love of living, so full of the myriad curiosities that made living a colorful vibrant thing.

"This one here. Over here—a big tall wooden one."

Doug heard her quick intake of breath, turned to her.

"Before the telecall, Doug. Before they took me. A helicopter came, from the electronics place…they brought that box, and I—"

In quick strides he was beside Mike and Terry, and everything inside him was suddenly churned up, cold, hot…

Mike had wrenched a section of planking loose, had reached inside.

"I got the label, Dad… High Speed Blower Rack, with Double Blower, Model 4-L532, two each—"

The final, hellish irony. As though it were not enough to fail, but to be mocked as he failed, as though Fate—or was it Providence?—could not close the incident without at least a gentle laugh at him, a cruel laugh to make light of all his confusion, his efforts and all that had driven him to make them. Doug wondered if there would be enough of the strength he would need, when he died, to laugh back.

The planking squawked as Terry pried with Mike's broadsword.

"Maybe it can help, Dad…maybe it can," Terry said, and he continued the prying. Mike pulled at it, and there were louder squawks as the nails protestingly surrendered.

Doug wanted to stop them, to tell them, but there could be such a little time left, and if it kept them busy there might not be time for them to become afraid.

He watched them as they ripped the top from the crate, eagerly began hauling out its contents.

Four large, wide-bladed fans, each perhaps sixteen inches in diameter, and each driven by a compact electric motor. They were coaxially mounted on tall, slender chromium plated racks and could be adjusted on them to meet any conceivable experiment in ventilation engineering.

Doug said nothing, let them continue. It might not even be necessary to tell them that their discovery was nothing more than two ingeniously designed air conditioning units.

He wondered why they had come at all. The Prelatinate Attorney's idea, perhaps, of a not-too-subtle jest. That, or even a veiled warning.

There was more squawking of wood and in a few moments Mike and Terry had each of the units placed beside each other on the cellar floor.

"There's other junk here too," Terry was saying. "Pulleys and stuff, Dad. And a sheet of directions or something. Here, look Dad...maybe it'll help."

Doug looked at the smudged sheet of plastisheet that Terry had thrust in his hand. Only simple diagrams, indicating the use and assembly of the pulleys for desired variations in blower speeds. Even the simple rheostat, Doug mused, was taboo...

He crumpled the sheet, let it fall to the floor.

And suddenly grabbed it up again, smoothed it, looked again at the last sentence! ...*each motor operates on regular household direct current of 250 Kemps, as authorized by...*

Two hundred fifty Kemps—and there were four of the motors!

"Dot! Dot those tools by the Contraption! And any scrap wire there—hurry!"

HE worked with inhuman swiftness of desperation. Dot knelt beside him, handed him tool by tool as he asked for it, as though she were a scrub nurse and he the surgeon, with a patient that might have but moments to live.

And silently, Terry and Mike, watched, eyes wide with wonderment. They watched as Doug equipped two of the motors with the large pulleys, the two others with pulleys of less than half their diameter. Then he linked them with the flat rubber belts.

"See if you can get the insulation off the ends of those wires—the ones a couple feet long are all right."

He moved the racks next to the bench, brought them close together and when Dot handed him the wire, he had the two motors on which he had placed the small pulleys denuded of their streamlined jackets. It was between those two that he made a simple connection in series.

"Terry, Mike—while I'm making connections to the Contraption, see if you can get the fan blades off their shafts."

Two connections—two simple connections…

He finished the second connection.

"One more fan to go, Dad—"

He plugged the two outer motors with the large pulleys into the wall outlets above the bench. Then his fingers waited on the switches.

"But Doug the fan motors will only work on house current—"

"Yes, that's right, but I've geared—pulleyed, I mean—two of them up, so that they'll turn the other two at least twice their normal armature speed. And the simple electric motor works—"

"—in reverse, too, doesn't it! If you turn it by mechanical means, it generates electric current!"

"That's about it. I ought to get about five hundred volts from each, with the pulley ratio I'm using. And they're both connected in series, so—a thousand volts, I hope. Childish, isn't it—"

There was sudden chaos above them.

"Doug—"

Terry dropped the last fan-blade to the floor.

Doug pressed the switches, and the two electric motors spun into humming, whirring motion, driving the other two at a speed he knew might burn them out in minutes. Then he closed the Contraption's main switch, and pulled Terry and Mike bodily to him with one arm as he held tightly to Dot with the other.

S-men swarmed down the cellar stairs.

CHAPTER TWENTY-ONE

A DOZEN men clad in white uniforms of the S-Council surrounded them, and there were weapons in their hands.

Senior Quadrate Blair understood. Partially, he understood. He had been reading a banner headline, and then suddenly—suddenly there had been an indescribable moment of utter dark, of awful timelessness—and cold. And there was still the cold, tangible and fluorescing in a green-blue flame about him. Through it he could see the white blurs—the men in white. S-men…

"Lisa—" He felt her beside him, crushing their two sons to her trembling body. He could see their faces, then—upturned to his, pleading, afraid. "The change. Somehow my counterpart, my imposing alter-ego has succeeded, Lisa! He has found his way back, and in so doing he has returned the four of us…"

And then the green glow and the cold was gone, and there was no more time to speak.

"Stand where you are! You have only to move to—*Madame Blair!*"

The leader of the white-uniformed band had half-succeeded in masking his initial amazement, but now the surprise on his heavy face was a naked thing. The others stood as statues to each side of him.

There was an awful moment of silence, and the weapon-muzzles held steady, even if the dozen hands that gripped them were momentarily incapable of flexing trigger-fingers.

And then the Senior Quadrate had found his full voice.

"There has of course been some error. S-men do not enter the home of a Senior Quadrate—"

And Lisa's voice cut across her husband's.

"They—Douglas, these aren't—aren't S-men! I recognize him—the leader! Mylor Kuun…"

"Of course, Madame," the heavy-faced one said rapidly. "The disguises—a desperate necessity, I assure you. There is very little time, however. Once informed of your escape from the hospital, and of the Senior Quadrate's violation of arrest, it was necessary to act at once to find you. Genuine S-squads cannot be much behind us. We're but one of a number of our groups in the search, and we came to your home only so no possibility might be overlooked. Yet I don't understand—" For a moment a look of puzzled doubt flickered on the underground leader's heavy features. His nervous gaze touched the strange array of forbidden equipment, which but moments before had been bathed in the green-blue glow.

"There will be time for explanations later!" Lisa said. She caught herself as she was about to add that what the agent was saying made little sense.

She put a protective arm around each of her still, frightened children. There must be great trouble or the group would not have so brazenly exposed itself and come here to her home. Something desperate enough so that added confusion might serve only to make a dangerous situation an impossible one.

"But I don't—you said violation of arrest," her husband was saying stubbornly. "I demand a thorough—"

"Your lives are in danger, sir. If we do not move immediately, it will very probably be not at all. Gundar Tayne is relentless, and is reported enroute from Venus to join this search himself."

"Tayne!" Blair's face blanched, then reddened. "The Taynes, you mean! Gundar and Larsen, with Larsen behind it—"

"Sir? You're being tracked down for—they say, for murdering Larsen. Please follow us sir, Madame..." The look of puzzled bewilderment deepened on the underground leader's face as he motioned his men in screening flanks surrounding the four. One of the men handed him a white bundle from a compact equipment-pack on his back.

"You had better get these on. We would say we have captured your boys—"

THEY were S-Council uniforms, and the Quadrate and his wife donned them quickly; Blair doing so more in hesitant imitation of Lisa's frantic haste than from the desperation of a situation, which he only half-understood.

Murdered Larsen Tayne? Then...yes of course. The other Blair. But why should the other Blair hate Tayne so? He was of a different Earth, of course... He would think like those of his own world. He would hate all this world stood for. Hate Tayne for his overbearing, brutish use of authority—criminal cleverness at deception.

Suddenly, he knew the confusion of panic for the first time in his life. Suddenly, his mind was a boiling thing, and all the brilliant solutions that had been forming in it with split-second rapidity were unexplainably invalid, wrong...

And then they were at a half-run, leaving the house, heading for a 'copter painted with the S-Council insignia, counterfeit serial code-numbers beneath it.

In moments the craft was airborne, and Washington was falling away below them, fading away behind. And now any small thing—an incorrectly acknowledged radio challenge—would undo them, the Quadrate realized, but that was only a part of this terrible gamble they were taking. Gamble, on their very lives, yes—only why? Why?

Slowly, bit by bit, the thing pieced itself together as they flew. A great forest stretched ten miles beneath them, faded, wilted at last into desert as the first shadows of a day dying crept silently upward to engulf them.

In low tones, he and Lisa talked with the heavy-faced leader, and they talked for a long time.

"If it were not for the boys—" Blair murmured finally.

"The boys will be safe with us," Lisa answered. She looked at them, and they were sleeping, hardly looking the part now of young warriors of broadsword and mace. "We will teach them a different way…"

He was silent for long moments. Then: "I cannot understand. I cannot, Lisa. That I have always believed as I have—and he, as we know he did. Yet that we should both have mortal hatred for the same man; he to the point of doing what I did not have courage to do. And now, regardless of what I believe, my own kind are hunting me down."

"They would have, had you had the courage of which you speak— the courage of that conviction. And was it, Douglas, simply a conviction about a single man?"

"I—I don't know." He looked through a port; it was night, and they were speeding silently westward. Then he was looking back to her, and deep into her eyes. He had never felt lost, alone, hunted before. There was something very wrong.

"With us, Douglas…will you try? To understand—with us?"

"Not because I am hunted."

"No. No. But now is the time for that wanting courage. Another man, too, hated a Tayne, and killed him. Can you help us kill the things that all Taynes stood for? In our way?"

Great mountains were looming before them, and the 'copter was beginning to lower into their darkened maw. And suddenly he felt a new strength in him from depths of his being that were opening to him for the first time. *Another man had killed Tayne. And could he—*

"But what of the other man?" he suddenly heard himself asking. "What have I done to him? What have I done to *his* world?"

"He must be a man of great courage." Lisa answered slowly. "I think—I think such a man will find a way to undo what you have done. For such a man, and for such others as he, there is always great hope."

"You will help me, Lisa."

"All of us, Douglas."

"Then that is all *I* shall need," he said softly.

The 'copter vanished into the mountains.

TERRY and Mike came running from Doug's den, a welter of books open on the floor behind them, which they had not opened.

Dot was coming from her bedroom. A pistol Doug owned had been in her hand, and she put it in its place in the open drawer from which she had not taken it.

"Dot! Kids—the living room! I'm in the living room! Dot!"

In a moment they were around him, and they were the Dot and the Mike and the Terry whose faces had been so familiar so long ago.

"I must've—he—I must've been reading this final—look, Dot, my God look—"

She saw the Page One streamer.

"Then he was—he was trying, here, he was trying, Doug... That was why. When I arrived, I had a pistol in my hand..."

The headline read BLAIR BILL GOES TO HOUSE TOMORROW. And in the three-column drop beneath it: *Unanimous Passage Seen—Senate Reported Favorable—President Says He'll Sign Immediately—Draft Of 13'S Would Begin Nov. 15—Soviet Terms Measure 'Fantastic'.*

"Doug—"

"He's begun it all right. How, I don't know, unless— And beneath the centerfold he read CLERGY LAUDS BLAIR BILL AT PARLEY HERE.

"Had them falling for it, had 'em mainlined all the way!" Doug said.

And then he was going swiftly toward the den, almost at a run.

He pulled a battered chair up to the big desk, lifted his telephone from its cradle almost in a single motion.

Quietly, Dot shut the door behind him. It would be a long time, she knew, before it would open again.

CHAPTER TWENTY-TWO

THE night was quiet, and the air was warm and still.

The man and the woman walked close together, and with slow, un-measured steps, as though the great, slumbering city was a garden, and they were exploring it for the first time.

They did not speak, for their eyes were wide, engrossed simply in seeing.

A soldier passed them, then a man who might have been a store-- clerk, a student, a salesman, a clergyman, a scientist.

A young couple approached from the opposite direction, saying quiet things to each other, perhaps deciding intimate, very important plans for some near future time.

They passed an all-night drug store, its gaudy light washing the sidewalk to the curb, limning the wide racks of newspapers and mag- azines, which told their stories in a dozen languages, on a thousand themes.

The streets were wide and empty, but they were not lonely, for in them were the silent echoes of the struggles and victories, big and small, that had been fought, won and lost in them in a day just dying, just to be born again in a few short hours.

The man and woman walked for a long time.

And Douglas Blair thought of what would not happen tomorrow.

Not tomorrow or, perhaps with great care and the forgiveness of the Almighty, not even the day after that.

THE END